"Well, now," she whispered. "If it's romance you want, then let's get on with the show."

Nick scooped her up and settled her against his chest. His kiss was warm and tender, and Laura felt an excitement building in her. Tonight would be a night of love, unlike any other.

He moved around with her in a circle, blowing out the candles as he turned. Then he carried her into the bedroom and lowered her onto the silky sheets. The light of the single candle she had left behind softly illuminated the room.

"One little thing," Nick murmured, reaching behind the bedside table. He gave a short jerk of his hand then held the unplugged telephone cord aloft. "Tonight, Laura Jensen, you're all mine."

ABOUT THE AUTHOR

Sharon Brondos decided to set her second
Superromance close to home in Wyoming. While
researching the book she learned almost everything
there is to know about golf—except how to swing a
club herself. Sharon, her husband—a pathologist—
and their three teenagers live at the edge of a
country club golf course. "I just have to look out
my window," says Sharon, "and there's the 16th,
17th and 18th green."

Books by Sharon Brondos

HARLEQUIN SUPERROMANCE
153—A MAGIC SERENADE
183—PARTNERS FOR LIFE

HARLEQUIN TEMPTATION
70—IN PERFECT HARMONY

These books may be available at your local bookseller.

Don't miss any of our special offers. Write to us at the
following address for information on our newest releases.

Harlequin Reader Service
P.O. Box 52040, Phoenix, AZ 85072-2040
Canadian Address: P.O. Box 2800, Postal Station A,
5170 Yonge St., Willowdale, Ont. M2N 6J3

Sharon Brondos

PARTNERS FOR LIFE

Harlequin Books

TORONTO • NEW YORK • LONDON
AMSTERDAM • PARIS • SYDNEY • HAMBURG
STOCKHOLM • ATHENS • TOKYO • MILAN

Published October 1985

First printing August 1985

ISBN 0-373-70183-7

For my husband, Greg,
who is learning to play golf

CHAPTER ONE

LAURA JENSEN TOOK ONE LAST PUFF from the cigarette and hastily flushed the remains away. She was thoroughly ashamed of the habit and blushed every time she heard herself advising a patient to quit smoking.

Time and time again she had told herself that as a physician she should set a good example, not a bad one.

But the food, the wine and the good company of her friends had weakened her resolve once more, and she had retreated to the ladies' room of the Linville Springs Country Club and barricaded herself in a cubicle for a few guilty puffs of nicotine. *Next* week, she promised herself, she would quit. For good.

She opened the bathroom door and noted thankfully that the lounge was empty. No one to smell the smoky scent of her fall from grace. She moved over to the mirror and checked her reflection critically.

The light was soft and flattering, and in its soft glow her black hair seemed to show a little less gray than usual. It might just be the style, she decided, readjusting the small combs that held her hair away from her face on either side. The dark strands fell in two midnight wings to her shoulders, curving under slightly where they touched her skin. Too bad she couldn't wear her hair loose like this all the time, but it wouldn't do to have it falling in her face while she was trying to examine a patient. Highly unprofessional.

"Maybe," she told her image softly, "you should have gone into modeling instead of medicine. Then you could smoke, wear your hair any way you wanted, and your friends wouldn't always be on you to take better care of yourself." She gave her reflection a wry smile.

No, the road had been long, hard and sometimes heartbreaking, but she wouldn't exchange her medical degree for anything. Helping people was in her blood, a natural inheritance from her country-doctor father. As far back as she could remember, Laura had longed to go into the same profession.

She took a tube of lipstick from her evening bag and looked back into the mirror. All right, maybe she was having second thoughts about returning to her home town in the middle of Wyoming ranching country and going into practice with her father. But she did enjoy medicine. Loved it more than anything else. *Had* loved it to the exclusion of everything else. Only now, in the last few months of her residency, was she realizing how narrow she had allowed her life to become. She pointed the lipstick tube at her reflection.

"You've gotten completely out of practice at relaxing and having fun, Doctor Jensen. What you need is—"

"What you need, lovely lady, is a little professional instruction." The deep baritone echoed off the flocked mauve wallpaper, and the entire room seemed to cringe at the male intrusion into strictly female territory. Laura whirled around and stared at the tall figure by the door.

The man leaned casually against the frame, his arms crossed and his head cocked slightly to one side. His eyes were half-closed, lazily sexy, and it occurred to Laura that she had been under that sultry scrutiny for several minutes. Long enough for him to have heard her talk out loud to herself not once, but twice.

"I thought this was the *ladies'* room," she said acidly, pleased when his eyes opened wide at her tone. Amber-brown eyes went perfectly with his auburn-brown hair and tanned skin. He probably wasn't a local, she decided. He looked too groomed, too elegant to be an oil-man or a rancher, the only kind of Wyoming male to sport a year-round tan.

"It *was* a ladies' room," the man said, flashing her a wide grin. He pushed himself away from the door frame and ambled across the room toward her, his hand thrust casually into the trouser pockets of his tuxedo. "But I've declared it *our* room for a few minutes, lovely lady."

"*Our* room?" Laura raised an eyebrow and willed herself not to smile back at the intruder. *This one's a lady-killer,* she decided quickly. *Smooth. Better not let him think his charm is having any effect.* His smile took on a warmer look, and she felt her mouth go cottony.

"My name's Nick Hawthorne," he said, stopping just short of invading her personal space. He seemed to hesitate and then went on. "I saw you from a distance, Laura. You disappeared in here, and I collared every person in the dining room until I found out who you were, and that you were here alone."

"I'm not alone." She tried to keep her voice cold. "I came with the Pattersons as their guest."

A light danced in his eyes. "You know what I mean, Laura," he said softly. He shrugged his wide shoulders. "You aren't with another man. That makes it all right for me to introduce myself to you in this bizarre way and to ask if I can claim the rest of your evening exclusively for myself."

Laura blinked. She was hardly a stranger to male attention, but this man looked as if he had just stepped out of a men's fashion magazine. She *wasn't* used to men like that. Not at all. Her male friends all seemed a little frayed around the edges. This one didn't have a thread loose.

And he was more than just handsome, she realized. He was compelling, standing so close to her, his smile warm. She took a slow, deep breath, using the time to organize her tumbling thoughts. But the spicy scent of the man filled her nostrils, drowning out the powdery, perfume smells that clung to the lounge like soft ghosts.

"You're asking me for a date, Mr. Hawthorne?" she finally said. "Don't tell me that you came to a Valentine's Dance all by yourself." She looked him over with a glance as bold as the ones he had been giving her. "I really find that hard to buy."

His laughter surprised her. "I had a premonition," he said, "that I was going to meet an angel tonight, and I didn't want to spoil my chances by being encumbered with a lesser being."

"Oh, really?" She kept her tone skeptical, but his words caused her a feeling of pleasure. She could read admiration for her in his eyes, and, lady-killer or not, it was flattering to have this handsome man obviously interested in her, even if just for an evening's flirtation. "I do hate to disappoint you," she continued, giving him a shadow of a smile, "but I'm a very ordinary being myself. No angel at all."

"Good." His expression changed to a cross between mischief and lechery. "I didn't want an angel in the spiritual sense. Only in the physical." He removed his hands from his pockets and took the lipstick from her fingers, setting it on the countertop. Then he touched her arm.

"Hey!" Laura took a step backward. "I didn't mean..."

"Neither did I." His expression sobered. "Sorry, Laura Jensen. I don't mean to come on like Don Juan. Force of old habit." He held out his hand, palm up, in offering. "All I meant to imply was that I recognized you as a person, a woman. Not a mythical male fantasy."

"Oh." Something deep in his eyes made her slide her hand into his. Something that seemed to reach out to her. Something that put frayed edges on this otherwise perfect man. Instantly Laura regretted the gesture.

His hand closed firmly around hers, and she was pulled close to his body. Mischievous lights danced in his eyes, and his grin turned wicked. "Come on, Laura," he said softly. "Dance with me."

"Don't be silly, Nick." She tried to free herself, but he slipped an arm around her waist and drew her closer. "Someone might come in," she protested.

"So what if they did?" He tilted his head slightly to one side as he asked the question, and his hand moved hers out into a dancing position. In spite of herself Laura put her hand on his shoulder in automatic response.

"This is ridiculous," she replied, trying to sound sensible but fighting a smile. "There isn't even any music."

"Oh, there's music," Nick murmured, turning her in a slow, dancing circle. "There's music in your face, Miss Jensen. Music in your soft, gray eyes. In the way your raven hair frames your face. In your creamy, satin skin which right now is blushing pink with embarrassment." His last words were accompanied by a return of the wicked grin.

"I'm not embarrassed!" Laura lifted her chin and glared at him. "I haven't been embarrassed for years...I think it was my first day in medical school," she added absently as he moved them in another circle.

They were almost a perfect match, she realized. She was only a little bit shorter than he was, and his solid muscular body fit easily against her slender one. She had never been much of a dancer, but his lead was sure and strong, and she felt almost graceful as he moved her around the powder room.

"Medical school?" The dance came to a halt. Nick looked as if she had hit him. "Don't tell me you're a doctor. That would be asking far too much!"

"Well, I am." She let her hand continue to rest on his shoulder. There was something intriguing about the way she could feel the play of his muscles underneath his tuxedo jacket. "I'm finishing up a residency in family practice. Why is that asking too much?"

Nick didn't answer. He just sighed deeply, seemingly in pleasure, and pulled her closer. She resisted for a moment, then relaxed. The warmth of him felt so good that it was foolish to pretend she wasn't enjoying herself. He began to hum softly, the tune sounding a little off key.

Okay, Laura told herself as she was swept gently around the room. By not really fighting him, she had agreed to the flirtation. And judging by the response of her body to his, she needed it. She let her hand slip across his shoulder to the back of his neck. His hair was soft, and when she gave the silkiness a gentle caress, he drew her closer until their cheeks rested together and his sideburns tickled her skin pleasantly.

"You know," she commented dreamily after a few moments, "we're both going to feel pretty silly when someone comes in."

"No chance of that." Nick's hand moved up her back, caressing her spine. "I told you I'd made it *our* room Laura. I stuck a sign on the door that says it's out of order. Anybody with a problem will have to go to the restroom downstairs."

Laura experienced a wave of astonishment. He had certainly gone to a great deal of trouble to ensure that he'd be alone with her. Why in the world would he bother? A man as charming and handsome as he was should have women waiting in line for him. "I'm curious," she said in a deliberately light tone. "Do you always take such pains to isolate your women?" This was only a game he was playing, she decided. Something to relieve boredom. Something like that. But he hesitated before he spoke, stopped dancing and pulled back to look at her with a serious expression on his face.

"I swear, Laura, I've never gone to this much trouble before." A small line appeared between his eyebrows. "When I found out you were here by yourself, I just decided I had to...make you my valentine."

As he spoke the corny words, Nick almost winced but he said them anyway. Said them, hoping that the lovely woman he held loosely in his arms would catch the spirit of what he was trying to say and not be put off by the words themselves. He watched emotions shift like soft clouds across her gray eyes and mentally crossed his fingers. He wasn't sure himself what he wanted from her, but he did know that ever since he had first seen her, he had been feeling a rush of inexplainable excitement.

He had almost not come tonight. Linville Springs was a great place for him to live, given his physical problem with humid climates, but socially it lacked the usual pool of single women he was used to fishing in. Actually, until he had seen Laura, he had planned on putting in the token appearance expected of him and then going home alone. But now....

"All I'm asking for is this evening," he added, sensing she was about to say yes. A smile twitched at the edges of her mouth, making the soft, full lips seem to pout, ready for a kiss. Nick restrained himself with difficulty. "If there's another guy," he went on, "he can't be too serious since he left you on your own on Valentine's Day."

She smiled, and he knew he was home free. "I have friends, Nick. But nobody sent me even a card." Her expression told him that she didn't mind the lack of romance in her life. Well, he could change that in a hurry.

"Good," he said aloud. "Then nobody will mind if I do this." He leaned down and placed a soft kiss at the corner of her smile.

She drew back, looking at him with an expression he couldn't read, and for a moment he was afraid that he had make a mistake. That he was moving too fast. That he had let his impulses take control and had blown it. There was something about her that made him feel unsure of himself—make him feel like a clumsy, adolescent lover. Then she smiled, and he felt almost giddy with relief.

"I think," she said, lifting one dark eyebrow, "that you'd have probably done that even if there had been someone who minded. Am I right?"

Nick laughed. "You've read my innermost thoughts," he confessed, realizing that she was indeed correct. It was just possible that even if she had been married, he would have been tempted. There really was something about her...

"Say you'll give me the rest of the evening, Laura," he pleaded. "Maybe you aren't a real angel, but you're the closest thing to heaven I've been near in a long, long time."

Laura hesitated, then nodded. The attraction between them was undeniable, and she had no reason not to agree to spend the evening with him. "Why not." Bob and Ellen wouldn't mind, and it would be much more fun to have a partner when the dancing started, than to have to wait around as she usually did at functions like this for one or another of her old married friends to get permission from his wife to escort her through a number.

And she had to admit that his light kiss had stirred her. His lips had been warm, and she had wished that the caress had been centered on her lips instead of on the side of her mouth. Kissing Nick Hawthorne would be a very pleasant experience, one that she hoped she would have before the evening was over.

Nick beamed, his pleasure in her acceptance obvious. "Great!" He stepped back from her, still holding her right hand. "I wasn't looking forward to spending another Valentine's Day evening all alone."

"No roommate?" Laura questioned, in a deliberately teasing tone. Immediately a suspicious expression darkened Nick's features.

"No," he said abruptly. "You have one?"

"Yes." Laura barely refrained from smiling widely. "His name's George, and he has nice brown eyes, just like you."

Nick frowned. "I thought you said you weren't involved, Laura." He sounded almost hurt.

"Are you jealous?" She was enjoying his discomfiture.

"No!" His frown deepened to a scowl. "It's none of my business how you handle your domestic life. Why should I be jealous?"

"George is a gerbil, Nick." She couldn't stop the laughter.

"A...what?" His confusion seemed to deepen, and she could tell he was struggling to regain his composure. He had been stung by the idea that she was living with a man. Interesting.

"A gerbil's a small brown rodent," she explained, relenting. "Like a hamster or a large mouse. George has been living with me since medical school."

"Oh." Nick let go of her hand and shoved his own back into his pockets. "A pet?"

"That's right. Everyone should have one. It's good for the psyche when you live alone. How about you, Nick? Any pets?"

He shook his head. "Like I said, I live alone. Not even a goldfish." He hesitated, and Laura had the impression that he wanted to say more on the subject. But then he smiled, the old, devilish expression back on his face. "You must think I'm some dull date," he said, taking her arm. "Come on, let's get something to drink and then go dancing."

"Just a minute." Laura retrieved her bag from the countertop and picked up her lipstick. "I'd like to finish my makeup, if you don't mind. Why don't you go take down your bogus out-of-order sign while I..."

"Your face, Laura Jensen, looks just fine as it is," Nick interrupted. His hand cupped her chin, the skin of his palm and fingers feeling warm and slightly rough. He leaned forward and kissed her lightly, this time right on the center of her lips. "That's all the decoration your mouth will ever need," he added softly.

"Very gallant of you," Laura mumbled, trying to sound casual, hoping to cover up the warm dizziness that had swept over her with his kiss. This was crazy! No man, no matter how sexy, should be able to make her faint with one little kiss.

"I mean it." Nick's eyes widened. "You're a natural beauty, Laura. It's almost a crime to cover any part of you with paint." His glance traveled downward, over the silvery silky evening dress she wore. "Or anything else," he added, giving her a slight leer.

Laura gave him a good-natured smile. "Lower your blood pressure, Nick. We just met, and while I may be a doctor, I don't intend to *play* doctor."

His eyebrows lifted. "I could swear that I heard you telling yourself you needed to have a little fun."

Laura felt a sudden suspicion. "Did somebody, one of my friends, put you up to coming on to me like this, Nick?" she asked, knowing she'd be disappointed if it was true, but certain that the events of the past few minutes had all been just a shade too romantic to be coincidence. It could well have been cooked up by her friend and fellow resident, Peter Vance. He and Anne, his wife, had known she was spending Valentine's Day alone. Maybe they had talked to the Pattersons, and between them they had all come up with this wicked, winsome gigolo to tease her into having a good time.

But Nick looked shocked. "You think somebody else set this up?" He touched a hand to his chest, flattening the ruffles of his dress shirt. "Laura, I told you. I saw you from across the room when I first came in and was jolted down to my socks. If there was any setup, I was the one doing it."

"It just occurred to me that you seem too good to be true." She fixed him with a steady gaze. "But I don't really mind, Nick. You're handsome, and you make me feel happy. Whatever the source, I'll just enjoy the Valentine's present."

Nick stared at her, too flabbergasted to speak. She had misread him completely, and he wasn't sure how to get back on track. His attempts to impress her—hell, to court her—were only giving her the wrong ideas. Now she had neatly reduced him to a joke sent by one of her friends. A treat to be enjoyed for the evening and then dismissed. Anger rose in him, and he controlled it with difficulty.

"I'm a man who saw a woman who attracted him intensely," he explained stiffly. "I don't see why you have so much trouble understanding that, Laura."

"Oh, come on." She sounded annoyed. "Don't go waving your ego in my face, Nick. Just because I figured the situation out..."

"You haven't figured anything!" He grabbed her shoulders and kissed her hard, regretting it instantly when her lips softened under his. Her response brought a surge of raw disire that shocked him so much he released her. He stepped back, muttered apologies coming to his lips.

Laura only looked amused. "That's supposed to convince me you're genuine?" she asked, her voice an odd mixture of warmth and cynicism. She lifted her hand and rubbed at her shoulder where he had grabbed it.

Nick felt a rush of anxiety. "I didn't hurt you, did I?" he asked, reaching out to touch her gently. He hadn't applied much pressure by his own standards, but she was so delicately built. Mentally he berated himself as an insensitive clod.

"It didn't hurt," she replied, her voice low and soothing. "But you're very strong, Nick. I don't think I've ever been held that...firmly before."

He felt a surge of relief at her words. Stepping a little further back, he spread his hands. "Look, Laura, I know I've handled all this badly. I should have waited and let Bob Patterson introduce us. But I was so...eager, that I.... Please, just give me a chance to start over."

Laura took a deep breath. He sounded so upset and looked so unhappy that she began to seriously doubt her assessment of him. Was he just a play-boy? A young man on the make? Someone hired to flirt with her? None of the patterns seemed to fit him at the moment. Shadows darkened his face, and the devilish light of mischief was gone from his eyes.

"Quit trying to catalogue me," he said softly, startling her by seeming to read her thoughts. "Don't diagnose me as if I was one of your patients. Don't do that, Laura. I may be crazy about you, but that's all that's wrong with me."

His smile, she decided, was one of the nicest she had ever seen. And remembering how his lips had felt on hers, she found the sight of them curving up in a friendly manner unbelievably exciting. "Well," she said slowly, "you did admit that you aren't behaving by normal social guidelines."

"I, um, I was trying to impress you." He ran a hand through his hair and appeared ill at ease.

"I'm impressed, Mr. Hawthorne." She rubbed her shoulder again, pointedly.

He held out his hands again. "Do I get another chance?"

Laura studied his eyes. How often she had wished she could read minds to help her diagnose disease. Now she needed to diagnose motivation, but all she could discern was a handsome man looking at her hopefully. Could all of his shenanigans simply have been designed to win her romantic favor?

"All right," she said carefully. "Maybe I did mis-judge you, Nick. But maybe you misjudged me too."

His eyebrows lifted in silent question.

"I'm not a member of this club," she told him. "I come to parties like this occasionally because I have good friends who think I'm too serious about life and need to be dragged out for a good time every so often. We all went to undergraduate school together, and they say I've gotten too buried in my work."

"They're probably right." Nick folded his arms across his chest, and Laura noted that the material of his coat sleeves strained against his enlarged biceps. "I did catch you talking to yourself."

"I do it all the time," she answered breezily. "Habit from living alone. Don't you do it?"

Nick didn't reply right away. He lifted one arm and put a finger on his chin. His expression became speculative, and he seemed to be sorting through a series of rapid thoughts. "Laura," he said finally, "do you have any hobbies? Any outlets besides your work? Anything you do just for the hell of it? For fun?"

The question surprised her. It was a subject she had discussed recently with Peter Vance, when he had admitted that his wife had been on his case to take up some form of outside activity that they could share. Listening to Peter had made Laura realize how narrow she had allowed her life to get in the seven years since she had started medical school. Study and work. Work and study. That was all she had. All she had been able to afford. But now that she was nearing the completion of her formal training...now was the time when, for her own mental and physical health, she should be trying to break out of the old grind.

"I guess I don't," she admitted. "My schedule up until recently has always been a backbreaker, and when I'm not working I'm usually too tired to think about recreation."

"Hah!" Nick pointed at her. "You're a workaholic, aren't you. You derive all your satisfaction from your profession. No hobbies. No exercise." His gaze traveled over her again, but this time there was no lasciviousness in it. He was studying her clinically.

"You smoke," he said accusingly. "I smelled it when I first stepped into the room, and there wasn't anyone else in here who might have lit up. I can tell just by looking at you that you don't have a proper diet. You're far too skinny."

"Hold it right there!" Laura raised her hands. "Don't lecture me. I'm a physician, remember."

The gleam of mischief returned to Nick's eyes. "Well, physician," he drawled, "can you heal yourself?"

"I'm not sick."

"But you aren't really healthy either," he countered. Before she could protest he had taken her shoulders and turned her so she was staring into the mirror. "Look at yourself," he challenged, pointing at her face. "You've got dark patches under your eyes, you're too pale, and you're thin enough to pass through a keyhole. What you need..."

Laura pulled away. "You seemed to like the way I looked a few moments ago. I don't need anything except for you to get off this subject."

Her annoyance didn't seem to faze him. His arm went around her waist and she was pulled back into position again, facing the mirror and pressed against his sturdy body. "Look," he commanded, pointing at the two of them. "Honestly look, doctor, and then tell me which of us looks healthier."

Reluctantly Laura obliged. He was right, of course. The honey gold of his tanned skin above the white collar of his dress shirt and black bow tie made him look the picture of vitality. The reddish highlights in his hair gave him an aura of energy and strength. She, by contrast, looked almost anemic with her pale skin and large, dark eyes.

"Speaking professionally now, Laura," Nick murmured, his breath tickling her cheek, "which one of us would you lay odds on getting through the rest of the winter without catching a cold or the flu?"

"You, of course." She pushed at the arm around her waist. "Now let me go."

"Listen to me, Laura." He put his other arm around her and hugged her close. His eyes, reflected in the mirror, were warm. "I saw you," he said, speaking to her reflection, "and I *knew* there was going to be something important between us. I admit I thought it was going to just be sexual at first, but now I'm convinced it will be far more interesting."

Laura made no verbal response but rolled her eyes in exasperation. This was getting crazier by the minute.

"There are too many neat coincidences," Nick went on, releasing her from the hug but moving his hands to her shoulders and continuing to regard her intently in the mirror. "When you stop and think about it, it's as if we were fated to meet."

"Oh, come on!"

"No, really." Nick's eyes gleamed in the soft light. "You're a doctor. I need someone who's a health-care professional. You obviously need someone to help you change your life-style...."

"I didn't ask to have it changed." Laura tried futilely to twist from his gentle but firm grasp.

"Yes, you did." He smiled in an engaging manner. "By coming in here to smoke, you admitted that you're ashamed of the habit. That means you'd like to quit if you could. Given the right motivation you will. And we both know that the kind of workaholic pattern you've gotten into is just the sort of thing that can bring on serious health problems once you start getting on in years."

Laura dropped her gaze from his. What he was saying was absolutely true. Her own father was a classic case. He was undeniably a good father and husband, but he did nothing else but take care of his patients. At all hours of the day and night. And he smoked too. It was rare for Walt Jensen to seat himself without pulling out his favorite old pipe for the lighting ritual. Laura gave a defeated sigh. He had blood-pressure problems and had been warned repeatedly about his heart. Could she be looking forward to the same situation twenty or so years down the line?

"I can make a difference, Laura." Nick's words were whispered seductively, and goose bumps rose on her skin. "Listen to me with an open mind, and I think you'll agree."

"Nick, what are you talking about?" She twisted around to look at his face. There was an excited light in his eyes that the mirror hadn't shown.

"You and me, Laura," he intoned, his voice sounding as if electric sparks were shooting off inside him. "I believe this is the start of something I've dreamed of for years. I think we're destined to become *really* good friends.'' He hesitated, and Laura was certain that he was experiencing a deep, inner excitement that had nothing to do with his earlier, lusty attraction to her.

He started to speak, then seemed to think the better of it. Releasing her shoulders he handed her the evening bag. He started to speak again, then ducked his head slightly, looking for all the world like an overgrown child trying unsuccessfully to keep a secret.

''Let's go sit downstairs, Laura,'' he said finally. ''I've got a proposition for you....'' His words trailed off, and he shook his head. ''No, that's not what I mean. I've just got to explain it all to you. Then you'll understand.'' He gazed at her intently for another moment. ''Who knows,'' he said in a low voice that sounded as if he were talking only to himself. ''Maybe someday, because of this evening, we may even be partners. Who knows?''

CHAPTER TWO

NICK HAWTHORNE WAS CRAZY, Laura decided as she
let him lead her into the club bar. And she was probably equally crazy to agree to stay with him, to hear
about this wonderful thing he was having so darn
much trouble keeping to himself. His manners, now
that they had left the privacy of the ladies' room,
were impeccable, however, and she noted by the
greetings he received from other patrons of the
watering hole that he was obviously well-known and
popular. He must be part of one of the wealthy min-
eral and oil families, she deduced. That would make
sense. He thought he was able to get away with the
kind of bizarre behavior he had displayed earlier because of his family's money and influence. She knew
the type.

He escorted her to a secluded table in the back of
the dimly lighted room and helped her into her chair
with easy gallantry. Almost immediately a perky
blond cocktail waitress appeared, to take their order, and it was obvious by her friendly attitude that
Nick was no stranger.

"You'll have the usual, right, Nick honey?" She
looked at Laura. "And the lady?"

"The lady will have a glass of white wine," Nick
said before Laura could speak.

"The lady will have a Scotch on the rocks," Laura corrected, leaning back in her chair.

"That's not good for you." Nick made an imperious gesture with his hand. "A glass of wine," he repeated to the waitress, who looked confused.

Laura moved forward in her chair and leaned over until her lips were nearly touching Nick's ear. "If she brings me wine, buster," she whispered, "I'll pour the whole glassful in your lap." Then she sat back, waiting for his reaction. He hesitated, eyeing her speculatively, but Laura kept her expression neutral.

He was certainly used to getting his way, she decided. Undoubtedly pampered and spoiled. She put her elbows on the arms of the chair and pressed her fingertips together. Well, he would have to figure out for himself just how far he could push her.

"Go ahead and bring her the poison she ordered," Nick finally said to the waitress. He sighed and sat back, still watching the enigmatic woman across from him. She might look as if she was all softness and submissiveness. She might feel like thistledown in his arms, but she obviously was going to be no pushover for the plans he had for her. He rubbed a finger across his upper lip.

"Would you really have dumped it in my lap?" he asked, trying to keep his tone casual, when what he longed to do was lean over and kiss the cool, haughty look from her face. Then the look softened, and she smiled, making his insides quiver.

"Probably I wouldn't have," she admitted quietly. "I just couldn't let you get away with ordering something for me that I didn't want. I never could abide white wine. It tastes like something unfinished to me. And I like to make my own decisions."

"Have most of them been good ones?" He sat forward, suddenly wanting to know everything about her. She didn't answer immediately but settled herself more deeply into her chair. The silver dress clung to her slender curves, and Nick felt his palms start to sweat. Lord, but she made him feel like a love-starved teenager.

"I haven't had too much trouble with my decisions so far," she said finally, staring off into space. A little line at the corner of her eye told him she was lying. "I've wanted to go into medicine for as long as I can remember. In a few more months I'll be finished with my residency and will go to set up practice with my dad in Advance. It's a small town north of here."

"You have no other options?" Nick asked the question carefully. His own ideas and plans were only half-formed, although he had lived with the dream in the back of his mind for years. The lady sounded less than enthusiastic about setting up shop with daddy, and she might, just might be responsive to overtures from him. If, that is, he could present it with some logic and structure. He smiled casually, trying to cover his excitement.

Laura tilted her head to one side. "Why are you interested?" she asked. "Does it have something to do with what you said about us being partners at some future time?"

His gaze seemed to intensify. "It does."

"Well." Under his scrutiny Laura began to feel like a microbe on a glass slide. "What's your pitch?" His eyes, she realized, had gold and green highlights in their amber depths. Like his hair, they weren't just one color. A complex man. There was probably much more color to his personality than she had seen so far. And he certainly seemed to be simmering inside with some idea, some secret that he was bursting to share with her.

The return of the waitress with their drinks interrupted any further discussion. Nick signed for the drinks, his impatient expression indicating that he could hardly wait until they were alone again. His drink, Laura noted, was clear and effervescent. Probably not even alcoholic, she'd be willing to bet. She lifted her own and took a sip.

"You drink much of that stuff?" His voice had an edge to it. "To relax after work?"

She placed the glass back on the cocktail napkin. "I'm more than aware of the dangers, Nick. I don't have a drinking problem. I don't have the makings of a drinking problem, and I really resent your mother hen attitude." *I ought to take out a cigarette,* she thought wickedly, *and really give him something to complain about.* But her own embarrassment about the unhealthy habit kept her from taunting him with it.

Nick chuckled, unscathed, it seemed, by her snappishness. "I'm sorry," he said. "It's just reflex action with me. I'm such a devoted health nut that I can't help trying to straighten everybody else out, the way I did myself."

"You had a problem? You don't look like a man who's spent one unhealthy moment in his entire life."

He lifted his glass in salute. "I appreciate the compliment, doctor. You are looking at a self-made model, however. I was a fat, pigeon-chested, asthmatic kid."

"You're kidding!" Laura let her gaze roam over him. If ever she had seen a specimen of aggressive health, Nick Hawthorne was it. Thick head of hair, clear eyes and skin, and a body that she knew from personal experience was rock hard. If there was any fat on him now, it had to be located somewhere in the vicinity of his big toe.

"I'm not kidding." He took another swallow of his drink. "I even have documents to prove it. Pictures. Medical records. Anything you need to be convinced that my program works."

"Program?" Laura took another sip of her Scotch. The smoky bitter liquid slid down her throat and settled warmly in her stomach.

Nick leaned forward and rested his forearms on the table, his hands spread out toward her. "It's not exactly a defined system," he said. "It has to be tailored to each individual. Like a custom garment. What would work for me might nearly kill you and vice versa. That's why I need someone like you to try it—for scientific input and advice."

"Nick, what are you talking about?" His eagerness was almost palpable, and Laura felt her curiosity growing. Unless he was putting on a terrific act, Nick Hawthorne was now sincerely interested in her as a professional, not as a member of the opposite sex. She wasn't completely sure she was happy with the change.

"I'm talking about preventive health care, Laura," he said, his eyes alight. "About tailoring life-styles and habits to fit known health needs. To *prevent* predictable breakdowns. To change and replace unhealthy foods, activities…."

"Hold on." She raised a hand. "Are you talking about taking proactive measures with sick people? Because if you are, that's already being—"

"No!" His hand hit the table with a slap. "I'm talking about getting to people *before* they get sick. Designing programs before any therapy is needed. Avoiding expensive posttrauma treatments. Guiding people into better health early in their lives so that trouble doesn't have a chance to start." He paused, but his nostrils were flared, and his eyes seemed to bore right into her.

"My, my," she murmured. "I believe you're a bit of a crusader, Mr. Hawthorne."

"Damn right." He settled back into his chair. "I've got a good idea, Laura. A great concept that could help all kinds of people. I just have to collect all the pieces to make it work."

"And you feel that I could be one of those pieces?"

"You could." His voice was quiet, his gaze intent. "I hope you will."

An uneasy silence settled between them, Laura sensed that he was waiting for her to speak, to ask more questions, to offer her help. But to even agree to hear him out was to compromise her commitment to her simple, structured future.

She had to admit, though, that what he seemed to be saying was very appealing. Her own training had included a hefty dose of the same attitudes that Nick had just expressed. The real problem was that the average individual wouldn't seek such advice as long as she or he had no adverse symptoms.

"Give me a hint." Nick slid his chair around so that he was sitting beside her. "I can see the wheels turning behind those lovely eyes, but I can't figure out if I'm winning or losing." He took her hand in his.

"I didn't realize this was a contest." Laura tried a teasing smile, but he didn't respond. His expression remained serious, expectant, and his hand gripped hers more tightly. Again, she was very conscious of his strength and of the odd roughness of his palm. Her small, narrow hand must feel like a child's to him, she thought.

"I just need for you to listen to me with an open mind, Laura," he said. "I've got a strong, instinctive feeling about you. I really believe you're the right person to help me with my idea." He paused. "My dream."

"Nick." Laura tried to pull her hand away from his. "Don't be so melodramatic. We just met. We don't know very much about each other. I can listen, but I can't make you any kind of promises."

"Yes, you can!" He leaned forward and put his hand on her shoulder. "All you have to do is agree to give me your body for six weeks."

"You're out of your mind!" Laura whispered the words, not wanting to make a scene, but his intensity was beginning to disturb her.

"I don't mean sex, Laura." He sat back, shaking his head. "I find you unbelieveably attractive, but that's not what's important now. I'm talking about my tailoring a health maintenance program for you like the one I designed for myself. If you stick with me for six weeks you'll be convinced that my system works, that you'll feel *much* better if you're in top physical shape and are eating properly."

"I'm in as good shape as I need to be," she countered, picking up her drink. "And I won't stand for anyone telling me what I can and can't ingest." She deliberately took a long pull at the scotch. Nick made an exasperated sound.

"Well, what would you have me do?" she asked, annoyed. "Go vegetarian or some such foolishness?"

"It would undoubtedly be healthier than the questionable diet I'll bet you're on now." Censure showed in his eyes, and his lips were pulled into a tight line. "I can just about tell you what your eating habits are. Lousy coffee and some kind of sweet pastry for breakfast—when you even *eat* breakfast—fast food hamburger for lunch, dinner..." He paused, finger on chin. "Dinner, you might eat at the hospital. That might be the only real nutrition you get all day."

"Give the man first prize." Laura glared at him for a moment, then felt a bubble of laughter in her throat. "Just listen to us," she said, reaching over and touching his hand. "We're fussing like an old married couple."

Nick didn't return her smile, and he pulled his hand away from her touch. "No, we aren't," he said slowly. "I've had firsthand experience, and I can tell you that married couples are far less civilized when they disagree." His expression was almost sullen, and Laura realize that she had inadvertantly touched a sore spot.

"Okay," she said in a light tone, hoping to ease his personal pain. "You were right on the money about my dietary habits. And I would like to quit smoking. But if I do agree to try this...thing of yours, would it involve a lot of time? That's one commodity I'm stingy with. I don't relate at all to some of the doctors around here who take off an entire afternoon or weekend to hit a stupid golf ball around on the grass. That's a waste of time to my way of thinking.'' She glanced around the room, noticing that several of the golf players she had been thinking of were present. They didn't look as if they were in very good shape.

''I didn't have golf in mind for you.'' Nick's voice was low.

''I suppose you play, since you belong to the club.'' Laura sat back in her chair. ''I'm sorry, but I really think it's the most senseless game I've ever seen. I have yet to understand how a grown-up can get so hooked on slugging a tiny white ball around on the grass with an undernourished hockey stick.''

Nick's smile reappeared. ''The grass is called the greens, and it's not a stick, it's a club. And not all of the balls are white. Even some professionals prefer orange or yellow.''

Pleased to have pulled him out of his dark mood, and happy to have him off the uncomfortable subject of her physical habits and fitness, Laura continued to voice her disapproval of golf. Nick didn't actually defend the sport, but he quietly corrected her whenever she paused.

''Hitting the ball is only the visual point of the game,'' he said. ''The real point is the skill you develop and the control you achieve over your own mind and body. It's a mental game as much as a physical one.''

''Then why not play something that takes less time?'' She warmed to her subject. ''You can develop mental skills in less time-consuming and expensive ways. Doesn't the equipment cost an arm and a leg? And membership in a good club like this one is astronomical I understand.''

''None of it's cheap,'' Nick admitted. He took a small sip of his drink, his eyes continuing to watch her with unconcealed amusement.

''Then how do you justify it?'' Laura indicated his elegant clothing as well as the country club as a whole. ''What kind of work do you do that makes you feel you can squander money on what is essentially a waste of time? Especially here in Wyoming, when the months you play have to be limited by the weather.''

''I never said I was a member of this club.'' His eyes danced.

''You must own the place then. Everybody seems to know you.'' Maybe he was the manager, she thought. And if so, how could he justify spending time exclusively in her company?

Nick folded his hands in his lap. ''I don't own it. A club like this is owned by the members and run by a manager operating under an elected board of directors.''

Ah-ha, Laura thought. Was that an admission? ''Well,'' she said, ''if you don't belong, then you either have to be the manager, or a guest like me. Which is it?''

''Neither.'' Nick reached into his jacket and took out a long flat wallet. ''I'm not a member. I'm not the manger or a guest. I'm just one of the hired help like our nubile waitress.'' He took a business card from the wallet and tossed it onto the table in front of Laura. "I'm the club's pro, Laura. I'm a professional golfer."

He watched the kaleidoscope of emotions play over her face. She had insulted him, and she knew it. Gleefully Nick decided to pursue the possibilities. She was a gentle lady, in spite of an occasionally sharp tongue, and it probably would make her feel bad if she believed he had been hurt by her downgrading the sport at which he earned his living. He wasn't, but he could play the part. It was taking advantage of a good soul, he cautioned himself, but he was determined, more determined than even a few minutes ago, to make her a part of his plans.

Trying to look at her objectively, he could see so many reasons why he should court her help as well as the woman herself. She looked the lady, so cool, so elegant. An automatic A-plus salesperson. Once he had her endorsement as a professianal, a physician, he couldn't lose when presenting his system to the public. Nick felt the excitement inside him start to simmer. What had started out as a simple if bizarre come-on had developed into an opportunity to realize his dream. Laura might just be the right catalyst, the key he'd been searching for.

Her slim hand touched his card, and he thought he could see her delicate fingers shaking slightly. A rosy flush stained the skin above the low decolletage of her evening gown, and Nick realized she was probably exerting a great deal of control over her embarrassment. Not a pushover, he reminded himself. This was a lady with a tight rein on her feelings.

"I am sorry, Nick," she finally said. "I've been really rude to you. Please forgive me." Laura picked up his card, noting that it was light gold beige, almost the color of his skin. His name and address were printed in unpretentious, square letters in a dark brown tone that matched his eyes and hair. After his name, were the letters PGA. The entire card indicated professionalism and pride, and she had just thrown verbal rotten tomatoes at his work. She looked up at him.

His features were unreadable. Absolutely nothing gave her a clue as to what he was thinking or feeling. He said nothing, simply stared at her. And Laura couldn't remember ever having felt so chagrined at her own bad manners.

"Nick," she said, touching his hand again. "I was speaking out of ignorance. I tend to get obnoxious when I feel on the defensive. You've struck a number of sensitive chords in me tonight, and I admit I'm feeling prickly. Hey, please say something to me!"

He cleared his throat, and his eyes continued to accuse her. "Well," he said slowly. "I've got to tell you that you have hurt my feelings. It may seem silly to you, but golf is my life. The game has literally made me into the man I am today."

"I said I was sorry," Laura repeated. She increased the pressure of her hand on his and leaned forward to brush a light kiss on his cheek. "What more can I do?"

The hurt glaze over his eyes vanished, and a triumphant gleam replaced the wounded look. "So you're really willing to make amends?" he asked, his hand turning over to capture hers.

Laura tried to pull back. "Within reason, Nick." She had stepped right into a trap, she realized. He had been feigning hurt so that she would offer to make up for it. She would have to watch herself very carefully. This was one tricky man.

"Oh, I intend to be nothing but reasonable, Laura." Nick grinned and leaned back, releasing her hand but regarding her with an air of triumph.

"Then why do I feel like a fly in a spiderweb?" Laura eased back in her own chair. They were, she realized, squared off like two fighters in a ring.

"Well, look." Nick drawled the words. "We did just meet. You don't have any more reason to trust me than I do you. But if you'll just agree to give me six weeks, I promise that you'll find improvements in yourself you never dreamed of. I won't ask you for anything more than the basic six weeks. After that, if you want, you can just kiss me 'bye and go on with your life." His eyes were half-closed, but Laura could sense that he was studying her intently.

"Six weeks," she repeated. It really wasn't much time. And since her schedule wasn't very demanding for a change, she could afford a little time each day to do whatever he suggested. And if he could at least get the nicotine out of her life, it would be worth it. There was also the definite appeal of being in contact with him. Nick might have some opinions she didn't agree with, but she couldn't deny that she liked his company.

"Just six weeks," he echoed. *Trust me*, his amber eyes said.

"Um." Laura tapped her fingertips on the table. "I do have office hours and certain times I'm expected to be at the hospital or at lectures. I can't just up an go whenever you want."

"I'll work around both of our schedules. That's the beauty of my idea. Individually designed for each person."

"Sounds like a lot of work." Laura traced a circle with a drop of moisture on the table.

"I have time right now." Nick gave her a quick smile. "I took the job as pro here for a number of personal reasons. One is that the weather in Wyoming being what it is, I have a fair amount of free time. Time I wouldn't have in a climate with year-round golf."

"I won't tolerate any interference with my job. If I feel that your program's affecting my performance, I'll quit immediately."

"Any effect will only be positive." He sounded extremely confident. "Think of it as an experiment." He pulled his chair close to hers again, and his voice was low and persuasive. "It can only have a positive influence on your practice. As you find things working well for you, you can begin to suggest, maybe even prescribe similar remedies for your patients." He slipped his arm around the back of her chair.

Laura eyed him askance. "What about those strange noises you were making about us being partners?"

Nick shrugged, the motion bringing his arm down onto her shoulders. "After six weeks you may be hooked. You may be a believer like me. Like I said, who knows?"

"You know I have plans for the future. My father is counting on me."

"And you're the only one who could possibly do the job?"

"Well, no," she admitted. "Anyone else in the family-practice program could do it, but..."

"Look." Nick's fingers touched her lips, cutting off her words. "We don't need to discuss this right now. All we have to do is agree that you'll let me design a program for you the way I did for myself. Simple as that. Not a thing more."

"No golf," she stated firmly.

"I wasn't even going to suggest it."

Laura bit her lip.

"Say, yes," Nick entreated.

The dimly lit room seemed to fade away, and all Laura was aware of was his face. Tanned, glowing with health, eyes watching her eagerly, expectantly. *Here goes nothing,* she thought.

"Okay, Nick," she whispered. "I'll do it." She felt no surprise when he leaned forward and, instead of replying, touched her mouth with his own.

His lips were soft and warm against hers. His hand slipped around to the back of her head, caressing her hair, and Laura found herself sinking slowly into a feather bead of sensual sensation. No fireworks, just a sense of peace and safety.

He ended the kiss slowly, coming back for one more tender joining before sitting up and releasing her. "You won't regret this Laura," he said. "It'll get rocky at times, and I can't promise you there won't be any pain. But if you felt what I just felt, you *know* we're on to something good."

Laura blinked. He could have continued the kiss and she would have made no objection. It had been a long time since a man's touch had pleased her so much, had brought her such a sense of being a woman. Nick Hawthorne, she realized, represented something she had kept out of her life for far too long, a desirable man who seemed to find her desirable, as well.

"Now," he said "let's get started." He held out his hand.

"Now?" Laura stared at him. Were they going to just leave the party and get to work immediately? She felt a wash of disappointment. Now that she had agreed to his program, was the romance going to disappear?

"I can't think of a better time to start." Nick took her hand and stood up. His expression was full of mischief.

Laura resisted slightly, but his tug brought her to her feet. "I guess you're the boss," she said. "But I can't imagine anybody leaving a Valentine's party to go work on a health program."

"Who said anything about leaving?" His arm went around her waist. "Right upstairs on the dance floor we can both get a respectable workout while having fun at the same time. Wasn't that one of the things you confessed to yourself that you were missing in your life?"

"Dancing might be fun," she replied, feeling a fresh surge of enthusiasm. So it wasn't to be all business after all. "But a workout?"

Something wicked flashed in his eyes. "I can tell that you've never danced with anyone like me, Dr. Jensen. If you don't think you'll use a few muscles, you've got a surprise in store." He gave her a little hug. "I'll just wear you right out."

"Well, we'll see." Laura rose to the challenge. "I may not look like much, but I've got staying power."

His eyes warmed. "Not nearly as much as you're going to have. I promise you that."

Laura didn't respond. There wasn't much point in trying to get in the last word, and she suspected that her efforts would be futile anyway. Nick Hawthorne seemed to have a way of turning *all* words to his own benefit.

CHAPTER THREE

FOR THE NEXT FEW HOURS, however, he proved himself to be as good as his words. Nick guided her around the dance floor until Laura was laughing and breathless. By midnight her muscles were trembling from the unaccustomed exertions, but she couldn't remember when she had had such a good time with a man. It was pure fun. Nick was master of every kind of dance step, and his athletic, graceful body controlled her and covered her occasional awkwardness. She was, she realized, truly enjoying social dancing for the first time. In the past it had been a bit of a strain, an effort, to match herself to a partner's moves. With Nick, every step felt right.

The only fly in the ointment had occurred during a break when she had excused herself to go to the powder room. Her old friend, Ellen Patterson, caught up with her there. Having noticed that Ellen was throwing her strange looks while she and Nick danced, Laura expected a strong reaction from the small, red-haired woman. But she had not been prepared for Ellen's dismay.

"Laura!" Ellen put a hand on Laura's arm. "What in the world are you doing with Nick Hawthorne?" Her blue eyes were filled with concern.

"Obviously dancing." Laura smiled at her friend. "What's the matter, El? I thought you and Bob brought me here to have a good time."

"Of course we did." Ellen hesitated. "But, Nick Hawthorne...?"

"All right." Laura crossed her arms over her chest. "Tell me what the problem is. I like him, Ellen, and if there's something seriously wrong, I'd appreciate knowing it. Is he married? Engaged? Living with someone?"

"No, no." Ellen made a vague gesture. "Maybe I shouldn't say anything at all. But he did...does have this reputation as a womanizer, Laura. I know, because Bob was on the board when he was being considered for the pro position here."

"Well, he was hired anyway, wasn't he?" Laura took a cigarette from the pack in her evening bag and lit it. Her nerves needed the soothing, even if her body as a whole didn't. "In a city the size of Linville Springs, if he womanized too much, word would spread in a hurry. Have you heard anything about him recently?"

"No," Ellen admitted. "But I did hear one of the sports commentators make a remark about him last spring when he was playing on the tour. Something about a remarkable number of his fans being young, female and attractive."

"So? He's young, male and attractive." Laura turned her head and blew out a lungful of smoke. "If I were a golf fan—which I am *not*—I'd rather watch somebody like Nick play than a lot of the guys I've seen on television, bending over to sink the putt of their lives. Silly game," she added.

Ellen continued to talk, admitting that Nick's amorous reputation was rumor, but cautioning Laura against expecting too much from the man. Laura insisted she wasn't expecting anything but a good time and a ride home. She didn't mention the agreement that she and Nick had sealed with a kiss. The agreement that would put them in close association for the next six weeks. After she finished her cigarette, the two of them returned to the ballroom. Ellen was quickly swept away by her husband, Bob, a burly man who looked more like an oil-field worker than the stockbroker he was. Laura smiled at her friends and waggled her fingers in a goodbye wave, then she returned to the part of the room where she and Nick had been sitting between dances.

Nick was nowhere in sight. That was funny, she thought. He had been quite insistent that he planned to wait right there until she returned. She felt suddenly weary, and her ears were protesting from the fresh onslaught from the band.

His coat and tie were draped over his chair, however, reassuring her that he did plan to return, and Laura sank into her own seat, grateful for a chance to rest. The conversation with Ellen had put her on edge, even though she knew her friend meant well. So what if Nick did have a busy romantic past. That had nothing to do with the two of them in the present, did it? Laura sighed deeply.

Thank goodness she didn't have to go to the hospital until tomorrow afternoon. She'd sleep all morning, as tired as she was. Leaning her head back, she studied the scene in front of her with half-closed eyes. Then the flash of a smile and the wild tossing of auburn-brown hair caught her eye.

It was Nick. He was out in the middle of the pulsating, dancing crowd, obviously having a grand time. She couldn't make out who his partner was, but she felt a sudden pang of jealousy. Don't, she warned herself firmly. She had only known the man a few hours, and he had every right to dance with anyone he wanted. Just because of Ellen's remarks she was getting herself all bent out of shape! She forced herself to relax.

But it was one thing to reason logically and quite another to sit calmly watching him doing his darnedest to charm a new partner. He must be a playboy, she decided reluctantly, never content with only one woman at a time. Probably she should be flattered that he had bothered to take as much time snowing her as he had. As she watched him, she determined to be an objective observer.

He was a sight to make any healthy female heart beat faster. With his coat and tie off, and the top buttons of his dress shirt undone, he had a go-to-hell dissarray that was downright appealing. He was glowing from his exertions, and he tossed strands of hair back from his forehead as he spun in a turn to pull his much shorter dance partner close to him. Cheek to cheek. Laura closed her eyes, remembering how exciting it had been when he had made the same move with her. How his sideburns had teased her skin, how his body had felt, moving so closely against hers, how the musky scent of him had grown more enticing as the minutes had passed. How her own body had tingled where his hands....

"Are you falling asleep on me Laura?" Nick's teasing voice broke into her reverie. Laura opened her eyes.

He stood by her chair, one hand resting on the back of it in a proprietory fashion. By his side stood a tiny, elderly woman whose miniature frame didn't look as if it had the strength to make it all the way across the dance floor, much less follow Nick's skilled moves. Her thin white hand was clasped in his large tanned one.

Laura smiled, feeling senseless relief to find that the woman couldn't possibly be considered a rival for the man's romantic inclinations. "I was just resting," she said, pleased that her tone sounded casual. "Thanks for keeping him busy," she said to the newcomer. "He warned me he'd wear me out, and I'm about ready to admit that he succeeded."

"It was my pleasure, Laura Jensen." The woman's voice was breathy but had an underlying current of strength. She wore a lacy, lilac gown, which at second glance Laura knew must be a designer creation. Professionally styled snow-white hair framed the heart-shaped, wrinkled face, giving further clue that this was an elderly woman of means. "One dance with Nickie Hawthorne is about all I can handle anymore," the little woman went on. "But I still insist that he share a few moments with me on occasions like this one. After all the years we've known each other, I deserve it."

"This is Isabelle Franklin, Laura," Nick said, introducing them. "She and her late husband were close friends of my parents. And *my* friends for as long as I can remember."

"That's because I knew you before you can remember, young man" Isabelle held out her hand to Laura, and the thin fingers trembled slightly. "I used to help when his mother changed his diapers," she

muttered as Laura took the offered hand. It felt
brittle and frail, as if Isabelle was just a shadow of a
person, but Laura sensed there was a strong personality inside the delicate frame.

"I'm delighted to meet you, Mrs. Franklin," she
said, standing up as they clasped hands. The woman
must be the widow of the oil magnate, Philip Franklin, a man who had given generously of his wealth to
a number of causes in the city and state, including the
Family Practice Center where she was completing her
training. If Isabelle had known Nick long enough to
have performed such services for him when he was a
baby, then maybe her own guess that Nick came
from a wealthy background hadn't been off track. If
Nick was rich and still preferred to work for a living, it raised her estimation of his character several
notches in spite of what Ellen had said.

"And I'm *very* pleased to meet you," Isabelle
Franklin told her as she sat in the chair Nick offered. "From what Nick was saying about you, I
wasn't sure you wouldn't come complete with wings,
harp and halo."

"No tales out of school, Isabelle," Nick said in a
warning tone. "I thought our communication was
privileged." He sat down on the chair draped by his
coat, but perched on the edge of it as if he expected
to get up at any moment.

Isabelle's faded blue eyes gleamed with a light as
mischievous as the one Laura had seen in Nick's. "I
never made you any promises, Nickie," she said,
leaning over to pat him on the knee. "Now, be good
and go get us something to drink while Laura and I
talk."

To Laura's surprise, Nick rose immediately to do his friend's bidding. Laura watched until his wide-shouldered figure disappeared into the crowd around the bar. Then she turned to Isabelle, a hundred questions in her mind, wondering if she dared ask them.

"He's a good boy." Isabelle's voice was soft and full of affection and her gaze was focused somewhere beyond Laura. "A good man," she amended, almost as if she were talking to herself. Lines appeared at the sides of her mouth, and her eyes seemed to mist slightly.

Laura sat quietly. She had always felt comfortable with the elderly and had enjoyed those moments when she sensed she was sharing years of memories and feelings with an older patient. It was like dipping into a rich well of human experience and, however briefly, being part of another soul. Isabelle seemed to stare into nothingness for another moment, then her gaze focused back on Laura.

"He can be a stubborn bully," she announced, "and he could make a saint lose her temper. But if you give him a chance, Laura Jensen, you might see the worth of him after a while."

"Mrs. Franklin, I..."

"I know." Isabelle reached over and put her papery hand on Laura's. "You just met him, you just met me, and I have no business telling you how fine my Nickie is." She sighed. "But I don't have all the time in the world, you understand, and I feel I must speak out when I have something on my mind."

Laura smiled. "All right, Mrs. Franklin. You go ahead and talk. I'll listen."

For the next few minutes Laura was treated to a capsule biography of the auburn-haired golf pro. And even when she made allowances for the source of her information, she found herself growing gradually more impressed.

Nick Hawthorne, she learned, had been born to a middle-aged couple who were longtime friends of the Franklins. His parents were dead, both succumbing to the heart diseases that Nick's proposed program could have prevented. Nick himself, she was told, had been spoiled and pampered. He was a rather unattractive boy until around the time of his fourteenth birthday, when he had suddenly taken charge of his life. He had declared independence from his parents' life-style, which included a great deal of leisure and rich living, and had established his own disciplined, sparten regimen.

"His father thought he had gone crazy," Isabelle confided. "But when the doctor informed the Hawthornes that Nickie was making intelligent and informed choices, they let him go his own way."

Laura listened, imagining what it must have been like for people raised to believe that if you could afford it, you should indulge in it, to be confronted by a child who had practically overnight become a health-food and exercise nut. They must have thought the elves had left a changeling in their son's bed, Laura thought, smiling to herself.

"As you can see," Isabelle continued, "he thrived. And when his father suffered a severe reverse of fortune, Nickie left college and started playing golf professionally, supporting his parents as well as himself with his earnings. He did very well, until..." The rest of the story was cut short by Nick's arrival.

The mysterious "until" must have had something to do with marriage, Laura thought, remembering the bitterness he had demonstrated earlier when she had brought up the subject. Looking at him now as he graciously handed Isabelle a small glass of sherry and herself a tall glass of ruby-colored liquid, Laura found it hard to believe that any woman could bring herself to hurt him. He was too likable. She took a hesitant sip of the drink he'd given her.

"It's just cranberry juice," he explained, sitting down, "with no-salt seltzer. You can drink all of that you want."

Laura gave him a wry grin. "Thanks a lot."

Nick leaned back and regarded them both from under half-lowered lids. "Well, Isabelle," he drawled, "did you manage to give Laura my entire history?" His tone was friendly enough, but it seemed to have a wary edge.

"I only told her what she needed to know to keep from tossing you out on your ear when you get too preachy, young man." She turned to Laura. "He tried to indoctrinate me a number of years ago. Fortunately that was when he was still on the regular tour, and I was spared his constant attention and nagging. You, my dear, won't be so lucky."

"What you mean," Nick interjected, "is that the lovely doctor is *very* lucky to have all of my attention. And if she likes what I do, I hope she'll think about joining me in expanding the system into an operation that will reach hundreds, maybe thousands of people."

Silence followed his little speech. Laura stared at him, wondering where he had found the gall to assume that she would even consider changing her plans for him. She could sense that Isabelle Franklin was equally surprised.

"Isn't that just a bit presumptuous of you, Nickie?" she asked, verbalizing Laura's feelings perfectly.

Nick looked at the two women. Decades apart in age, they both had the same qualities he admired. They were both women of strong character and obvious class, women he could be proud to call friends. His gaze lingered on Laura. And maybe more than friend. He smiled and spread out his hands.

"You know me, Isabelle. I don't like to stop the ball once it's rolling. I haven't made any secret of my ideas. Laura knows..."

"Laura knows that she fell for a sucker-play and ended up agreeing to a six-week experiment," Laura informed him. "Nothing more." Her pale, aristocratic face was set in a defensive expression, and he could see storm clouds in her gray eyes.

Nick warned himself to back off. He knew she liked him. The way her body and lips had responded to him without protest had told him that. But he needed to be a little more subtle about winning over her mind. "You're right, of course," he agreed. "It is premature to be talking any farther into the future. Excuse my eagerness, Laura. I don't mean to hold you to anything but our present understanding."

"Good luck," Isabelle said sarcastically to Laura.

But to Nick's relief, Laura laughed. "I suppose I should expect to be hustled a bit," she said, smiling warmly in a way that made his insides tingle. "From what little I do know, I understand that golf can be a hustler's game. I guess I'll just have to keep my wits about me, that's all."

Nick relaxed. As long as she could keep this sense of humor, all would be well. Once again, he mentally pinched himself, not sure that this wasn't all a dream. Laura Jensen seemed too good to be true. Funny, those had been the same words she had used about him.

He sat back and directed the conversation in such a way that Isabelle seemed to be drawing information for herself from Laura. In fact, he was logging every detail for himself. The band had taken a break, and the room was relatively quiet, enabling him to pick up on nuances in her speech.

She had never been married, he discovered, a fact that didn't surprise him. She had a freshness about her that marriage would have eradicated. He thought briefly of his own experience, then shoved the bitter memory aside. That was a long time ago, and it didn't need to haunt his present.

Medicine was her life, but once again Nick detected a note that made him feel her heart wasn't really set on moving back to the small town that had been her home. It struck him that she was going back out of loyalty, and no other offer had provided greater appeal. Optimism stirred in him.

And plans, as well. He would finish the evening as it had begun, a flirtatious date. But tomorrow Laura Jensen was going to find herself dealing with a different man. She seemed to be a serious, matter-of-fact person at heart, and he would be the same. He'd shelve all notions of seducing her, although giving up the idea of romantic involvement pained him. That could wait. The important thing for the near future was to convince this lovely, intelligent woman that his idea was a good one, to show her that the system could work, and then to persuade her to come into his camp. After that, well...

"Watch yourself, Laura," Isabelle was saying. "I can tell that Nickie's been thinking while we've talked. And every sensible human being within a mile should run for cover when that happens."

"How unkind, Isabelle." Nick affected a wounded expression. "I was just worrying about Laura."

"You were scheming, you rascal." Isabelle's tone was affectionate and teasing, but she was hitting close to the truth. Maybe, he decided, he'd made a mistake in introducing the two women.

But Laura seemed to enjoy the banter, and it wasn't until several minutes later that Nick was able to interject the comment that tomorrow was going to be a busy day for them and that he should be getting her home.

"I really hate to leave you, Isabelle, love of my life," he said, standing and stretching. "But Laura needs to get all the sleep she can. Tomorrow's the first day of training for her, and it's liable to be a bit tough."

Laura looked up at him. "I thought tonight counted as a workout. Why's tomorrow going to be so difficult?"

"Because you aren't used to it yet." He held out his hand. "Remember that I never promised it would be easy."

Laura felt only a twinge of apprehension. This evening had been fun, and she was sure she could handle whatever he had planned, only if for the reason that it would keep her in his company. The longer she was with Nick Hawthorne, the more she found she liked him.

They escorted Isabelle back to the couple who had brought her to the club, and Nick promised to keep her informed of Laura's progress. Isabelle said she would be in and out of town, but she was interested and intended to keep track of her Nickie in any case. When they parted, Laura gave the older woman an impulsive kiss on the cheek.

"She likes you," Nick said in a warm tone as he helped Laura on with her coat. "Isabelle is old enough and powerful enough that she doesn't feel obliged to be nice to people she doesn't find interesting and attractive. I think you scored high with her."

"I like her." Laura turned to look directly at him. "I wasn't trying to score. I just enjoyed her company. Just like I enjoy yours."

The directness of her words seemed to have a strong effect. Beneath his tan, Nick appeared to blush. He hesitated, then smiled. "Are you always this honest, Laura?" he asked.

"Unless I have a very good reason not to," she replied, "I tend to say what I think. Doctors sometimes have to be diplomats, but I don't think they should ever deceive. It's not a good way for anyone to live."

Nick didn't reply, but the pressure of his hand on her back told Laura that her words had meant something to him.

The air, when they emerged from the noisy, humid cocoon of the country club, was frigid enough to make her gasp for breath, even though her body was warm enough in the heavy fur coat that had been a graduation present from her parents. Nick, on the other hand, wore only a light topcoat and didn't seem bothered by the weather.

"I like the cold," he commented as he led her to an old station wagon parked under an amber street-light. "No little allergens running around in the air when it's this cold."

Allergens? His comment made Laura wonder, as she settled onto the seat, if Nick was one of the many allergy sufferers who sought relief in the dry, Wyoming climate.

He was. Before they had driven three blocks he was sneezing lustily. "It's just your coat," he said as Laura fumbled in her bag for Kleenex. "I've been off my medication because of the weather, and I guess I'm unusually sensitive," he explained, sneezing again.

Laura handed him a tissue. "Want me to drive?"

"No, I'll be okay." His voice had a determined edge, and when he had taken several deep breaths of air from his opened window, the sneezing fit seemed under control. Laura began to speculate silently on the possible effects of such a highly allergic condition on the life of a professional golfer.

He must suffer miserably, even while under med-ication, she decided. What kind of determination would make a man constantly expose himself to that sort of physical discomfort? Even humiliation. Sup-pose he sneezed during a vital shot?

Nick sniffed and rolled the window back up. "I can hear the wheels going in your head, doctor," he said. "I suppose you're wondering why a chronic allergy patient is in my line of work."

"It did cross my mind." She sat as far away as possible, hoping that her coat wouldn't trigger another attack. "It does seem a bit like asking for trouble, if you don't mind my saying so."

Passing headlights illuminated the ironic smile on his face. "I've tended to do that, Laura," he said. "Sometimes I think I deliberately search out the toughest way to go. A personality defect, I've been told."

"Only if you're bullheaded." Laura remembered her own struggles with personal achievement. "Otherwise I think it's a sign of strength." She was rewarded for the compliment by the sound of his pleasant laughter.

"When I get to feeling down on myself, Doctor Jensen," he said, "remind me to come in for a counseling session with you. You certainly know how to pick a guy up. What time do you have to be at work tomorrow?" he asked abruptly.

"I might not actually have to go in at all," she replied. "My partner, Peter, is on call. Unless he has a problem, I'm free for the day."

"Your partner?" There was an edge in Nick's voice.

"Peter Vance," Laura explained. "We've been friends for years. We're assigned to the obstetrical rotation together. That's my house, third on the right from this corner."

Nick made the turn, adjusting the station wagon skillfully as the back wheels slid slightly on the icy street. He pulled into the driveway and parked, shoving the gearshift up and stamping on the emergency brake. "We need to talk for just a minute, Laura," he said, staring out of the front window, not looking at her.

"Talk away." Laura tucked her hands into her coat pockets. "I'm all ears." The evening certainly wasn't turning out the way she had imagined.

Then Nick turned and looked at her, and although the streetlight was dim, she had no trouble reading the intensity of his expression. Nick Hawthorne was feeling some strong emotions.

"If we hadn't agreed to work together on your health program," he said in a low tone, "I guarantee you, Laura Jensen, fur coat or not, I'd be trying my darnedest to seduce you right now." He took a deep breath. "You know, you're just about the most beautiful woman I've ever had the privilege of driving home in my car."

Laura looked at him steadily. "I think I'm flattered."

He reached out and touched her cheek. "Maybe you *are* the most beautiful."

She took her hands from her pockets as he slid across the seat toward her. His kiss brushed her lips, and she put her arms around his shoulders, letting the fingers of one hand touch the soft hair at the back of his neck.

"You're a sweet man, Nick," she murmured. "You make me feel very good."

He made a sound deep in his chest, and his arms went around her, pulling her close. "There's a whole lot more I'd like to be making you feel," he whispered. Then his lips covered hers.

This time, Laura found herself plunged into a whirlpool of sensation. It was as if all the small, tender touches he had given her that night had only been tinder for the fire that suddenly blazed within her. Yielding to her feelings, she melted against him and opened her lips for a deeper kiss.

For a moment, Nick seemed infected by her passion. He clasped her tightly and eased her back, taking her mouth with his tongue in a rushing thrust. His breathing came in quick rasps, a counterpoint to hers in the otherwise silent winter night.

Then he seemed to gain control. He eased his embrace, and his tongue became a silky, teasing thing that tasted and caressed her mouth, stroking and tantalizing until Laura felt her desire build to an unbearable level. She wound her hands in his hair and twisted her body more closely to his. Now it was only her breathing that sounded raspy in the night. She was both fulfilled and horribly frustrated, and her body cried out for all of him, hating the heavy winter clothing that kept them apart. Had it been summer, she thought, Nick Hawthorne would have been in serious danger of being seduced by her.

Gasping, they finally broke the kiss. Nick laughed softly, but she thought she could hear the catch of passion in his voice when he spoke.

"I was going to suggest you take a warm bath before going to bed," he said. Then he sneezed. "But I think we both could use a cold shower instead."

Laura eased away, digging out another tissue from her bag. "I forgot about the coat. Allergic reactions don't do much for the libido, do they."

Nick blew his nose. "That wouldn't have stopped me, if I thought the time was right, Laura." The firmness of his tone convinced her that he meant what he said.

He opened his door and got out, coming around to assist her. Laura took her keys from her purse as they made their way up the driveway to her front door. Her legs still felt shaky from the bout of passion.

"I'll be by in the morning," he said after he opened her door. He put his hands on her shoulders and gazed into her eyes. "We've really got something exciting ahead of us, Laura. You can feel it, too, can't you?" She nodded, unable to frame a reply and unsure whether he was referring to their agreement or to the kiss.

"I won't kiss you again," he continued in a tender tone, "because I know that if I do, I won't stay outside where I belong tonight." He grinned. "Besides, we'd probably stick together like wet fingers on an ice-cube tray in this temperature."

The comic image made Laura laugh. "I'd hate to have to explain that to people I know in the emergency room"

Nick's smile widened, and he blew her a kiss. "Sleep well, Laura. I'll see you in the morning." Then he was gone, moving through the arctic night and slipping into his old car. Laura stepped into her house and closed the door against the chill. But she watched out her window until the last traces of the cloud of his exhaust had dissipated into the night air.

CHAPTER FOUR

THE RAUCOUS RINGING of her telephone woke Laura. Groping for the receiver, she rubbed her eyes until they opened, then she muttered her name into the receiver and rolled onto her back, trying to decide which universe she had awakened to.

"Yo, Jensen!" It was the cheerful voice of her resident partner, Peter Vance. "How's my good buddy this fine Sunday morning?"

"Is it morning?" Laura stared up at the silver slats of sunlight that made the ceiling look like the barred cell of a prison. The only time the sun came into her bedroom that way was early, *very* early in the day. "It's still dawn, Peter. You remember, the time of day when people who aren't on call get to sleep?"

"Hey, were you still in the sack?" He sounded contrite, but she could detect a wheedling tone underlying the apology. "I'm sorry, Laura. I just assumed you had one of your quiet Saturday nights and got to bed early. Listen, I'll call back later. Don't worry about it, the kids won't mind."

"Wait a minute." Laura sat up, glancing at the electric clock on her bedside table. "What about your kids?" The time was six-thirty.

"Well..." Peter's voice was hesitant. Laura had a flashing image of her friend's face—a lean, angular face that could break into a feature-fracturing smile.

Peter Vance was a wonderfully caring physician, but he was also a natural-born con man.

"Well, Anne and the kids..." His voice trailed off. Anne and the kids, Laura thought. The three most important people in Peter's life had lately been taking a poor second place to his practice.

"What's the problem, Pete?" she asked.

"The boys are in a play at Sunday school," he explained. "I forgot all about it until Anne...reminded me this morning. Things are pretty quiet, and I was wondering...?"

"I'll cover for you, of course." Laura flipped off the blankets, noting without surprise that she was dressed only in her underwear. After Nick's abrupt departure she had found herself too drained to do anything but remove her outer garments and fall into her bed. "I don't have any special plans for today, and I don't mind at all. Just drop the beeper over in case I have to go out for milk or something."

Peter's yelp of gratitude nearly burst her eardrum. Laura hung up while he was still listing all the holidays he would cover for her.

She stood and stretched. Nick had made no promises, and she could hardly turn down a friend with family problems. She gave a sudden squeal of agony as her overtaxed muscles protested. Oh, boy, she thought. Nick's dancing must have worked her harder than she had realized. A hot shower, some aspirin...maybe she could face the day after that.

She struggled into the bathroom, grimacing with annoyance as she practically had to back into the shower stall to close the door. Two and a half years crammed into cramped living quarters in this small house had been just about all she could stand. In

July she was planning to buy her own house instead of renting a cracker box. She could find a place back in her home town with as much room as she desired. She cranked on the taps, then listened to the old pipes groan and complain before granting her a meager trickle of hot water from the corroded shower head.

She managed a thorough shower, however, turning her body under the thin stream and finding a new sore muscle with each swipe of her washcloth. She must really be in bad shape. If Nick had been sincere, maybe an exercise program that fit her life-style was just the thing she needed.

The thought of him and the sensations his warm lips and muscular body had created in her suddenly filled her mind. His appeal was strong, and she hoped he didn't intend to limit their relationship to health and exercise. In spite of Ellen's warning, she found that she was intrigued by the romantic possibilities. Her heart started to beat faster, and she felt an unaccustomed excitement sweep through her. Quickly she turned the water from hot to cool.

After she had finished, she stepped into the tiny bathroom and wrapped herself with a towel, pausing in front of the steamed-up mirror to comb her hair back from her face. It had been a long time since she had had any romance in her life. Since Nick had made the first move, she was certain that the second would soon follow. In a way, his reputation took some of the pressure off her. If he tended to have short-term relationships, that would keep him from interfering with her plans to leave in July. Probably she could chalk his "health plan" and a talk of a long-term professional relationship down to a sophisticated seduction. She slipped out of the towel and into a bathrobe, then reached for the hair dryer.

The sound of the doorbell made her turn in surprise. Peter was early. Maybe he had decided to drop the beeper off before he went home to get his family. Drawing the robe more snugly around her, she hurried to answer the door. When she opened it, she barely suppressed a gasp of astonishment. Instead of Peter's lanky form, the tall, sturdy figure of Nick Hawthorne greeted her.

"Good morning," he said, smiling at her. "You're tougher than I thought. I fully expected to have to scrape you out of bed." The air around him seemed to shimmer with sparkles of frost, sunlight and his own superenergy. He looked as fresh and alert as if he'd slept for a full eight hours.

"What in the world are you doing here so early, Nick?" she asked, taking in his sweatpants and dark green ski jacket. He had running shoes on his feet and no hat on his head. "You didn't jog in this weather?" she added, stepping to one side and letting him into the living room.

"Slow jogging," he said. "Helps me control my breathing. I didn't even break a sweat."

"You're out of your mind." Laura closed the door. "You could freeze your lungs in this kind of weather."

"I said I went slowly." He grinned and set the two bags he was carrying down on the coffee table. One was a soft sports bag and the other a briefcase. "I wanted to get over here before you had a chance to eat breakfast, and I needed the exercise. Now, take off that robe. I need your measurements." He reached into the briefcase and took out a tape measure, paper and a pencil.

"Measurements?" Laura pulled the robe tighter.

"Relax." His smile was slow and amused, and the light she had seen the night before was dancing in his eyes. "You don't have to be naked. Go put on something thin. I just need to know where I'm starting from with you—with your body. Otherwise I won't be able to chart where I want to go with it. Understand?"

Laura sat down on the sofa. "No," she said.

Nick shrugged out of his jacket. "This is going to be just like any scientific experiment, Laura. I need before and afters to make my point. If people don't know what you were like before, how can they appreciate how much..."

She hugged her arms across her chest. "Why don't you just use yourself? You said that you'd changed dramatically."

He reached into his briefcase and took out a folder, which he tossed onto the coffee table. "Too dramatically," he said in a casual tone. "Take a look and you'll see what I mean."

The folder contained about a dozen snapshots of an adolescent boy whom she had no difficulty identifying as a younger Nick. His hair was redder and longer, but the fire in his eyes was unmistakable. The body, however, was that of another person, soft and obviously overindulged. It wasn't Nick.

"You have come a long way," she commented, looking up at him with renewed respect. As a physician she would have predicted that that boy would grow up to be an adult with an increasing list of physical problems, probably ending in death or crippling illness in his mid to late forties. The natural process had been reversed by a determined will.

He stood in her living room, shrinking the small area with his physical presence. His T-shirt did nothing to conceal his well-muscled torso and arms. Wide shoulders, broad chest, flat stomach and trim hips. No, not what she would have predicted from the pictures.

"You're saying that your own example is extreme?" she asked. When he nodded, she tapped one picture with a fingernail. "Maybe an extreme is what you need to convince people. I know I'm impressed."

For a moment he grinned, then his expression grew serious. "I don't have the right kind of documentation for myself," he said, sitting on the sofa beside her. "I can say this is me." He waved at the snapshots. "Maybe even get someone with a good eye like yours to believe me. But I want to accomplish wonders, not miracles. I need a less dramatic case; a doctor, a busy professional, who can integrate my program into her life. That would impress the kind of people I want to reach."

Laura listened as he went on to explain that although his final plans were yet unformed, he had visions of a nationwide network of locations where people could go to receive the kind of training he planned to give her. He would need a large amount of financial backing, he pointed out, and for that he required attractive, convincing promotional material. As he spoke, he made it clear that he had great admiration for her, but Laura could find no trace of the romance of the night before. Intrigued by his words, she couldn't help but feel a pang of disappointment at this distancing.

"See," he said, taking a chart from his briefcase. "Here's where I need to log in how you're built now." He pointed to a stylized drawing of a female figure. "And here is where we'll see how you've improved in six weeks." He pointed to a second figure.

Laura took the chart. It was similar to ones she used in her own work, except that the emphasis was on the exterior of the body instead of the interior. There were places for chemical analysis, but the thrust was the development of the outer body and the way improvement there would affect the person as a whole. Regarding it as a scientist would, she had to admit she was impressed. Regarding the situation as a woman, she felt only confusion.

What did Nick Hawthorne want from her? She glanced sideways at him. He smelled clean, of soap only, without the spicy scent of men's cologne that had surrounded him last night. He had shaved, but here and there she could see the gleam of a reddish whisker he had missed. In a hurry? To be with her?

"Let's see," he muttered, making some notations on the chart. "You're female. Unmarried. How old are you?"

"Twenty-nine." Laura leaned forward to watch him write.

"Weight?" Nick scratched one eyebrow with the eraser of his pencil.

Laura shrugged. "About one-fifteen, I think. It's been a while since I weighed myself."

He penciled the numbers lightly on the chart. "We'll weigh you in on a scale. If you top one-twenty after a full meal, I'll be surprised. Height?"

"Five-nine."

"Do you do *any* kind of regular exercise?" He shifted his weight and scratched his eyebrow again.

"No," she admitted.

"Any regular sex?" His voice was neutral, his gaze directed at the chart.

Laura sat up straight. "That's none of your..."

A rapid knocking at the front door cut off her indignant words. "Laura," a familiar male voice called out. "Let us in. The boys and me are freezing our buns off!"

Nick glared at the door and then at Laura. "Just who the hell is that?" he asked, his brown eyes almost black.

"It's just Peter." Laura rose. "Remember, I told you about him last night." The sudden show of temper surprised her. Why should he care who came knocking at her door?

"And the boys?" His tone was metallic.

Laura narrowed her eyes. "Oh, yes, Mr. Hawthorne, I run a regular little love nest over here every Sunday morning. Like to meet my clientele?" She strode to the front door and opened it to reveal Peter and his two blond sons, all three dressed in identical blue suits. The boys chorused hellos and ran into the house, heading for the jar of cookies Laura kept for them in the kitchen. They ignored Nick.

Peter didn't. He stepped into the house, shut the door and glared at the man on the sofa. "Who's this?" he demanded, a decidedly "big brother disapproves" look on his lean face. The boys came noisily back into the living room but stopped and were silent when they saw the hostile tableau.

"Funny." Laura pushed back a stray lock of hair and looked from one man to the other. "Nick was just asking the same thing about you and the boys,'' she said to Peter.

Nick rose slowly to his feet. He had made a big mistake, he realized. Drawn the wrong conclusion entirely. This man was her friend, nothing more. He stepped around the coffee table and offered his hand.

"I'm Nick Hawthorne," he said, managing what he hoped was a cordial smile. "You're Peter. Laura told me about you last night."

"Peter Vance." The man returned his handshake, and Nick managed to resist showing how much stronger he was than the lean physician. Vance was tall, but without much of a build. Not unlike Laura. Probably, Nick guessed, he expended all his excess energy in nervous concern over his patients.

"Now that you've shaken hands," Laura said, "you can each retire to your respective corners." Her voice dripped sarcasm, and Nick forced himself to laugh.

"Hey, the guy's your friend," he said, gesturing openly. "I'm sorry I misunderstood...."

"Are you and daddy going to fight?" One of the small tow-headed boys spoke up, directing his question to Nick. All three adults started to deny any hostility, but the second boy's clear voice cut through the chorus of words.

"Mom and dad got into a fight early this morning," the youngster said, his round little face puckering into a cross between a self-conscious grin and a scowl.

"It wasn't a fight, Davy," Vance said abruptly. "It was a discussion." He reached out and drew the child close to his side. "Sometimes grown-ups sound like they're mad when they're only trying to solve an important problem."

Nick listened cynically to the conversation. And sometimes, he reminded himself, grown-ups sounded mad. because they hated each other's guts. Maybe someone ought to tell the kid that, before he had to find out on his own the hard way.

But as he listened to the thin doctor talking to Laura, he had to admit that the guy did sound as if he had more of a problem and less of a disaster than Nick's own experience. The wife wanted more, not less of him. That couldn't be so bad, could it?

"It's the old 'I don't see enough of you and the family needs you,'" Vance was saying, including Nick in the conversation. "Chronic problem with a doctor and his family. Sorry I took my temper out on you, Hawthorne, Laura's my good buddy, and I guess I felt I needed to act a little bit like a big brother."

"It's okay," Nick replied, noting that Laura seemed pleased with his efforts to be civil. "It's good to know she's got such a good friend. Now, when you hear her complaining about me for the next few weeks, you can take it with a grain of salt, since you've met me and know I'm not some kind of sadistic ogre." Vance's eyebrows lifted questioningly.

"Nick's putting me on an exercise program," Laura said hastily. "He's got this terrific idea for a proactive health system." She hesitated. "I'm his first guinea pig."

"Second," Nick corrected, seeing the light of alarm in the blond man's eyes. "I was the first."

"You're a big man, mister," the boy, Davy, interrupted. "How'd you get muscles like that?"

Nick chuckled and bent down until he was at eye level with the child. "When I was a little older than you, son, I started doing some special exercises. And I quit eating cake and cookies. Stuff like that."

Davy made a face. "Doesn't sound like much fun." His brother chorused agreement.

"Come on, kids." Vance's voice sounded tight. "We've got to go. Sunday school will be starting..."

"Are you and Doctor Laura going to get married?" Davy asked Nick. Nick felt himself flushing under the kid's steady gaze.

"We're friends, Davy," he replied. "People can stay friends without getting married, you know." He straightened and glanced at Laura. She was smiling slightly, obviously amused at the boy's direct question.

"My mom says..."

"We'd really better get going." Vance put his hand on his son's shoulder, cutting off what was probably going to be a significant social statement. "Thanks for covering for me, pal," he said to Laura. "I owe you one." He nodded at Nick. "Nice to meet you, Hawthorne."

Nick stood back, watching while Laura shepherded the three out the door and waved to a blond woman who waited in the car out front. Vance's wife had a nice smile and a pretty, open face. Nick had trouble picturing her in a bad temper, but then, he reminded himself, looks could be deceiving.

There was Laura, for instance. Last night she had radiated elegance and sophistication. This morning, clad in an old pink bathrobe, her raven hair damp and combed straight back and her pale skin clean of any makeup, she looked like a natural beauty, a woman...

...A woman he could pull laughing into his arms and tumble back into bed for...

No! He reminded himself of the decision he had made overnight to keep the relationship on a professional level in spite of his strong attraction to her. There were enough beautiful women around, but few of them had the training or potential for helping him with his program that Laura did. To blow it on a romantic affair that might not last would be disastrous. So it was hands off. He turned around and shuffled the papers on the coffee table.

"Nick." Laura's hand settled on his back. "I don't want to be nosy, but would you mind telling me why you carry such a chip on your shoulder about marriage? I could actually see the bitterness in your eyes when Peter was talking...."

"I was married," he blurted harshly. "It didn't work out." He made a cutting motion with his hand. "Let's get on with the business of measuring you. I haven't had breakfast yet, either."

Laura gazed at him for a moment longer. Behind those eyes lingered some ghost that she wanted badly to see, to help him exorcize. He was almost defensive, which made her doubly curious. It was like watching a patient try to hide or deny a serious symptom of illness. Nick was hiding a vulnerable part of himself.

But she simply smiled and turned toward the bedroom. He would have to tell her when he was ready. Forcing a diagnosis or a confidence were equally foolish, she knew. "I have an old bathing suit somewhere," she said. "Will that do?"

"For now." The tone of his voice told her that his humor had returned. "But we'll have to get you some proper exercise clothes, including a leotard and tights."

Laura paused in the doorway. "Just how much is all of this going to cost me, Nick? I don't have a lot of money to throw around."

Nick looked up at the ceiling. "Let's see. Clothes, if we stay on the conservative side and don't get into designer stuff, may ultimately run you around a hundred or so. Health club membership—"

"Health club! Now wait a minute, Nick!"

His smile was wicked. "You want to run outdoors with me in weather like this? I'm used to it, but you'd freeze your chassis off."

"But I can't afford..."

"*I* can afford it." His smile was reassuring. "Don't worry. As long as I can use the results for legitimate marketing purposes I can even deduct what I spend getting you into shape from my taxes. How's that for a deal?"

Laura could think of no further objections. They had an agreement, after all. She excused herself and shut the bedroom door behind her.

Nick watched the door close with a growing sense of satisfaction. Laura was being pleasant and tractable, and as long as he was able to keep his mind on business and off other things, he was certain to be successful. It was too bad the golf season would start shortly after they were through with the experiment, but somehow he would manage to juggle his job and the tournaments he had agreed to play with this chance to get his dream off the launching pad. Laura could be persuaded to stay with him, he was sure of

that. She was too good to waste her life in some
backwater cow town, maybe married to some leather-
faced rancher.

He shook himself free of the unpleasant fantasy
and looked around the living room for the first time.
With Laura in the room, he hadn't bothered to study
anything else.

It was a cracker box of a house. Hardly as big as
his apartment. The sofa appeared to have been sub-
jected to at least two generations of heavy sitters, and
the coffee table had deep scratch marks in the surface of the wood, although both pieces of furniture
seemed clean. The only other furniture in the room
was a small, cluttered desk and a cheap-looking
bookcase filled with thick, hardback textbooks.
Probably, Nick surmised, her father had made a decent but unspectacular living, enough to send his
daughter to medical school but not enough to get her
used to a life of luxury. It would be nice to give her a
taste of the rich life, he mused, remembering places
he had been as a child and the home in which his
family had lived before his father's financial
problems.

Dream on, he scolded himself. What little he had
managed to accumulate had disappeared five years
ago down the well of mismanaged matrimony. Even
if his long-term plans were successful, and even if
Laura Jensen continued one way or another to be a
part of them, it would be a long time before he could
be considered a rich man again. Of course, there
were worse problems.

He picked up the sports bag which was loaded with
health foods, and hefted the straps onto his shoulder. He ambled over to the closed bedroom door and

gave it a rap with his knuckle. "How're you doing in there?" he called, grinning to himself when Laura's musical voice told him to keep his shirt on, she'd be out in a minute.

Not only was she beautiful, he thought as he wandered into the kitchen, but she was personable. Brains as well as beauty. How could he have gotten so lucky? He glanced around the kitchen.

How the hell did she work in this place, he wondered, tossing the bag onto the postage-stamp-sized table. Hardly any cupboard space. No room at all to lay out a decent feed. He opened the refrigerator.

Milk, orange juice, some lunch meat. The pickings were pretty slim. He started to fill the fridge with the food he had brought. Tomorrow he would have to make a run by the natural food store. The larder would have to be stocked, and that would mean having to get a key from her.

And *that* would mean having to get her to trust him. Nick sighed and shut the refrigerator door. When it came right down to it, his entire dream depended on getting Laura and people like her to trust him, to believe that what he was suggesting could improve the lives of people all over the country, to accept that good health could be as powerful against sickness as any drug.

He straightened, then stopped when a rustling noise caught his attention. Curious, he searched for the source of the sound.

It was coming from the top of the refrigerator, from a small, wire-topped glass cage. Bright brown eyes stared down at him, and a delicate, handlike paw rested against the glass wall. Nick picked up the cage and set it on the table.

"You must be George," he said softly, not wanting to startle the little beast. George looked up at him through the wire mesh, his long, silvery whiskers twitching and his tiny paws tucked against his creamy fur chest.

He did look like some kind of mouse, but much more appealing. Nick pulled out a chair and sat down. He tilted his head to get a better view. George followed his every move. When Nick put his finger on the glass, the small brown animal came over to it, trying to sniff it through the glass.

"Hey, George." Nick took a packet from the pile of dried food in his bag. "You want a sunflower, fella?" Gingerly he lifted the lid of the cage and dropped in a sunflower seed. George ran over to it and grabbed it in his paws. He ate the offering with obvious relish. Nick grinned.

"Want another one?" He put his hand in the cage, a seed held between his thumb and forefinger. George hopped over with no hesitation and took the seed. Then he sniffed Nick's hand, the long, delicate whiskers at the sides of his nose tickling Nick's skin. Delighted, Nick began to laugh.

"For a man who doesn't even own a goldfish, you're acting as if you've been handling gerbils all your life."

Nick looked up, then had to quickly look back at George to catch his breath.

Laura stood framed in the doorway, looking as if she had just stepped out of an advertisement for a tropical paradise. Her hair was still slicked back, emphasizing the fine bones of her face, and she had put on only enough makeup to make her large gray eyes even more luminous and her full lips more luscious. Her arms and long legs were bare, her skin creamy satin. The rest of her body was covered by a turquoise-blue bathing suit. Sort of covered.

Nick took a deep breath and swallowed hard. George came over to the side of the cage and stood up, resting one paw on the glass and looking for all the world as if he were asking where the hell the rest of the sunflowers were. Nick tossed him a handful and put the lid back on the cage.

"Is something the matter?" Laura came into the room, concern written on her face. Nick forced himself to laugh easily.

"Nothing's the matter," he said, putting the cage back in its place on the refrigerator. George was greedily chowing down, his little body hunched over his treasure trove of seeds. "Nothing's wrong at all," Nick continued, turning back to her with a smile. "I'm pleased to report that I don't seem to be allergic to George." His hands felt suddenly damp, and he resisted the urge to rub them on the seat of his sweatpants.

Laura's smile was a flash of sunshine. "I'm glad to hear that. I'd really hate to have to choose between the two of you." She glanced at the food on the table. "What's all this stuff?"

"Sustenance." Nick picked up a packet of raisins and tossed it into the air, catching it backhand as it fell. "This 'stuff' is going to be what you eat and drink for the next six weeks."

"Oh, Nick." She held out her hands in a pleading gesture. "I'll go crazy if I only get to eat things that are good for me! No hamburgers? No Danishes?"

"Only the kind I fix." He took her hands in his and discovered they were soft and cold. He realized she must be freezing in that skimpy swimsuit. "Don't worry, Laura," he added with as much warmth in his voice as he dared. "You won't starve under my system. In fact, at first you might think I'm feeding you too...." He let the words trail off as his nostrils were suddenly assailed by the sharp mustiness of cigarette smoke. Making an angry noise in his throat, he pulled her close, trapping her slender wrists with one hand and taking a handful of her hair with the other. He sniffed the hair suspiciously.

"You sneaked a smoke, didn't you," he said, hurt that she would have committed such an act almost in his presence. "If I hadn't been so damn fascinated with George, I would have wondered why it took you so long to change from nothing into nothing."

"So, what if I did?" She glared at him, "They're my lungs, after all."

Nick held her for another moment, then released her. Fleetingly he considered the possibility of grabbing her and shaking some sense into her. But physical force was not his way. Using logic would be equally futile. She knew better, yet she persisted. Only an emotional appeal might have a chance of succeeding.

"Let's sit down and talk," he said quietly. "Go get on your robe so you don't freeze. I think we need to get a few ground rules straight before we go any further."

CHAPTER FIVE

LAURA OBEYED HIS ORDERS without protest. She knew she was blushing with guilt. Smoking the cigarette had been stupid, and she should have known that Nick would sniff it out. But it had helped ease the attack of nerves she had experienced at the prospect of appearing before him clad in only a few square inches of lycra and a smile.

He hadn't seemed particularly impressed, however, she thought as she slipped on her bathrobe, except for a second when he had looked up from George. Just for a moment she had seen an expression on his face that had made her tingle inside. But he had become distant so quickly that she wondered whether she had imagined it.

She walked back into the kitchen, fully expecting a stern lecture. Instead, Nick was sitting slumped in a chair, a mournful expression on his face.

"I have to have your full cooperation," he said, after she had seated herself. His hair was disordered and looked as if he'd been raking his fingers through the auburn strands in frustration while she had been out of the room. Laura felt her resistance melt.

"I'll really try, Nick," she promised, reaching over to touch his hand with hers. "I was just nervous, and I still don't believe that one little cigarette now and then—"

"But it isn't now and then, is it, Laura." He sat up and grabbed her hand in both of his, a passion not born of desire gleaming in his eyes. "It's whenever you get uptight, or think you need to relax. And that means you're using it as an emotional crutch. Suppose you do go back home and set up practice now, tomorrow. Don't you know you'll be under tremendous pressure there? Local kid. Think you'll get the respect your father has right off the bat?" He shook his head. "Take it from me, no way. You'll have to earn your own reputation, and that will mean pressure. What's an occasional indulgence now might become a real killer of a habit."

Laura jerked her hand free. He was right, but it stung her to hear it. "All right, Mr. Righteous," she snapped, "I suppose you have some magic formula that will give me the backbone I need to kick it. Well, lay it out for me!"

Nick relaxed in his chair. "No formula, no magic tricks. Just a lot of concern on my part, and some patience and suffering on yours." His eyes softened their hard expression. "But nothing I can do will work until you decide that you're willing to let it hurt for a while. Once you've made that choice, I can help you."

His gentleness brought the sting of tears to her eyes. "Nick, why are you doing this?" she asked. "Yesterday we didn't even know each other, and now, here you are, offering to change my life. Why?"

He looked away. "I've told you"

"But…?"

Nick stood abruptly. "Where do you keep your pans?" he asked. "While we're talking, I might as well get started on breakfast or it'll be lunchtime before we eat. Where are the pans?''

"In the oven. There's not enough room in the cupboard, and I rarely use the oven." She got up and showed him. But as he followed her, Laura found his nearness irresistible. She turned into his arms and put her hands on his shoulders. To her surprise, he stepped back.

"On second thought," he said, his voice sounding strained, "maybe I'd better get the measuring over and let you get dressed." He lightly grasped her wrists and eased her hands off his shoulders. "That squawk box Vance brought you might go off any time. I wouldn't want to keep a lady waiting to have a baby just because I hadn't given you a chance to get some clothes on." He smiled, but it was a shallow effort, and Laura could detect tension at the corners of his eyes.

She said nothing, but turned and walked into the living room. Flinging the bathrobe onto the sofa, she lifted her chin and gazed challengingly at Nick. "All right measure me."

Nick swallowed hard. Except for the fashionable bathing suit, she could have been some kind of primitive love goddess, standing there in the pale sunlight that streamed through the front window. Her dark hair gleamed, the few silver strands only adding to the halo effect. Like an aura of sensuality, he thought.

He forced himself to walk past her and retrieve the tape and the chart. If he could only accomplish this task without breaking down and taking her into his arms, he would know he could handle the rest of the experiment. He had resisted when she had turned to him in the kitchen. He could do it again.

But his fingers shook as he wrapped the tape around various parts of her body. His fingers shook and his heart pounded, and his breath seemed thick and gummy in his chest and throat. He coughed several times, trying to cover his agitation.

"Frog in your throat?" Laura asked innocently as she raised her arms so that he could measure her chest. Her gray eyes were watching him. He could feel them like a soft caress, but he didn't look at them.

"Just a little congestion," he muttered. "Maybe I should cut out the outdoor jogging until it gets warmer."

"Probably a smart idea." Her voice was noncommital, neutral.

Damn it, Nick thought. She knew the effect she was having on him. Why bother hiding it. But he had to play the game through. Once in bed he could kiss objectivity goodbye. There would be no way for him to maintain the kind of control he knew he had to have to get her to complete the program properly.

So he gritted his teeth and choked down his passions, reminding himself that this woman was far more valuable to him as a friend and colleague than as a lover.

Laura submitted patiently to the measuring and prodding. Nick's touch was deft and sure, and even though she thought she could detect a slight tremor in his fingertips, he showed no signs of desire and no particular appreciation for her body. It was as if she were a neutral object, separate completely from the person who had seemed to arouse his interest and desire the night before. Confused and a little hurt, she decided to cover her feelings.

When Nick coughed again, she calmly suggested that if his cough didn't clear up by the next day, he should consider seeing a doctor. "At least go over to the public-health clinic and get your throat swabbed," she said. "There's a lot of strep going around this time of year. Have you been in contact with school-age children lately?"

Nick was on his knees, taking final measurements of her calves. "The last kids I was close to were the Vance boys," he said. "You know, the little guys with the curiousity about our arrangement."

Laura started to laugh. It hadn't occurred to her that the openness of Peter's children might have needled Nick. "They do tend to speak their minds," she said. "Anne and Peter raised them to be very honest."

Nick made a grumbling noise and rose to his feet. "That can be carried too far," he muttered. "If I had kids..." He turned and started marking up the chart.

Laura slipped her bathrobe back on. "If you had kids, what?" She sat on the sofa and tucked one bare leg up underneath her. "How would you want to raise kids, Nick?"

"Kids should be raised in a stable, nurturing environment," he said, not looking at her. "I won't ever have them because I can't provide that. Now, go get dressed. I'll get breakfast." He put the chart down on the coffee table and left the room.

Well, Laura thought, listening to the sound of pans being banged around in the kitchen. *I seem to have hit another nerve.* Nick liked the subject of children no more than he did the one of marriage. Interesting.

And he did still feel desire for her. She would be willing to bet on it. She rose and went into the bedroom.

His pretended indifference puzzled her. Since her undergraduate years when she had been forced to make a heart-rendingly painful choice between love and her career education, Laura had been satisfied to date but to keep deep emotions at arm's length. She posed no threat to Nick Hawthorne's free-wheeling life-style, so it seemed strange that he hadn't followed through on the moves he had started last night.

She took off the swimsuit and put on fresh under-clothes before pulling on a blue turtleneck and gray slacks. Although the weather was still frigid, the sun was out, and by late afternoon the air would have warmed considerably. No point in overdressing.

A quick brushing set her hair into its usual page-boy style, but she hesitated to pull it back with an elastic. Maybe if she had to go in to the hospital, she would. Otherwise, it wouldn't hurt to let it hang free.

A warm, yeasty fruity aroma began to tease her nostrils, and her stomach reminded her that it had been many hours since her last meal. She headed with anticipation toward the door.

Nick had proved himself as adept in the kitchen as he had been on the dance floor. Laura gratefully settled in to devour a large breakfast of grapefruit, granola and whole-wheat toast dabbed with a spread, which Nick declared to be salt free and low in cholesterol. She could have all she wanted, he declared, since she didn't need to lose weight but gain several pounds.

"Of course," he added when she reached for another piece of toast, "I intend for that weight to show up as muscle, not fat." When Laura asked him how, she was rewarded with a wicked grin.

SEVERAL HOURS LATER Laura was wishing she had never set eyes on Nick Hawthorne. Wishing that his show of wounded feelings hadn't lured her into making *any* kind of agreement with him. Surely he had to be the most insensitive, sadistic male she had ever had the misfortune to know.

"Just a little more, Laura." His voice was gentle and encouraging, but it didn't make her feel any better. In fact, it acted as an irritant. Laura groaned and pushed upward on the silver metal bar with all her strength. The bar refused to budge.

They were alone together in the weight-training room of the health club to which Nick belonged, and to which he declared Laura would belong come Monday. Using his apparently considerable influence in the sports community in Linville Springs, he had persuaded the owner of a sporting goods store to allow Laura and himself a private shopping spree to outfit her. Then he had let the two of them into the health club several hours before the regular Sunday opening. Finding the light switches with an ease that spoke of great familiarity with the place, Nick had directed her toward the women's locker room.

"Go change into this," he said, indicating the pink sweat suit he had bought for her. "We're going to really work out for the next hour." His expression indicated that he was looking forward to the experience. Naively Laura decided that she was, too. Her attitude quickly changed.

Working out, she discovered, meant doing things that hurt. Doing things deliberately that made her hurt, made her sweat, made her use muscles she had never learned about in anatomy class. For the first time in her life she was being forced to do physical instead of intellectual labor.

"You'll get it." Nick put a finger under the bar. "Just concentrate and push." His voice radiated encouragement. To her amazement, Laura felt the bar begin to move upward. Then she realized that the power was coming from Nick's finger. With his *finger* he was able to lift more weight than she could with both her arms. She shoved angrily, and the bar slid all the way to the top of the machine.

"Way to go!" Nick sounded jubilant. "Okay, now do that again."

"I can't." Laura sat up and glared at him. "My arms are shaking so badly I don't think I can lift a feather, much less this torture device."

But her negative attitude didn't seem to have any effect. Nick merely smiled and patted her shoulder. "You're doing just fine. In a few weeks you'll be doing three full sets and laughing at how easy it is."

"No, I won't."

"Do it again now." His smile remained, but his tone hardened. "It isn't going to kill you."

Laura sighed and eased herself back down on the bench. "It will," she muttered rebelliously. But when she shoved, the bar slid smoothly upward. In her astonishment, she let it drop with a jarring clang.

"See?" Nick's expression was one of pride. "I knew you had it in you."

Under his coaching she "had it in her" for another five presses, then her tormentor relented. He helped her into another section of the weight machine and taught her to do leg work, which she found considerably easier.

"Women tend to have more of their strength in the legs," he explained. "But after a while you'll find that your upper body will toughen up, and you'll be amazed at how strong you'll become without really building muscle the way a man would."

"That's a relief to know," she said sarcastically, eyeing his chest and shoulders. "If I ended up with a build like yours, my patients would run screaming away from me."

"You get the female version," Nick said, his tone more affectionate than it had been all day. "It's strong, but a lot prettier to look at." He handed her a towel. "I want you to go next door into the exercise room now. Do those stretches I taught you. It'll help prevent some of the soreness."

"Where are you going to be?" She had expected him to hover over her and make sure she performed all of her appointed tasks. That he would trust her to do them on her own surprised her.

"I need to do some lifting myself," he explained. "And if I mother hen you over every detail of your program, you're not going to integrate it into yourself. Remember, you are doing this for you. Not for me."

"I tend to get confused at times. Sorry."

Nick smiled at her caustic comment. She had done better than he had expected, but he wanted to be careful with his praise. Several years of teaching golf had convinced him that it was as wrong for a coach to overdo the compliments as it was to pile on the criticism. Encouragement was what she needed. Encouragement, an occasional prod in the backside and a chance to discover for herself the pleasures of physical well-being.

He shooed her out and drew a sigh of relief when her slender form disappeared from his sight. He could be in her presence only so long before his resolve to keep the relationship out of the bedroom fell by the wayside and he gathered her up in his arms, bad temper, sweat and all. Bringing her to the club when no one else was around had been designed to spare her embarrassment during her first attempts to lift weights, but it wasn't doing anything for his libido except to stoke the fires. The thought that the two of them could be swirling around naked together in the Jacuzzi made him break out in goose bumps.

No sex, he warned himself again. A romance would only undermine his authority. He stood and adjusted the weights. He would have to work the need out of his system. Pushing iron was a whole lot more sensible than pushing against sheets. Nick eased himself down on the bench and started shoving the bar up.

In the exercise room next door, Laura dutifully went through the series of contortions that Nick had shown her. Each move pulled her already stressed muscles, and she watched herself grimace in the mirror attached to the wall. She made a face at herself and turned her back to complete the exercises.

There had been a mirror in the weight room too, she remembered. Although she had enjoyed watching two Nicks move around during the few breaks he had given her, she couldn't imagine for the life of her why anyone would want to watch while they exercised. If her own experience was typical, the sight wasn't a pretty one.

Grumpily, she finished her exercises, wondering once again why she was putting herself through this ordeal. If Nick had wanted a physician to endorse his system, why couldn't he have picked someone who liked doing this stuff, for goodness sake? Why her? And why in the world was she being so cooperative?

Deep down she knew why. In spite of everything, she did like him. Liked the way the sunlight seemed to dance in his eyes. Liked the way he looked at her, and the way it made her feel when he did. Liked watching the graceful way he moved, using his muscular body more like a dancer than a sportsman. Cutting the truth to the bone, she had to admit that she just plain liked Nick.

Frowning at the self-confession, she picked up her towel and straightened her clothes, preparing to go back into the next room. It was all right to like him, she conceded to herself, but she'd have to be careful not to let it go beyond that. First, there was his reputation to consider. And then there was the certain knowledge that she didn't want to find herself pinched into the crack between loved ones and work the way her friend Peter was. No, if she was going to fall in love, it had better be with someone back in Advance. Someone who would fit into her professional plans without any fuss. It was already obvious that Nick Hawthorne would not do that.

He had a truckload of his own ambitions. Anyone who hitched to him would hitch to his star, as well. Maybe that was what had gone sour with his marriage. Whatever the reason, his bitterness was a safety factor for her. She had no objection to romance, but any kind of long-term relationship would be out of the question.

But when she stepped into the weight room, the sight of Nick—stripped of his T-shirt, his magnificently molded torso gleaming with perspiration as he lifted a heavy barbell—jolted her down to her toes. He was facing the mirror but didn't look as if he was seeing himself. His eyes were unfocused, staring off into some interior universe of his own, and his face was devoid of any expression. He lifted the bar slowly up and down, and Laura marveled at the strength that it must have taken him to do it with such control.

She moved quietly, not wanting to disturb his concentration, and sat down on the floor by the door to watch.

He raised the bar, and the muscles in his arms, chest and back strained. He lowered it, and she could see cords standing out on his neck. A trickle of perspiration ran down the side of his face. Such feats must involve a triumph of mind over body, she decided. The effort must have been tremendous, but Nick worked on until she had counted ten repetitions. On the last one his composure finally broke, and he grimaced as he lowered the bar to the floor. Then he saw her, and his expression changed to one of pleasure.

"Done already?" he asked, picking up his discarded T-shirt and ambling over to her. "You must have zipped right through those stretches." He sat down next to her and used her towel to wipe his face and chest.

"I zipped right through them like a tortoise," she replied. "I hurt all over already. I can hardly wait until tomorrow. Tell me, how much weight were you hauling just now?''

Nick shook his head. ''Trade secret. And don't ever fall into the mistake of comparing what you can lift with what another person does. You're competing only against yourself. Nobody else.''

''I didn't know I was competing at all.'' Laura closed her eyes. Heat from his body was radiating over her like a sensual blanket, and only the memory of the way he had avoided her embrace earlier kept her from touching him again.

Nick didn't reply to her comment, and they both rested in silence for a few minutes. Laura listened to the sound of Nick's breathing and tried to imagine what her reaction would be if he touched her now as he had the night before. *I'd probably ignite like a piece of dry tinder*, she decided. Physical activity increased rather than decreased desire, it seemed. Or maybe it was just the company she was keeping.

''I'll bet you a milk shake I can tell what you're thinking.'' Nick's voice cut through her thoughts, startling her. She opened her eyes and looked at him, feeling a little guilty about the notions she'd been entertaining.

''I didn't think milk shakes were allowed to health-food devotees,'' she snapped, trying to cover her embarrassment with a display of temper. ''All that fat and carbohydrate and artificial...''

''Nothing about the shake I'm offering is artificial.'' Nick heaved himself to his feet. ''Come on. We'll go over to my place for lunch. Then I want you to lay out your schedule for me so I can sit down and figure out a program for you. You aren't always as

free to come and go as you are today, are you?'' He
held out a hand to her.

''No.'' Laura took it and allowed him to pull her
to her feet. ''This is my day off, even though... Oh,
I ought to take the beeper back to Peter as long as
we're going to be out. Church will be over in a little
while, and he might not want to hang around the
house just to be near the telephone.''

Nick laughed. ''Tell me, what did doctors do before the invention of paging devices?''

''Hung around the house so they were near the
telephone,'' she replied.

They showered in their respective locker rooms
and met in the entrance lobby just as the manager
was opening the club for regular hours. Nick intro-
duced Laura as his protégée to the slightly balding
but well-built man. She felt a bit uneasy at the label,
but accepted it for the time being without protest.

Later, when they were in his station wagon on the
way to the Vances' house, she remembered his challenge. ''You never did tell me what you thought I was
thinking,'' she said, glancing over at him. Even in the
washed-out silvery February sunlight, his skin
glowed bronze. The man would never look unhealthy, she decided. No matter how sick he was,
that inner dynamo would keep him looking great. A
real diagnositic challenge.

''You were thinking about sex,'' he said, a smile
curving his lips. ''Or at least about something sensual. Exercise has a way of doing that to many people, I've discovered.''

''Oh, really?'' Laura kept her tone disdainful. ''Is
that how you've managed to make your many con-
quests? Get them all sweaty and then make your

move?'' She was angry and hurt that he would talk about the subject when he had so pointedly avoided sharing any affectionate intimacies with her all day. It was difficult to equate this friendly but distant man with the almost overbearing suitor who had led her dancing less than twenty-four hours before.

His smile faded to a frown. ''I'm not apologizing for my past, Laura. But don't judge me by what you've heard. I thought we were getting to be friends.''

''We are!'' She reached over and touched his hand, surprised when he let go of the steering wheel and returned the touch with a quick squeeze.

''I was trying to tease you,'' he explained. ''I thought friends could do that without getting all cat-clawed.''

''I'm sorry.'' She returned his squeeze. ''Remember, I get rude when I feel backed into a corner.''

''Apology accepted.''

They talked companionably the rest of the way to the Vances' home. Nick pulled into the driveway of the ranch-style house, and Laura told him to wait. ''I'll be right back,'' she said. Then she jumped from the car and ran up the walk with an agility that surprised her, considering the physical energy she had already expended.

Anne Vance answered the door. The blond woman was effusive in her thanks to Laura, and she refused to take a ''no'' answer to an invitation to lunch.

''Bring your friend in with you,'' she said insistently. ''From what Peter and the boys told me, he sounds like the kind who will do justice to a home-cooked Sunday dinner.''

Laura hedged, aware that Nick's peculiarities might cause everyone embarrassment, but finally she agreed to at least ask him. Anne Vance was a small person, but she had a persuasive way about her.

Nick accepted without hesitation. After apologizing for his casual garb—he had changed into a clean pair of jeans and a green polo shirt which were in his locker at the club—he settled in with the ease of an old friend of the family.

During the meal, Laura noted that he tactfully passed up gravy and biscuits and helped himself to an unusually large helping of salad. Otherwise he was a perfect guest, complimentary to the cook and entertaining to everyone without actually dominating the conversation. Even Peter, who had obviously not been too pleased by Nick's inclusion, seemed to warm to the man, laughing heartily at some of his golf stories.

At the end of the dinner, Peter asked Nick to explain exactly what he was doing with his program for Laura. The boys left for the playroom, and Laura got up to help Anne with the dishes. Better to leave Nick on his own, she decided. She was so unsure at this stage about what was going on that she would probably only muddy the waters.

"Pete has his older-brother coat on today," Anne commented dryly when they were alone in the kitchen. "Your new friend is absolutely charming, but be forewarned. I'm afraid that we're both feeling a little concerned for you."

"What *is* this?" Laura turned on Anne. "First Ellen Patterson. Now you two. Nick and I are just friends, for goodness sake. And if we get to be anything else, remember, I am a grown woman, perfectly capable—''

Anne's light laugh interrupted her. ''Don't get all ruffled, Laura. I guess 'concerned' is too strong a word. Pete and I just hope you find someone to settle down with. Nick Hawthorne doesn't strike either of us as the type you need.''

''Who says I need a type at all?''

''Come on, Laura.'' Anne smiled. ''You know what I mean. You plan to spend your life in Advance.'' Her tone became slightly wistful, and Laura remembered that her friend had grown up in a Nebraska town similar to her own hometown. ''Can you see an urbane man like that being satisfied with a social life revolving around the PTA and church? Does Advance even have a golf course?''

''There's a putt-putt,'' Laura retorted, and both women started to laugh. Laura repeated that no one needed to worry. She liked Nick and hoped he could help her quit smoking, but that was the extent of their relationship.

She and Anne chatted amiably while they finished cleaning up. Although they had only met when Laura and Peter had started the family-practice training, their similar backgrounds had enabled them to become friends quickly. In fact, Laura realized as she mused over the concern Anne and Peter had for her, they were more than friends. They had in a very real sense become the sister and brother she had never had.

''Mom!'' Tommy Vance's young voice interrupted Laura's thoughts. He and his brother came into the kitchen. ''We can hear daddy and Mr. Nick all the way down in the playroom through the heat registers. It sounds like they're having some kind of fight." The boys' faces reflected fear spiced with a slight eagerness.

"You two have fighting on the brain." Anne ruffled both tow-haired heads. "You've been watching too much television."

"Your father and Mr. Hawthorne are probably just having a discussion," Laura interjected. The dishwasher was running noisily, and it was possible that the discussion was vehement enough to be heard through air ducts but not loud enough to disturb them in the kitchen. "Why don't we go see what's going on?" she suggested.

The four of them went into the living room. When they didn't find the two men there, they proceeded to the den, guided by the sounds of raised voices. There was indeed an exchange of ideas going on, and it didn't sound entirely peaceful.

Nick looked up from the article in the medical journal that Vance had literally thrown at him minutes before. The sight of Laura filled him with a sense of relief. He had told Vance about his ideas, only to be battered in return by a barrage of medical jargon. He needed Laura for rebuttal against thick heads like her friends. He knew the concept but not the scientific details that would convince health professionals.

"Are you two solving some major world problem?" The tone of Anne's voice held a heavy dose of castigation. "The boys thought you were fighting."

Peter's shoulders hunched slightly. "We were talking about Hawthorne's crazy scheme, and I—"

"It's a dream, Pete," Laura said interrupting. "And it's a good one. Nick just needs time and some concrete proof."

Her vehemence surprised Nick. To have her come to his defence on her own pleased him immensely. He stood up and took her hand. "Peter's got some good points," he conceded, not wanting to let the hostile sparks that had flashed between himself and the other man affect the women and the boys. Anne relaxed visibly, but although he held Laura's hand, he couldn't sense her reaction to his peace gesture. Then he turned to look challengingly at Vance.

"But next time we get into it," he said, "I intend to come armed with facts and figures you can't blow holes in. I admit I've got a long way to go, Vance. But I'm going to get there, believe me." Laura's hand stirred in his, a movement that seemed to indicate encouragement, and Nick suddenly felt absolutely certain that the words he had spoken were prophetic.

Laura listened to his little speech with mixed emotions. That he had come over and taken her hand had pleased her, and she sensed he had been relieved of some tension when she had entered the room. But his brave words bothered her. Beyond the six weeks training, there was nothing she could do to help him. Or was there? Suddenly she wanted a cigarette very badly.

CHAPTER SIX

LAURA DID NOT, HOWEVER, give in to the temptation, then or in the days to follow. Something of
Nick's sense of purpose had rubbed off on her, and
in spite of the agonies it cost her, more mental than
physical, she stayed true to his every dictate. She had
made an agreement—an agreement sealed by a kiss
her lips could still remember.

And memory was all they had to go on. Nick
seemed as determined to keep her body at arm's
length as he was to fine-tune it into shape. Once in a
while, usually when they were both relaxed and tired
toward the end of the day and had managed to get
together in spite of their busy schedules, she could
see him slip and she caught a glimpse of something
deeper and warmer than friendship. But if he did feel
more for her than he had declared, he covered it well.
One thing Nick Hawthorne had by the bushel was
willpower. She saw that in everything he did. And
everything he didn't do.

Once she had presented him with her work schedule, it had only taken him a few hours to put together a program for her. At first glance she had been
sure it would be too rigorous, involving as it did
weight training three times a week and aerobic dance
three other days. Sundays, she got off. But as the
weeks progressed, the exercise became part of her

everyday life, hardly more of a bother than making rounds with a senior physician who liked to hear himself talk too much. And once in a while, when she knew Nick would be joining her, she actually looked forward to the workouts.

He had distanced himself from her exercise schedule, leaving her weight workouts to the professional coach at the health club, a cheerful hulk of a man who presided over the room with the barbells and silver metal torture devices. The man had a great deal of admiration for Nick and lost no opportunity to talk to Laura about the golfer's prowess as an all-round athlete when Nick wasn't there. Her aerobics instructor was a hyperactive teenager who didn't say anything to Laura about Nick but who lost no opportunity to be close to him when he showed up. Nick was pleasant to her, nothing more, and Laura managed to resist the urge to behave childishly and declare to the young woman that Nick was hers. After all, he wasn't.

But as time passed, she began to wish more and more that he was, or at least that something of the magic of the first night would return. Since he made most of her meals for her, there was a domestic nature to their relationship that could have slipped easily into romance, but it was quite clear to her that Nick wasn't interested. If the atmosphere between them started to warm up, he invariably came up with some kind of excuse to leave, and Laura was reluctant to push anything.

To add to her emotional confusion about Nick, she found that only Anne Vance accepted her relationship with him with little criticism. Her other friends made no bones about disapproving.

Ellen Patterson called a few times every week, pretending that she phoned for a friendly chat, but it became obvious to Laura that Ellen was keeping tabs on a man she considered to be a country-club Lothario. It took a great deal of willpower for Laura not to make it clear to her old friend that all the lust in the relationship seemed to be on Laura's part. Nick had been more than a perfect gentleman, much to her disappointment.

Peter also turned out to be very thickheaded about undertstanding what she and Nick were doing.

"I don't like the man," he announced one afternoon while he and Laura were comparing notes on patients. "He's using you, and you're letting him do it with both of your eyes wide open."

"Just how do you figure?" Laura made a note on a chart. "His program's working. I look better. I feel better. And I haven't had a cigarette in weeks."

"There's something weird about him, Laura." Peter looked genuinely troubled. "Something strange about the way he treats you."

Laura took a sip of her herb tea. The rich aroma of coffee that filled the small room serving as the residents' lounge was making her taste buds tingle, but she knew that after the clean flavor of the tea, the coffee would hit her tongue like battery acid if she tried a cup. Nick had managed to wean her off caffeine as well as nicotine. "He's using me in an experiment," she said patiently. "I'm his guinea pig. I suppose that gives him a right to treat me a little differently."

"Differently!" Peter rubbed a hand over his lean face. New lines had been etched in his forehead since the first of the year, and Laura suspected they had been put there because of his disagreement with Anne about where they should finally settle down to live.

"Differently," Peter repeated. "He treats you...I don't know. Like some damn toy. Like he owns you or something."

Laura stared at her friend. He had been given the opportunity to observe her and Nick together, since they had been dinner guests of the Vances several times since the first Sunday lunch. Perhaps Peter had insight that Laura lacked because of her emotional confusion.

"Just suppose," Peter continued, warming to his subject, "that he really is on to something. Suppose he's going to go places with his ideas. What do you get out of it besides a pat on the head?"

"Maybe that's all I want." Laura picked up a chart and pointedly directed the conversation into less personal matters. But she did ponder Peter's comments.

Because of his casual treatment of her, by the end of the third week Laura had come not to expect anything from Nick. When he announced that the following Monday he would be leaving town to participate in a tournament, she took the news without turning a hair. He had obligations, and she understood that. Her own plans were loose, and she decided she would take advantage of the time to herself to make a short pilgrimage home.

She called home on Friday and let her parents know she was on her way. For a change the roads were clear of snow, and she made the two and a half hour trip with no difficulty. The look of delight on her parents' faces when she stepped from the car reminded her of the changes that had taken place in her life since the last time she had been home at Christmas.

"Honey, you're positvely glowing!" Her mother, Adele, a small round woman from whom Laura had inherited her dark hair and gray eyes, embraced her warmly.

"You look wonderful," her father agreed. Walt Jensen's lined face lit with pleasure as he looked at her. "This is the healthiest I've seen you, sugar, since you left for college."

Both parents eagerly questioned the reason for the changes, and Laura teased them for a while. She relaxed into the atmosphere of family and friendship that home brought to her, letting the sense of safety and security she had known since childhhood wrap itself around her. Of course coming back to Advance was the only sensible future for her. Nick was an interlude, not even a romantic interlude. This was her reality.

"Well, I met this man," she said finally in response to her parents' questions. Then she began to explain Nick and his experiment. Although she tried to make it clear that she was going to be involved with him for only a few more weeks, she could see that what she was saying had stirred the parental waters.

"He's just a friend," she repeated firmly. "Not a boyfriend. I'm helping him do a study of the benefits of diet and exercise on a healthy person. I ran a battery of tests on myself when we first started. At the end of the six weeks, I'll run another set. The changes and the record he's keeping of my diet and exercise will be demonstrable proof that Nick's on to a good idea.''

"Of course he is.'' Walt Jensen frowned. "Any physician worth his salt would agree with him. But how does he plan on selling it to the public?''

Laura shrugged. "That's not my problem. I only signed on for six weeks.'' And, she thought, he'd given no indication that he wanted her for any longer. She folded her arms across her chest. Even up here in the warmth of familiarity of her home, the idea of a time when Nick would no longer be in her life made her feel sad.

Her mother came over and gave her another hug. "Well, whoever he is, I'm grateful to him. You look one hundred percent better, honey. Now you go and and visit with your father. I'm going to make dinner.'' She gave Laura a kiss and left the living room.

Laura bit her lip as she watched her father move over to his desk and take out his pipe. Nick would have a fit if he saw someone with Walt's health problems smoking. Some of his crusader's spirt must have rubbed off on her.

"If this man's such a good friend, why didn't you bring him along.'' Her father's tone was neutral, but Laura recognized parental probing when she heard it. "We do have the guest room he could use, remember?''

"Oh, he went out of town Monday.'' Laura brushed her hand across the familiar soft corduroy sofa cushions. "And he won't be back until early next week.'' In fact, when she thought about it, Nick hadn't named a return date. Maybe, she thought glumly, it just depends on how much fun he's having.

"What does he do for a living?" Walt's blue eyes squinted as he lit his pipe, making him look decidedly suspicious.

"He's the golf pro at the country club." Laura suddenly felt that she needed to apologize for Nick's profession, but she kept the words unspoken. Her admiration for him as a person had overridden her prejudices against his occupation. Her father would have to draw his own conclusions.

"Golf pro." Walt seemed to be digesting the information. A cloud of pale gray smoke issued from his lips. "And he's an expert on health care?"

"No, of course not." Laura gestured with one hand. "That's where my knowledge comes in. He wants me to..." She let the words trail off, realizing that she really didn't know what Nick wanted from her. She had been going on his oblique remarks the night they had first met, but nothing had been said since then to make her think he wanted more.

"Wants you to what?" Walt's tone was quiet, but Laura heard an edge in it.

"I don't know." She shrugged again. It was so difficult to explain Nick. So difficult to explain the feelings she had about him. "We haven't made any plans. I suppose that if he has a pitch, I'll hear it when the six weeks are over."

"I just bet you will." Her father's voice was almost a whisper. Then, to Laura's relief, he changed the subject, easing back in his chair and filling her in on the local gossip and telling her every medical event that had happened in Advance since Christmas.

The rest of the weekend passed peacefully, although Laura could detect an undercurrent of tension and curiosity. Her parents seemed to feel that

Nick meant more to her than she had admitted to them, and she had to admit to herself that she did miss him. It wasn't a painful ache, but every so often she would feel that if she turned around, he would be standing behind her, a wide and roguish grin on his handsome face. On Saturday afternoon, when the weather showed a promise of spring, she went horseback riding by herself and thought about him.

Nick was a mystery, a puzzle, one that intrigued her deeply. She let her horse pick its own path through the winter-stunted sage and pale gold buffalo grass and allowed her mind to travel free.

Suppose the way he had been treating her was a sham. What if he actually felt the same way he had the night they had met, when it was quite clear that romance was uppermost in his mind? Laura took a deep breath, savoring the familiar smell of horse and prairie earth. What if Nick Hawthorne not only liked her, but was falling in love with her?

Laura laughed, and her horse flipped his ears back at the sound. She soothed him with a pat on the neck.

"I'm not laughing at you, Buster," she told him. "I'm laughing at myself. Sometimes I get the craziest ideas."

But what was love anyway, she mused as they ambled between a stand of huge rocks dumped there millenia ago by a glacier with indigestion. Since Nick had been married, he must have felt love for the woman at some time, even if he felt only bitterness now. And if he was falling in love with her, Laura couldn't understand why he didn't tell her.

Maybe he didn't tell her because what he felt was nothing beyond a superficial physical attraction.

That would make more sense, given the way he had behaved. She watched her shadow move along the face of one of the gray monoliths. Nick had come on to her, then realized he was more interested in her help with his system than he was in her body, and therefore he had kept his distance. Actually, that was rather thoughtful of him.

So why did she find his attitude so deeply disturbing. Remembering the emotion she had felt during the last kiss they had shared in his station wagon told her the truth. She might not be in love, but what she felt for Nick was strong. Stronger than she could ever remember. And if he didn't share that feeling, at least to some extent, she'd be crazy to act on it. His rebuff would be devastating to her.

"So," she said aloud, giving Buster another pat as she spoke, "I get to be emotionally mixed up, and Mr. Hawthorne...Mr. Hawthorne has a guinea pig who wants to be...his lover." She whispered the last words, wondering at her own bluntness.

Well, it was time she was honest with herself, even if she couldn't be with Nick. He had managed to win her affections...by the way he had behaved when they had met, by the gentleness and consideration he had shown her while she struggled to adapt to his system, by the diplomacy and thoughtfulness he had shown to her friends, in spite of Peter's less than charitable assessment of him. Little things, like the relationship he had established with her pet, tugged at her heart strings. Could the man be so friendly, so kind, and still not care? It didn't make any sense.

None of it made any sense. Laura gave the reins a gentle pull and headed Buster back home. The horse showed an unusual reluctance to turn around, and she sensed he had enjoyed the outing. Her friend, Myra, who was keeping Buster for her, probably didn't have time to take long, leisurely walks. Juggling a family and a job as the local Justice of the Peace undoubtedly left Myra little time.

"Well, Buster," Laura murmured, "I'll be back in July, and I promise to take you on one of our strolls at least once a week, no matter how busy I get. It's good for both of us." She tried to conjure up enthusiasm at the thought but found that she felt strangely empty instead.

Sunday morning she went with her parents to the community church, hoping to revive her anticipation for the time when she would once again be part of the community of Advance. But she found that she was impatient with the leisurely pace of living that her old friends and neighbors seemed to follow. Not one person imparted the sense of energy and excitement that she had felt in Nick. After the service she visited and chatted, but inside she was burning with a desire to get on the road and head for Linville Springs. She couldn't expect to see Nick, she knew, at least not right away. But he was going to come back to town eventually, and she was looking forward to seeing him again, maybe to test her emotions and find out if it was Nick or her future that was causing her this agitation.

Sunday afternoon she left as soon as she could and fairly sped along the familiar road back to the Springs. The sun was veiled by high thin clouds, and the shadows cast on the land by the occasional jutting hill or rock formation were purple and surreal. The landscape rolled beneath a worn, tattered blanket of old snow, the buffalo grass poking through it like straw. In a few days, she thought, the snow would melt completely. Spring was starting to make its slow arrival, and then summer would come taking her away from Nick for good.

By the time she drove into the city, her feelings were in a complete tangle. The sprawl of the urban setting was welcoming and made Advance seem sparse and desolate. Unfair, she thought. It wasn't the city. It was Nick.

She drove past the hospital, unable to stop, even though she knew she should check for messages. Instead she made a beeline for her house, arguing with herself whether or not to call Nick. If he wasn't home, it would only disappoint her. If he was...

He wasn't! Laura slammed on her brakes just in time to avoid rear-ending the station wagon parked in her driveway. He was here!

Laura felt her heart start to pound like a triphammer. What was he doing here? She forced herself to sit still and take long, slow breaths. She had to be composed when she saw him. She had to calm down so that she could analyze her own feelings.

Then Nick came roaring out of the house. "Where the hell have you been?" he yelled, waving his arms in the air. He jerked open the car door and swept her into an embrace. Stunned, Laura hesitantly put her arms around his neck.

"I was worried," he murmured, burying his face against her neck. "Hell, I was frantic. I got back last night and you weren't here. You weren't at the hospital. This morning I managed to drag your parents' telephone number out of Peter, but I called all morning and no one answered."

"We were at church." Mystified, Laura tried gently to get free, but Nick held her all the more tightly. She could feel his heart beating through the yellow polo shirt he wore and could hear a little sigh in his chest after each breath he took. Were his allergies acting up and was he laced with medication? That would help explain his strange behavior.

"So you were at your parents!" He broke the embrace but kept a tight hold on her shoulders. His expression was angry. "Why didn't you leave me a note?"

She glared back at him. "I didn't know it was required."

"Didn't you know I'd be worried?" Now Nick looked hurt.

"No. As a matter of fact I didn't think you'd care one whit! You certainly didn't give me a clue as to when you were going to be back. Why should I have..."

Nick's mouth covered hers, cutting off her words. His right hand left her shoulder and tangled in her hair, holding her so that she couldn't have escaped his kiss even if she had wanted to.

But escape was the last thing on her mind. Astonishment, yes. Excitement. The kiss had begun awkwardly, because she had been so completely unprepared, but once she realized that Nick was in fact kissing her, she responded eagerly. Suddenly the questions that had plagued her before no longer mattered.

His kiss became deeper and more passionate, and his arm went around her waist to draw her close to his body. Laura put her arms around his neck again, this time unhesitantly. His muscles rippled as he pulled her closer, and Laura gave herself up to the wonderful feeling of being embraced by such a strong man.

Nick knew that he had blown everything, but he didn't care. Having her in his arms and feeling her respond to him made up for anything he might have lost by giving in at last to his true emotions. The lonely days and nights he had spent away from her had convinced him that Laura meant a great deal more to him than he had thought. It had been one thing to keep himself in check, knowing that he could be in her company almost any time he chose. It had been quite another to leave her and then come home and find her gone.

She molded herself to him as if they were lovers, and his inflamed senses reeled. An ocean's roar filled his ears, and he lost his sense of balance for a moment. He staggered, but came up against the fender of her car. Leaning against it for support, he allowed himself to finish the kiss, tasting the sweetness of her mouth with his tongue.

She was everything he wanted. He suspected it before. Now he knew it. The stroke of luck that had brought her to him on Valentine's Day was not an accident. It was fate.

He broke the kiss slowly, gazing at her half-closed eyes and finding in them a reflection of the same desire that he felt. Her arms remained around his neck, and even when he relaxed his embrace, her body stayed pressed against his. Warm, he realized. Warm and willing.

"You missed me," he said. It wasn't a question.

Laura gave him a little smile. "Isn't it pretty obvious?"

"You had the weekend off." He touched her cheek. "Why didn't you tell me? You could have flown into Phoenix…"

"You didn't ask." Her tone was reproachful. "I had the distinct impression you were going off to do you own thing, and I was not invited." She looked away from him. "I didn't want to cramp your style."

"Laura?" He put his hand under her chin and gently forced her to look at him again. "I thought we were friends. How could you think I wouldn't want your company?"

Her gray eyes were suddenly swimming with tears. She pushed away from him and moved around the opened car door. Puzzled, Nick followed.

"What's the matter?" he asked. "We *are* friends, aren't we, Laura?"

She shoved a suitcase at him. "Yes, Nick, we're friends," she said, her voice sounding shaky and angry. "Let's go inside. I don't want to put on any more of a show for the neighbors than we already have."

That made sense, he realized. He didn't care if the world saw them kissing, but Laura had a certain standing in the community, and he supposed that she was worried about her reputation. Because of his former determination to keep their relationship as businesslike as possible, he had never stayed at her house long enough to start tongues wagging. But that was going to change.

He followed her into the house, admiring her figure as he did. She hadn't filled out too much in the last month, but where she had was in all the right places. His palms itched to touch her gentle curves.

He closed the front door behind himself and turned, hoping to catch her in another embrace. But she had gone directly into the kitchen.

"George is fine," he called, trying to lure her back out. "He was the first thing I checked after I made sure your body wasn't stuffed in a closet or cupboard."

"You aren't my keeper!" She reappeared in the doorway, and there were pink splotches high on her cheeks. "You don't have to worry about me," she added in a softer tone.

"Maybe not." He spread out his hands, willing her to understand his feelings. "But I did, Laura. I worried myself right out of the tournament. I missed you so badly that by Saturday afternoon I couldn't have sunk a putt if the ball was teetering on the lip. My nerves were so frazzled I actually had an asthma attack for the first time in years."

"Oh, Nick." The anger faded from her face, and her expression was full of concern. She left the doorway and came over to him. "Are you all right now?"

"I sure am." He touched her cheek again. "Seeing you is all the cure I need."

She stepped back, raising one dark eyebrow in that haughty expression he had come to know so well. "Excuse me if I seem a bit confused, Nick," she said. "But as I recall, except for the first night, you've reacted to any kind of intimacy from me as if I had the plague. I don't understand."

"Listen, Laura." He beseeched her with his hands again. "Let me explain. I was doing that for your own good. I figured that if we went to bed together, I'd lose my status, my authority with you, and you wouldn't take direction from me nearly as seriously. If I were your lover, I decided, I couldn't be your mentor.''

She looked exasperated. "You mean all this time…?"

"All this time I've been going slowly crazy wanting you. I didn't know how bad it was until we were really apart. Then I came back, and you weren't here…"

She still looked skeptical. "You could have gone out with other women. We have no ties on each other."

Nick felt himself blush. "I didn't want to go out with anybody," he explained. "And this week when I… Well, let's just say that I discovered I can't be satisfied with anyone else but you. Laura, I…" He let the words trail off. She had turned on her heel and stalked into the bedroom, slamming the door behind her.

He stared at the closed door, a feeling of rage stirring inside him. The last time a woman had closed him out, he had ended up in divorce court, a deeply humiliating and expensive experience. He balled his fists and took a long, shaky breath.

But Laura wasn't his ex-wife, he reminded himself, forcing the anger to subside. Compared to Caroline, Laura was a pool of crystal clear water, not a swamp of schemes and plots. His ex-wife could suck a man's soul and self-respect right out of him. Nick took another long breath.

"Hear me out, Laura," he said loudly. "I made a mistake or two, but you've got to give me a chance to show you how I really feel. Don't shut me out. I can't handle that!"

Laura listened to the sound of his voice. He couldn't handle it? Well, he ought to understand that she was having some problems, too. His confession that his indifference was all pretend was more troubling the longer she thought about it. He had been trying to manipulate her, just as Peter had suspected. The more she considered that fact, the angrier she became.

"Laura?" A fist pounded on the bedroom door. "Did you hear what I said?" His voice sounded thick, and he hit the door again, causing the hinges to strain. Laura stalked to the door and jerked it open.

She caught him with both of his hands raised over his head. He was obviously intent on breaking the door down, but as she glared at him, he seemed to deflate and slowly lowered his arms.

"You could have just opened it," she said dryly. "I didn't lock it."

Nick grinned suddenly. "Tearing it off the hinges seemed more romantic."

"Maybe so." She fought the urge to return his smile. "But it would have been expensive, and if you just blew a tournament, you hardly need to waste your money repairing this place." She gestured around the small room.

"Laura, I wouldn't have cared if it cost me a million dollars." His smile was gone, replaced by an expression of intense emotion. "I was miserable all week long, and it was because I couldn't be with you. You're like some kind of precious elixir, and I'm dependent on you for my very life."

"That sounds awfully melodramatic coming from the Nick Hawthorne I thought I knew."

His expression darkened. "Okay," he growled. "I'll show you the *real* Nick Hawthorne." And he reached for her.

CHAPTER SEVEN

LAURA DIDN'T STRUGGLE or try to resist. It didn't matter that he might have been with other women during the tournament. Nor that he had acted as if *she* had been at fault by not keeping him informed of her whereabouts.

What mattered was that his arms held her tightly. That his body pressed against hers with hungry need, that his lips covered hers with a rough yet tender passion, and that his heart beat in harmony with hers. Laura molded herself to him and gave herself over to the tide of desire that rose within her.

Maybe it wasn't exactly the romantic ideal she had dreamed about, but it was real. Maybe it wasn't love that made his heart beat so fast and hers race to catch up, but the sweet pressure that pulsed within her was no fantasy. She wanted Nick, and there was no doubt left in her mind that he wanted her.

His kiss finally put to rest any doubts she might have had of his desire for her. He must have had to struggle to suppress the need he was releasing now, and she felt overwhelmed by his passion—over-whelmed and unable to meet it fully in spite of her own feelings.

Nick's lips caressed her throat, and one of his hands gently tugged the hem of her shirt out of the waistband of her jeans. Laura felt the cool touch of air and then the heated warmth of his palm against her skin.

"Oh God, Laura," he murmured. "I want you. I didn't even know how much I wanted you until now." His fingers caressed the skin beneath her breast.

Laura struggled for rational thought. A few moments more and the two of them would undoubtedly be half-naked and making clumsy love on her bed. This wasn't the way it should happen.

Then, to her surprise, Nick slipped his hand out from beneath her shirt. He still held her, but his embrace had loosened, and she could have easily stepped free.

Nick's eyes were wide and shimmering with passion, but Laura thought she detected other emotions in his expression, as well. Confusion. Maybe even a touch of fear.

"Not this way," he said huskily. His breathing was too rapid, and she was certain she heard the rasp of rales after each breath.

"Nick, are you...?"

He released her completely and stepped away, turning his back to her. His wide shoulders stretched the fabric of the yellow polo, and the chords at the side of his neck stood out as he raked his fingers through his hair.

"This isn't right," he said, not looking at her. "Here I go, mauling you, and, hell, I don't even know if you like me."

"Nick, I..."

"I'm treating you like a golf groupie who's throwing herself at me." He turned, self-loathing marring his tanned features. "I'm sorry, Laura. Please forgive me."

"I don't think I was putting up much objection to what went on." Shakily she tucked her shirt back into the waist band of her jeans. "I can't see that you owe me any kind of apology."

"Well, I do!" He shouted the words. Laura stood her ground as he rushed back to her and grabbed her shoulders. "Laura, you're worth so much more to me than any other woman I've ever known. I want you, but beyond that, I need you. And you're too precious to be used the way I..."

"Nick, settle down." Laura put her hands on his arms. "You're upset, and you don't need to be. Come on, let's go back in the living room and talk about this like civilized people. I can't think with you hulking around and lunging at me like Conan the Barbarian."

Nick laughed abruptly. "That's an apt choice of words. There's nothing I'd rather do than throw you on the bed and slake my passion with you." His shoulders seemed to sag slightly. "Unfortunately I'm not a barbarian. Ravishment isn't in my game plan."

"That's just as well." Laura smiled as she led him from the bedroom. "I don't think the furniture would hold up for a no-holds-barred sexual wrestling match."

He grinned in the old, wicked way. "We could use the floor."

"Oh, go sit down." She gave him a friendly shove in the direction of the sofa. "I'll go fix us something to drink. Something soothing. We could both use a little calming down."

"I don't feel like calming down." Nick slouched on the sofa and grabbed an orange throw pillow, which he hugged to his chest. "I feel like getting more excited."

"I'll be right back." Laura felt a wave of friendly affection for him that was completely unlike the passion that had possessed her a few minutes before. "Don't do anything unnatural with that poor pillow." Nick's ridiculously exaggerated groans of passion followed her into the kitchen.

She lingered over preparing the herbal tea, trying to sort out her own feelings as she was sure Nick was doing in the solitude of the living room. He had fallen silent, and she heard him stand up and move over to the window. She could imagine that he was staring out, not seeing the quiet neighborhood street but considering the implications of what he had done and said.

For herself, his declaration of passion had come as both a relief and a problem. If he really did feel that way about her, it put a whole new series of complications in her life which wouldn't end in two weeks when the agreed-on period for her exercise program was over.

She hadn't committed herself in any way. Nick had done all the confessing. All she had admitted was that she had missed him. Nothing more. She hadn't resisted his caresses, but that could easily be explained by saying that she trusted him to come to his senses before anything serious happened.

Liar, she scolded herself. You wanted it as much as he did. You just had a small twitch of uneasiness over the speed and power of the whole thing. You don't much care for being so completely in someone else's control, do you.

All right. Suppose they did become lovers. Nick was going to be in and out of town with his golf, and when the weather warmed up, he'd be overwhelmingly busy dealing with the short Wyoming golf season. And she would be gone by July. Could either of them afford the kind of pain a love affair like that would bring?

It was so easy to think logically. She had always been terrific at that. But she was far less adept at deciphering her own feelings. As she poured the boiling water into the pot, she tried to imagine what it would feel like when she and Nick had to part company for good.

The sense of emptiness that swept over her was so strong that she almost dropped the teapot. Had he really come to mean that much to her in just a month? And what would it be like if they did have an affair and her affection was deepened by the shared pleasure of physical intimacy? She wasn't sure she wanted to know.

"Are you planning the NATO defense strategy in there?" Nick's voice interrupted her moody thoughts.

"Just taking care with the tea," she called. "I'll be right out."

"You'd better be. The pillow and I couldn't work anything out, and I'm seriously contemplating giving up my standards and sinking to barbarism. A sense of honor can keep a guy together for only so long, you know."

Another wave of affection swept over Laura. How could she possibly resist or refuse him when he could charm her so. Torn between smiling and sighing, she lifted the tea tray and went into the living room.

Nick was seated on the sofa, and his eyes seemed to fire as she bent over to place the tray on the coffee table. Laura sat gingerly next to him and began to pour the fragrant, steaming brew.

"After I left on Monday," Nick said softly, "I tried to see how long I could go without calling you, without having any contact with you." He clasped his fingers together. "I nearly lost my mind, Laura. My insides hurt, and I couldn't think straight."

"Maybe you had the flu."

He glared at her. "I'm baring my soul to you, dammit. Don't get all medical on me."

She handed him a cup. "Just trying to help. Sorry."

"It was the same way you said you felt about the cigarettes," he went on, apparently mollified by her apology. He held the teacup in his big hands and stared down into the dark liquid. "Like there was something that you had been able to turn to for a long time and suddenly it wasn't there anymore. Sometimes...sometimes I'd look up and think I saw you out in the gallery..."

"The what?"

"The crowd." He waved a hand. "You know, the bunch of people who follow a golfer around the course. Most of the guys have at least a smattering of special fans. The headliners have multitudes. Anyway..."

Laura listened silently to his recitation of the miseries he had suffered by her absence. What he said was astonishingly close to the feelings she had experienced in Advance, though of a greater intensity.

The times she had turned, expecting to see him, or thought she had heard his voice calling her name. She gave a little shiver and felt goose bumps rise on her skin. This was getting weird.

"Maybe working on your system has linked us psychically," she said, only half joking. "I told you I missed you this weekend, and it was a lot like what you're describing."

Nick's eyes widened. "Laura, tell me exactly how you feel about me. Please, be honest." He put his cup down and held out his hand.

Laura looked down. Here it was. Time to make a choice. She could lie....

Nick watched her face closely. Learning to read people was a technique he had picked up early in life. The only time he had made a serious error in judgment was with the other woman he thought he needed. It wasn't going to happen again.

But there couldn't be any deceit behind eyes as clear and open as Laura's. She was struggling, but she would tell him the truth. He knew it.

She put her cup down on the table beside his. "I can tell you for certain how I don't feel," she said. "I don't just like you, Nick." She glanced at him and then looked away. Rosy spots of color appeared on her cheeks.

"I like lots of people," she continued. "I have friends, both men and women. I can't categorize you as a friend."

"Why not?" he felt a sinking sensation.

"It's so different with you." She sat back, folding her hands in her lap. "'Like' just seems to be too weak a word to describe the way I feel." She stared off into space.

Nick waited, hardly daring to breathe.

"I'm...very attracted to you," Laura said. "I feel a great deal of...affection for you."

His heart started to pound so hard he was afraid she'd hear it and be startled out of her mood.

"I just don't know, Nick." She gave a long sigh. "I have to confess that I fell for you the first moment I saw you, and that the feeling has only grown stronger as time has passed. I don't know what I'm going to do when I have to leave."

"Don't leave!" The words burst from him, and he couldn't have stopped them if his life depended on it. Her visit home must have reinforced her plans to set up practice with her father. What an utter fool he'd been to go off and leave her!

"Nick." Her eyes were filled with sorrow. "I have to."

He put his hand on the back of the sofa and leaned toward her. "Do you want to? Tell me the truth."

The question agitated her. She squeezed her small hands together, then pulled them apart, then folded them again on her lap. "I...I have to admit that I've occasionally had misgivings about..."

"You'd never fit in," Nick interrupted. "Maybe it was okay for you when you were growing up. Maybe it would be an okay situation for someone who was settled with a family. But, Laura, you'll dry up all by yourself." A sudden suspicion flashed through his mind. "Unless you've got someone waiting for you?"

To his relief, she laughed. "No one's waiting for me. The only bachelors in Advance right now are either old enough to be my grandfather or still school boys. No, Nick, the only competition you've got is my sense of duty to my dad."

"Then let me offer you an alternative." She had almost admitted that she loved him. No better time to offer her a permanent place in his dream. He knew it was the same type of emotional blackmail he'd used to get her to try his system in the first place, but the ball was rolling, and he knew that now was the right moment to bring the subject up. Leave her alone at this point to brood, and he might lose the edge forever.

"Stay with me, Laura," he said, ignoring the astonished look on her face. "You have your medical degree. In July you'll be through with your training. Stay with me and help me put together a package that will sell my system. I can support us both—" He broke off, realizing that it sounded as if he was proposing marriage, something he had sworn never to do again as long as he lived.

"I mean," he corrected himself, "I'll pay you a salary. You'll work for me on the project and would be free to travel around with me to help promote it. Contact people to raise money for it."

"I'm a doctor," she stated, her expression indignant. "Not some salesperson. Some peddler!"

"I can teach you. Together we..."

"No!" She stood and made an emphatic gesture with her hands. "I'm going to do what I was trained to do. Help—"

"Help people," Nick interrupted, taking her arms and making her look at him. "Laura, stop and think how many people you'll help by helping me. Forget your feelings. Forget what's happened between us this afternoon. You could be on the leading edge of a nationwide program for preventative medicine.''

Laura stared at him, a dizzy sensation suddenly filling her head. The future, which had once seemed to stretch before her in a safe, predictable, if somewhat tedious line, had taken a jarring turn. Now there was a fork in the road. One way was safe, secure—and stifling. The other...

''I can't,'' she moaned, turning away from him and going back to sit, huddled, on the sofa. ''I can't just throw away everything I've worked for and go off chasing rainbows with you.''

''You won't be chasing any rainbows.'' He came over to kneel on the floor in front of her. ''Look, I know I've come on too fast and too strong.'' His hand touched her knee. ''I've had it all bottled up inside so tight that when I finally let it out, it was overwhelming to you.'' He patted her leg. ''Think about it, Laura. We've got plenty of time.''

''That's easy for you to say,'' she muttered, moving her knee away from the warmth of his palm. ''No one's asking you to give up *your* job and gamble your future on the word of a virtual stranger.'' She saw the hurt look in his eyes and hastened to touch his cheek to soften her words. ''I mean, we really don't know that much about each other, Nick, except that we're...attracted to each other.''

He moved up beside her on the sofa, and the nearness of his body made her tingle. ''That's how we started, remember, Valentine?'' His finger pushed a stray lock of hair off her cheek.

Laura felt a thrill at his words. She remembered, all right. Remembered, and had relived and puzzled over that first night time and time again during the last month. Now he was telling her that it had been the only time he had allowed his real feelings to show.

Her musings on horseback hadn't been so far off after all, she thought. Maybe he didn't actually love her, but he was far from indifferent to her, and he wanted much, much more from her than he had indicated. She tried to make some sense of the choices before her, but his nearness made clear thinking impossible.

"Don't worry, Laura," he whispered, putting his arm around her shoulders. "This is going to work out better than you can possibly imagine."

She closed her eyes. "You have no idea the things I can imagine."

"I can guess." His voice was low, a silky sigh, and his kiss brushed beneath her ear. "I bet you've imagined this," Nick breathed. His lips moved to the curve of her neck and shoulder and teased aside her shirt until the sensitive skin was bared. His kiss sent shivers through her. "Have you dreamed of this?" he asked, his voice serious, but when she looked at him, she saw mischief in his eyes.

"You're trying to seduce me," she said accusingly. "Don't be so darned sure of yourself, Mr. Hawthorne. I might go to bed with you, but that won't mean I'll throw my career in with my body."

Nick sighed and sat back. "Why did I have to pick a woman with the face and body of an angel and the mind of a corporate pirate." His expression was cheerful.

"Look who's talking pirates." Laura folded her arms across her chest. "You've been emotionally flimflamming me from the very beginning."

"A justified accusation." Nick patted her shoulder. "From now on, I promise to let you know exactly how I feel."

Laura raised her eyebrows and looked at him askance.

"On my honor." He put his left hand on his heart and raised his right hand. For a moment he grinned at her, then his expression became serious. "I mean it, Laura. One thing I don't do is make promises lightly. Did I mislead you about the way my system would make you feel?"

"No. I do feel much better," she admitted. "And the cigarette thing only bothers me occasionally."

"Keep saying no," Nick advised. "The urge may never go completely away, but by refusing to give in to it, you gradually weaken it to where it won't bother you much."

"Is that a promise?"

"This is a promise." Nick leaned over and gave her a kiss. "I'll keep your lips too busy to smoke."

Laura half shut her eyes. His face was close to hers, and he was gazing at her intently. She wanted very much for him to continue his caresses. "They feel a little bit like they're smoking right now," she whispered, putting one hand on his wide shoulder and teasing the hair on his neck with the other.

"And how do *you* feel?"

Laura leaned her head against the back of the sofa. "I feel sexy," she said.

"Let me see what I can do to relieve that," Nick murmured. He gathered her into his arms, and his kiss was so loving Laura felt as if she was melting. Only the insistent ringing of the telephone in the bedroom stopped what she had hoped would be a prolonged interlude.

Reluctantly she unwound herself from Nick's arms. "I'd better get it," she said. "I'm not on call until tonight, but you never know." Nick's expression told her that he was as disappointed as she was, but he released her.

"I suppose I'll have to get used to this," he said mournfully. "It could make things tough, never knowing if you're going to get to finish what you've started."

"I doubt if you'll ever have any problems," Laura called as she disappeared into the bedroom. Nick smiled wryly to himself as he heard her pick up the telephone and speak quietly to whoever was on the other end.

No, he decided, with Laura there would never be problems. It was obvious that she was willing to be his lover and that she was not completely decided about going back to Advance. A little more of the right kind of persuasion and she'd be his. They'd be lovers, and they'd be partners.

He took off his loafers and lay down on the sofa, indulging himself in fantasies of what lovemaking with Laura would be like.

The days without her had been torture. His emotional turmoil and loneliness in spite of any number of very friendly females, plus the asthma attack, had convinced him that for his own sake he had to change the relationship. He needed Laura for much more than friendship.

But he stopped shy of considering making her more than his lover. After his first experience, another marriage was out of the question for him. He had seen all too clearly how a woman could change once she decided that an alliance didn't suit her.

It had been like watching a horror film. One minute Caroline was a sweet, loving wife, and the next she was a witch who lost no opportunity to hurt him with her words and actions. For weeks he had felt as if his soul was bleeding and raw. He missed qualifying for several important tournaments and spent the play weekends drinking himself into a solitary stupor in his motel room rather than go home to face his wife. Finally one of his buddies had taken pity on him and told him the truth. Caroline was having an affair with an attorney, and the two of them were plotting ways to get the best divorce settlement possible out of Nick.

The pieces had suddenly fallen together. Caroline's strange behavior had been an attempt to induce him to abuse her, but even she hadn't understood how strongly he disliked violence and how far he would go to keep from inflicting pain on another human being.

Laura's reappearance brought him out of his somber reverie. She had tears in her eyes, and she was reaching for her jacket. Nick sat up quickly.

"What is it, Laura?" he asked, slipping his loafers back on. She probably wouldn't cry over a patient. There must be a problem with someone she loved.

"It was Anne," she said. "She and Peter had a big argument this afternoon, and he...left." Her expression indicated that she could hardly believe what she had just said. "Anne has no idea where he is. She called the hospital, the center and then me."

"She should try the bars." Nick's tone was dry. He pushed off his shoes and leaned back on the sofa. "That's where a lot of confused men go when their wives have bitched them out of the house."

Laura stared at him as if he had suddenly grown horns. "That's not how it was, Nick Hawthorne. Anne wants their family to be closer, not to be driven apart. Peter's been putting his work ahead of everything else and everybody's suffering."

"That's probably true. Wherever Vance is, I know just how he's feeling right now." Nick closed his eyes, remembering.

"Then you go find him," she snapped. "Talk some sense into him. I'm going over to be with Anne." With those words, Laura turned and stalked from the house. Nick stood up and started after her, then realized he was in stocking feet. By the time he had managed to get his shoes back on, she had pulled out of the driveway and disappeared down the street.

Damnation, Nick thought. As if he didn't have enough trouble trying to work things out with Laura. Okay, he'd find Vance, and the guy would, by hell, listen to him.

Listen to him. Nick paused, a flash of inspiration going off in his brain. Maybe this wasn't such a bad turn of events. Maybe the Vances' problems would be the key to solving his own. Plans and schemes raced through his mind, and Nick left the house whistling.

CHAPTER EIGHT

"IT'S BEEN COMING for a long time," Anne said, her voice shaky from crying. "I admit I've been nagging him, but I couldn't stand to see him growing more and more distant from us."

Laura put her hand on Anne's shoulder and patted soothingly. "Don't blame yourself," she said. "You probably accidentally said the wrong thing at the wrong time. You know how moody men can be."

"He says he wants to stay here." Anne gestured with her hands. "He wants to borrow a ton of money, buy office space near the hospital and go into a single private practice. If he does that, we'll never see him."

She was right, Laura realized. Linville Springs was a growing community, and a new doctor would have no trouble working himself into an early grave if he tried to handle a practice by himself. Peter had to be out of his mind.

"When Nick finds him," she promised, "I'll tell him I agree with you. A man who cares as much for his family as Peter does should never consider that kind of medical career."

"It takes one to know one," Laura replied. "Come into the kitchen. I'll bet you could use a cup of tea."

ON SUNDAY EVENINGS the number of places a man could do any serious drinking were fairly limited in Linville Springs. Nick moved from one to the other, surveying the bars for his quarry, and finally located the man in a motel lounge. Not too stupid, he thought. If he planned on getting smashed, he wouldn't have to drive anywhere.

Vance was sitting alone in a shadowed booth, a half-empty beer in front of him. From the number of wet rings on the table and the sodden condition of the cocktail napkin balled in Vance's hand, Nick calculated that the beer was far from the first of the evening. The man wasn't used to this, he observed. Nobody tried to get wiped-out drunk on beer. You ended up bloated and sick instead. Now, vodka...

He slid into the booth, sitting on the other side of the table from the doctor. Vance looked up, focused his glazed eyes on Nick, then spoke.

"What the hell are you doing here, Hawthorne?" he snarled. "This's a private table."

Nick signaled the waitress. "Bring the man his check, will you please," he said when the woman came over. "I'm driving him home."

The waitress gave him a relieved look and hurried away to get the check. Peter Vance leaned back, an angry expression playing across his slack features.

"Now wait a minute," he slurred. "I'm not goin' anywhere with...."

Nick moved quickly, sliding around the section of booth that separated them and gathering a handful of Peter's shirt in his fist. He pulled the smaller man close until their faces were inches apart.

"You have two choices," Nick said, keeping his voice low and conversational. "Come with me, let me get you sobered up and you can sleep at home in your own bed, next to your loving wife, or give me a hard time and you can sleep at the hospital alone, in considerable pain." He raised his eyebrows inquiringly. "Which is it going to be?"

Vance seemed to shrink. "I don' wanna fight."

"Good." Nick released him and straightened his shirt. "Neither do I. Now let's get out of here."

It took several hours, but Nick finally got Peter Vance in presentable, if somewhat rumpled shape. He called the Vance house and reported to Laura that the prodigal was on his way back to the nest, considerably subdued.

"You might want to make sure the kids are out of the picture," he cautioned. "Their old man's still in rocky shape. Not much of a role model at the moment."

Laura assured him that the boys were already asleep. She had fixed supper for the three of them. Anne was too upset to eat. "I told them that their mom and dad had a kind of flu bug that occasionally hits married grown-ups, and that they didn't need to worry. I was taking care of their mom, and you were fixing up their dad."

Nick chuckled. "We're quite a team. Did they buy it?"

"Well, they're asleep, anyway. Maybe we ought to consider adding family counseling to the service you plan to offer."

"No way." Nick heard his own voice take on a hard edge. "I flunked the course myself. I could never give anybody else advice about marriage. I'm just bringing the body home."

After they had finished talking, Laura hung up the phone and hurried into the den to tell Anne the good news.

"Nick said he was a little ragged around the edges, but okay," she said. Then she watched with astonishment as Anne's eyes filled with tears again.

"I really appreciate all the two of you have done," Anne whispered. "But it doesn't solve the problem, does it? We have to work it out between the two of us."

Sobered, Laura had to agree that Anne was right, and she prayed that her friends could handle the situation better than Nick apparently had. There was such bitterness in his voice every time he mentioned his marriage.

But when Nick arrived with the much-subdued Peter, he seemed unusually cheerful. He announced he had a suggestion to make that might solve a number of problems, the Vances' disagreement among them. He allowed Peter a few minutes to apologize in private to Anne, but none of Laura's probing or questioning could get him to tell her what he had in mind.

"I want everyone to hear it together," he said. "I think it'll have more impact that way."

Finally, the four of them gathered in the den. Peter sat next to Anne on the couch, his arm around her shoulders and her hand held in his. Clearly, they had made up, at least for the time being. Nick remained standing, and Laura settled into an easy chair.

"I know you're all wondering why I called this meeting," Nick quipped, grinning at the three of them. He was, Laura realized, having a fine time. Anne looked dazed, and Peter looked terrible. He was watching Nick like a frightened animal. What, she wondered, had happened between them before they had arrived here?

"Well," Nick went on, clasping his hands behind himself and rocking back and forth from his toes to his heels. "I think I've put together a solution to all of our problems."

"Listen, Hawthorne," Peter interrupted. "My wife and I are perfectly capable..." His words trailed off as Nick's smile grew chill.

"I didn't say you had to do what I'm going to suggest," Nick replied. "I just want the three of you to think about what I have to say."

"The three of us?" Laura felt a growing alarm. "How did I get into this?"

"I want Peter to consider taking your place in Advance," Nick explained. "It would give him a situation that would keep him near his family and would free you up to work for me without feeling guilty about deserting your dad. In fact, you'd have done a good thing for everyone involved."

"Especially you." Laura stood up to confront him. "This would just fit right in with your wishes, wouldn't it."

Nick shrugged innocently and looked aggrieved. "Did I start the fight? All I did was provide a solution."

Laura started to berate him for his nerve, but Anne interrupted her. "What's he talking about, Laura? I don't think I completely understand."

"Laura plans to set up practice in her home town," Peter explained, his voice dull. "That way, when her father decides to ease up or retire altogether, she'll be there to take up the slack. It wouldn't be very challenging professionally, but it would be..."

"Easy!" Anne interrupted. "It would be an easygoing schedule for you. You could take time to learn a hobby. Do things with the boys." Her voice softened. "With me."

Laura listened to the conversation, and her feelings became more and more mixed up. Nick had no right to make such a suggestion, even if it was a good one. It would make sense for the Vances to consider such an option. As for herself, it would loosen the tie of loyalty that kept her feeling bound to return home. And she had to admit an outsider like Peter would command more immediate respect than she would, since most of the people she would be treating had known her as a small child.

But Nick had used the situation to make things work his way, and that made her angry. She tried to summon up the right words to wipe the smug look from his handsome face.

"I'd have to have some guarantees," she said coolly. "I couldn't just step off into thin air with you or anyone else. Your plans are so...unformed, so far off in the future, and I'd have to have some kind of income."

"There's going to be an opening in the ER staff," Peter interjected, his voice sounding more alive.

"You wouldn't be building a practice that you'd have to desert if Hawthorne's brainchild ever got going. And you'd have predictable hours and an income.

Anne, Laura noted, was looking at her husband with delight. "Oh," she whispered, "I'm beginning to believe this was all meant to turn out this way." The glance she gave Nick was grateful, the one to Laura, pleading.

Laura realized she was caught. There was no way she could back out of the corner Nick had painted her into. No way, unless she wanted to look like a selfish, uncaring bitch. Although she was infuriated by his high-handedness, her feelings of affection for Nick were very real and deep. He had manipulated her again, but more people might be happy because of it.

"I'd have to check with my dad." She sat back down in the easy chair. "He might have some problems with the idea, and it is his town."

"We'd need to visit," Peter said. "See if we thought we could work together."

"We'd have to go up there some weekend," Anne added, "to make sure the boys would like to live there."

As Laura watched the two of them talk, a sense of inevitability took hold of her. Nick came over to her side and hunkered down on his heels by her chair.

"If you don't get the emergency room job," he said quietly, "I'll split my salary with you until we start to get off the runway with the system."

Laura gazed at him. "Have you always managed to juggle things to suit yourself, Nick? If I didn't know better, I'd swear you staged this whole affair to make me fit in with your schemes."

"I'm not scheming," he replied. "I'm planning, and I want you included in those plans."

Before she could respond, Peter came over to them. "It's late," he said, extending his hand to Nick. "You two have done a great deal for us tonight, and I want you to know that we're both really grateful."

Nick stood up and shook the offered hand. "I was glad to help out. When I was in a spot something like yours, I came near to pickling myself before a friend reached in to jam a cork on the bottle. Believe me, it's no way to find an answer."

"I know that," Peter admitted. "It was a stupid thing to do."

Anne came over and took her husband's arm. "At least it stirred us up to look for other answers besides arguing."

"We've all got a lot to think about," Laura said, realizing that of the four of them, she had the scariest decisions to make. "Excuse me, all of you, but I've got to run by the hospital and make late rounds. As it is, I'll probably have to wake up..."

"Don't worry." Peter gave a wry chuckle. "When I decided to go make shredded wheat of my brain, I asked Linda Turner if she'd cover for me. I forgot to tell her you came on in the evening."

"Laura, I want to talk to you." Nick took her elbow firmly. "Let's go for a drive. You can pick up your car later." He led them through hasty goodnights and directed her out of the house.

"I'm not so sure I want to talk to you," Laura said as he opened the door of the station wagon for her. "It always seems to get me deeper into trouble when I do."

"It only gets you involved." Nick smiled at her. "And that, lovely lady, is not a bad thing."

Maybe not, Laura thought glumly as they drove through the residential area of town then out onto the main highway. But it certainly had shaken up her life and ordered existence.

Nick drove along the highway in silence for a long time. Finally he spoke. "Okay, out with it. What do you think of my idea?"

"Which of the many are you referring to?" She was tired and in no mood to pretend politeness.

"About Peter." Nick sounded tense. "It really is a perfect solution, don't you think?"

"For you, maybe." Laura braced herself as he took a sharp turn off an exit ramp. "Where are we going?"

"Just some place I like to go when I have to think." He headed down a two-lane road that led into the foothills near the south tip of Linville mountain.

Laura looked out of the window and studied the rugged countryside. They could be hundreds of miles from civilization instead of five minutes. The road passed by acres of sagebrush and scrub grass prairie, then climbed into the hills. The moonlight washed everything gray, but Laura knew that in another month or so, tiny wildflowers would start to peek out of cracks in rocks and along the side of the road where the sun had warmed the earth the most. Then in June, for a short moment of glory, the entire landscape would boast green grass and pastel blooms.

But now it was dreary and depressing. She regretted letting Nick bring her here, and she was simmering with resentment.

He drove until the road became gravel, then he pulled off, parking where they could overlook a small lake. The place was on the east side of the hill, and even in the moonlight, the vista of the lake, prairie and hills was impressive. If Laura had been in any other kind of mood, she realized, she would have responded with pleasure to the location. As it was, she sat in sullen silence on her side of the seat.

"Okay." Nick gripped the steering wheel with both hands. "I know it's late and you're mad at me, but please don't sit over there as if you were made of stone."

"Give me one reason why I shouldn't." The words came out more harshly than she had intended. He had helped her friends after all, even if she had trouble accepting his methods.

"I'll give you one reason." His tone was as testy as hers had been. "There are probably hundreds I could think of, given time. But the one that springs to mind is that if Anne hadn't called you when she did, we'd probably still be sending up smoke signals from that little bed of yours. When I started kissing you that last time, I didn't intend to stop, and I don't think you did, either."

Laura stared out the window. He was right. She had wanted him and had been ready to make love. But that moment seemed a lifetime ago.

"Nothing's changed, Laura," Nick said, seeming once again to read her thoughts. "Please come over and sit close to me." His tone was tender, firm yet not demanding. Laura felt her anger start to ebb, and she released her seat belt and slid over until her knee touched his.

"All right," she said, looking directly at him for the first time since leaving the Vance's house. "I'm over. What did you bring me out here to talk about? What couldn't wait until tomorrow?"

"This." Nick leaned over and kissed her. His arm went around her shoulders, and he stroked her cheek and throat with his other hand. His caresses were gentle, and Laura felt her tense, tired body relax slightly.

"We could have kissed at home," she said after a while. "There wasn't any point in coming all the way out here."

"Um-hm," Nick nuzzled her neck. "If you'd gone home in your car, and I'd followed you, I bet there would have been a less-than-even chance for me to apologize for putting you on the spot like I did, let alone get to do what I'm doing now." He nibbled her ear.

"Apologize?" Laura felt the tingle of goose bumps on her skin. "I didn't realize the word was in your vocabulary. I thought you rearranged entire lives to suit your purposes then went on from there."

"I knew you were ticked off." His hand went to her waist, and his fingers began to tickle her. Laura squealed and struggled, trying to avoid the tormenting touch, yet finding herself breathlessly enjoying the teasing.

"Cut it out, Nick," she cried, twisting in his grasp. They laughed and wrestled, and then she was lying on the seat and Nick was above her, and it was no longer a funny child's game.

In the moonlight, his eyes seemed black and his hair strands of pure midnight. Laura felt her breath catch at the desire she saw reflected in his eyes. He held her gaze with his own for a long, long moment, and then he looked away and sat up.

"Another apology," he muttered. "I swear I didn't bring you out here for an adolescent roll on a car seat."

Laura sat up and straightened her clothing. "Maybe I wouldn't have minded," she replied, hearing the huskiness in her voice.

There was a touch of cynicism in Nick's laughter. "You've got to watch that willing nature of yours, woman. If you're not careful, it's going to get you in trouble."

"No trouble I can't handle."

Nick raised his dark eyebrows. "You're sure?"

Laura turned so that she faced him directly. "I may not like everything you do, Nick, but I thought I expressed myself pretty clearly this afternoon. I want to be more than your friend. I want to be your lover, as well."

Nick stared at her. Her words astonished him, and he wasn't quite sure why. He had offered her nothing and had made no commitments, yet here she was, offering him what *he* wanted with no strings attached. "Laura," he began, "I...."

"Don't say anything." She put her fingers on his lips. "And don't do anything but drive me back to my car. Too much has happened today for either of us to handle this sensibly. I've told you how I feel. Unless or until you're ready to do the same, don't try."

Her words only made him feel more confused. If she were anyone else, he would have lied to smooth over the moment. But Laura was honesty personified. He couldn't bring himself to say anything he didn't feel.

And he wasn't sure what he felt for her. All he was certain of was that he couldn't stand to think of the future without her.

"If you really mean that about wanting us to be lovers," he said slowly, "mind explaining why you seem to be having trouble throwing in with me and my plans?"

"Because your plans are still whistling in the wind, Nick." Her voice was low, her tone kind. "I said there were things about you I didn't care for. Your dreams are good, but they don't seem to have substance. I can't see myself living on your doled-out money and promises."

Her words stung him. Nick reached down and started the engine. It seemed so simple to him. Why couldn't she just believe in him?

He pulled onto the road and tromped on the gas pedal, making gravel fly. It was childish, he knew, but some perverse emotion made him take the narrow, winding road too fast. He would slow down, he told himself, only if she asked.

But Laura remained silent the entire way back to her car. He knew he should say something, do something to break the tension between them, but his mind was muddled and his heart felt like a heavy, leaden lump in his chest. If only they were near a bed somewhere. Then he wouldn't have to say anything, just romance her until the questions and problems all drifted away on a tide of ecstasy.

But that was the way he had tried to handle problems in his past relationship, and look where it had gotten him. Laura was asking for more. Hell, she deserved more. He pulled to a stop behind her car on the Vances' street. When she moved to get out, he stopped her by placing a hand on her shoulder.

His touch sent a shock through her. Laura had been convinced that her bluntness about her feelings, both positive and negative, had either put him off or angered him. She had planned to leave without a word. She'd said enough already.

But something in his eyes made her settle back in her seat. Nick was obviously caught in some deep inner struggle.

"You're right," he said, the words coming slowly. "I haven't offered you anything concrete. All I can ask is your trust. I can't see myself making anything of it without you, so I'm asking you to go out on a limb for me."

Laura's eyes stung with sudden tears. "Nick," she said, "I'll have to think about it. I'll have to give it some hard, serious thought."

He gave her a little smile. "That means no spend-the-night party until you're sure, doesn't it."

"I guess so."

Nick sighed. "Why do you have to be beautiful, intelligent, honest *and* high-minded all at once?"

"I didn't say I wouldn't sleep with you." Laura leaned over and kissed him lightly. "I just don't know about doing it while we have this other aspect of our relationship unresolved."

Nick kept his hands on the wheel, but a light crept into his eyes. "I bet I could get you to change your mind."

"I bet you could, too." Laura scooted across the seat. "That's why you're going home to your bed and I'm going home to mine."

"Spoilsport." His face was downcast, but his tone was good-natured. Impulsively Laura scooted back and gave him an affectionate hug and another kiss. Then she quickly got out, hurried to her car and drove off into the night.

Nick sat in his car outside the Vances' house for a long time, his eyes staring off into the future and his mind madly scrambling for ideas.

He had been stupid and hopelessly naive to believe she would readily go along with him. She was a capable, independent woman. She had confessed an honest affection for him, but she didn't need him. That was clear.

If he couldn't put together something definite soon he was going to lose her. The thought made him go cold inside. He'd been able to quick-step her along till now, but that was because none of his dealings with her had seriously interfered with her life, only improved it. He leaned his head back on the seat, recalling the way she had looked that afternoon when he had held her in his arms.

Her loveliness was the same as it had been when he had first met her, but now there was an added vibrancy. The shadows had disappeared from beneath her eyes, and her face had filled out enough to give her a more youthful appearance. He could imagine how good she'd look doing a television advertisement for his system: Hello, she'd say. This is Doctor Laura Jensen, and I'm here to talk to you about the Hawthorne System.

Dumb name. He was going to have to come up with something catchier. His idea was good, but if he couldn't sell it to the public he might as well plan on spending the rest of his life sneezing his way through tournaments and teaching duffers how to improve their handicaps. Not a bad future, but not an exciting one, either.

He stewed for a while longer, then leaned forward to start the station wagon. He glanced at the Vances' house before pulling away from the curb and reminded himself to call Peter the next day and encourage him to follow up on the idea of moving to Advance. If he couldn't get Laura to agree outright to join up with him, at least he could try to maneuver her into a position where it seemed logical for her to do so.

Because of the lateness of the hour, when he arrived at his apartment building he made as little noise as possible retrieving his key from the potted plant at the end of the hall and letting himself into the sparse rooms that were his home. He made his way through the darkness to the bedroom and turned on the bedside lamp.

The bed looked big and wide and lonely. He stripped off his clothing, berating himself for letting her go. If he had pressed a little more, she might be here with him now.

No, that wasn't the way. She might come to his bed, might spend a while loving him, but then she'd be gone. He had to figure out how to make her want to stay for good.

He took a quick shower, shampooing his hair to rinse out the smoky smell that still clung to it from the bar. Tomorrow, he promised himself, he would spend several hours drawing up a strategy. The prospect both scared and stimulated him. Laura was good for him, he realized. He could have messed around for years, just thinking about doing something. Now, because of her, he was going to take some definite steps. When he finally settled into bed, there was a smile on his face. Yes, Laura Jensen was definitely good for him. And she was going to be even better for him very shortly. Nick drifted into sleep, lascivious fantasies of Laura slipping through his mind.

Laura, on the other hand, found sleep impossible. Her emotions kept her tossing and turning until dawn, and when the golden slats of sunlight started to edge across the ceiling of her bedroom, she sat up and groaned aloud in frustration. Raking her fingers through her tangled hair, she pressed her palms on temples that throbbed and ached.

This was crazy. How could she let herself become so upset? She had made no one any promises. She was free to make any decision she wanted. Her dad might be disappointed, but both of her parents would want her to do the best thing for her own happiness. And if that meant going in with Nick...

Nick. She flung aside the bedclothes and shrugged into her bathrobe. Every morning for a month, unless he had told her the night before that he wasn't coming, he had appeared at her door shortly after dawn to fix them both breakfast. But this morning there was no sign of him.

She padded into the kitchen, shivering a little at the emptiness there. George stirred in his cage but showed no interest in her. It took Nick with his sunflower seeds to rouse the little animal out of his day-time stupor.

Laura set the kettle on the stove and rummaged through the well-stocked refrigerator for the yogurt. One thing for sure, Nick Hawthorne had definitely changed her eating habits. The idea of her old breakfasts of coffee and sweet rolls made her want to gag.

She was sipping herb tea and stirring hot whole-wheat cereal with a wire whisk to keep it from lumping when the phone rang. She quickly removed the pan from the heat and ran into the bedroom.

"Hello, Nick?" She pressed a hand to her racing heart. "Where are you? I started breakfast...."

"I have no idea where *Nick* is." Walt Jensen's voice sounded testy over the phone. "Your mother and I were worried because you didn't call to tell us you'd arrived safely yesterday afternoon. I thought I'd try to catch you before you left for work."

"Oh, dad," Laura laughed in embarrassment. "I'm sorry. I got sort of...caught up in things around here and forgot. I'm sorry."

"Was this Nick one of the things you got caught up in?"

"Dad...." Should she mention Nick's suggestion?

"I don't mean to pry, honey, but what you said about him kind of worried me. He doesn't sound like the sort of man you should be looking for."

"I'm not *looking* for a man, dad. Nick is a friend who's helped me get a better hold on certain aspects of my life. And speaking of that, if you've got a minute, I'd like to mention an idea that came up while I was over at some friends' house last night."

Fighting a rising sense of disloyalty, she sketched a picture of the Vances' situation for her father. Emphasizing the fact that what she was making was only a suggestion, she asked if he would be willing to consider someone besides herself to fill the job in Advance.

Walt listened, responding often enough to give her courage to continue. He sounded disappointed but at least ready to consider alternatives, if she truly felt they were in her best interest. Nick's motives, however, were another thing.

"Don't let that smooth-talking, country-club boy fool with you, honey," he said. "You make certain that anything you decide to do is because you want it that way. Not because he conned you into thinking you wanted it."

"I won't, dad. I...." The sound of her front door opening and Nick's booming greeting interrupted her.

"Sorry I'm late," he called, slamming the door. "But I've been on the phone with some great—" He broke off when he saw that she had hurriedly covered the mouthpiece.

"It's my dad," she whispered, shooing him out of the bedroom with her hand. Nick faded toward the kitchen.

"Laura?" her father asked. "I know you're a big girl now, but do you mind telling me what a 'friend' is doing in your house this time of day? It seems to me..."

"He comes over to fix breakfast." Laura left her explanation at that. She chatted for another few minutes, hoping she hadn't upset her father too much. Then she hung up, anxious to see Nick and learn what had filled him with such enthusiasm.

CHAPTER NINE

"YOU DID WHAT?" Laura stared at Nick's grinning face in complete disbelief. She had known the man had nerve, but she had no idea that he would go so far. "You really do have to be out of your mind!" she snapped.

"I knew you'd be delighted with the news." His smile didn't fade. "Actually, it wasn't my idea to call Selkirk. I spoke with Isabelle, and she gave me his home telephone number and a great deal of encouragement. I got him just as he came in from his morning jog. He remembered my parents and said that all I needed to do at this point was draw up a tentative presentation and get it off to him. He sounded extremely interested."

"Nick," she protested, "you have nothing to offer him. He's one of the financial emperors of the country. You'll need to have a sophisticated, professionally drawn-up proposal, otherwise a man like Andrew Selkirk is going to laugh and toss your stuff in the trash can."

"That's not what he said." Nick seemed undisturbed by her prediction. "Laura, you've got to have a little more faith in your fellow human beings."

"You're impossible. You don't know if the tests I'm going to run on myself will show any marked change. You don't even know if I'm going to be around to work with you.''

"That was your father on the phone?''

"Yes.''

"Didn't you call him up to tell him—''

Laura flung her hands up to her chest. "He called *me*. He was worried because I didn't phone yesterday when I got home.''

Nick's confidence faded slightly. "But you did mention the idea of Peter going up there instead of yourself, didn't you?''

Laura moved over to the stove. The cereal was cold and gummy in the saucepan. She scraped it into the trash and started to prepare a fresh batch for both of them. "If I did, Nick,'' she said in a level tone, "it's my business, not yours.''

"Wrong!'' He turned her around to face him. "Last night you accused me of whistling in the wind. Now I've taken steps to get a financial backer, and you don't seem the least bit impressed. What do I have to do to get your approval, woman?''

"Quit making plans for my life without asking my permission!'' She glared at him.

Nick seemed to deflate. He released her arms and turned away. "My dream's no good without you, Laura,'' he said. "I can't think of it anymore without you in the middle of the picture. I'm sorry if that makes me the villain in your life.''

Impulsively Laura went over to him and put her arms around him, laying her cheek against his broad back. "You aren't a villain to me, Nick. You're something much finer. But I won't tolerate your pushing me places I'm not ready to go.''

"Not even if I need you there so badly that I know I'll lose the will to strive for my goal if you aren't involved?" He glanced at her over his shoulder, his eyebrows raised inquiringly.

Laura started to laugh. "Nickie Hawthorne," she said, imitating Isabelle Franklin's breathy voice, "you really are shameless."

"Well, I try." He turned and embraced her loosely. "What's for breakfast, cookie? I'm starved. We can continue the fight over a good meal."

While they ate, Nick explained more fully what his contract with Andrew Selkirk meant. One of Selkirk's enterprises was a line of vitamins and health-maintenance products. That, plus the fact the man was personally interested in fitness, made him a natural for supporting Nick's program. As Laura listened, her respect for Nick's business acumen grew. He might be fast and loose with her plans, but he didn't miss a trick on his own.

"You're liking what you hear," Nick stated. "Admit it. You can see all kinds of possibilities, can't you."

"I will admit that it all seems a little less of a pipe dream and a little more real," she conceded. But a thread of suspicion had begun to weave its way through her thoughts. His plans were sounding so real that she wondered if his interest now lay more in her contribution to his program than in herself. Just how did he feel about her?

And how did she feel about him?

Laura wrestled with her thoughts after he left, finally concluding that she didn't know. She wasn't sure if she cared enough for him to throw caution aside and jump on board his dream, even though it had become more than simply an interesting topic of conversation. She did know that she didn't care very much for the idea of a future completely devoid of his presence. He had embedded himself firmly under her skin, but how close he'd managed to burrow toward her heart remained in question.

She arrived at the Family Practice Center around eight-thirty, just in time to greet a slightly green-faced Peter Vance as he walked slowly through the glass entrance door.

"I've seen you looking livelier," she said.

"I've felt better," Peter admitted. "That was a stupid stunt to pull, and you want to know what embarrasses me the most about it?"

"You owe Nick?"

"Exactly." Peter's expression was sour.

"About his suggestion..."

"Hey, listen." Peter reached into his mail slot and retrieved several envelopes. "Anne and I talked it over after you two left, and we agreed that it was unfair of all of us to jump on the idea like we did. The answer for us is to find a place like Advance, but not to take your place."

Laura picked up her own mail. "Maybe I wouldn't mind," she said. "I talked about it with my father this morning."

Peter expressed amazement, then launched into his usual criticism of Nick. Laura listened without comment. Since Peter was unaware of the latest development, his judgement was questionable. On the other hand, his emotions were not as involved as hers were, so it wouldn't hurt her to hear him out. In fact, it might help her make the decision.

"He's smooth," Peter told her. "He's very good at getting people to do what he wants. You just be careful you don't end up somewhere down the line holding the short end of the stick. If you make a commitment, be sure that he makes one, too."

A few minutes later Laura was sitting in the small cubicle that served as her office, reviewing the charts of the patients she would see that morning in clinic. She tried to keep her mind on her work, but the combination of a sleepless night and the questions humming around in her brain kept her from being as alert as usual. When the nurse came in to tell her that the first patient was ready for her, she had given the charts only a superficial review.

"I'm sorry, Mrs. Fox," she said to the nurse. "I didn't get to look at all the notes. Is there any particular problem with any of the ladies I'm going to see this morning?"

"Only the usual problem," Mrs. Fox replied cheerfully. "They've all gained too much weight, and only two of them seem upset about it."

A light seemed to go off in Laura's head. Here was a chance to perform a simple experiment of her own. If some of her patients were willing, she'd put them on diets similar to the one Nick had designed for her and see if it helped keep the weight gain problem under some control. That would give him another bit to put in his proposal.

Listen to yourself, she thought. *You're acting as if you've already agreed to join up with him. As if the two of you really are going into partnership on this.*

But the idea excited her, and she found that not two but four of her pregnant patients were interested in trying the diet. She made notes on each of them and planned to ask Nick's help that evening.

She also stopped in at the emergency room and asked for a job application. It wouldn't hurt, she told herself, to keep all her options open.

NICK SPENT MOST OF THE MORNING working in his office in the pro shop at the country club. The day was cold but sunny, and the usual March wind was quiet for a change. About a dozen hard-core players had shown up to use the course, but Nick had declined invitations to join them. He wanted to get ahead in his scheduling of local tournaments and events for late spring and summer. If things with Laura continued to work out, he wanted to be as free as possible.

He even composed a memorandum to the club board of directors, suggesting they consider hiring another pro, at least for the heavy summer season. He even offered to take a cut in his own pay to offset the extra expense.

His conversations early that morning with Isabelle and then with Andrew Selkirk had acted like a tonic on him. Nick felt confidence about the future growing within him like a strong, solid thing.

He would keep making plans as if Laura was definitely committed to him. It would be like the dream he had had as a child to be a healthy, strong man. He would pursue some activity, some lead daily, to ensure that his plans with Laura would succeed, in the same way that he had adjusted his life as an adolescent to ensure that he would turn out the way he had as an adult.

At one point during the morning he put down his pencil and paper and leaned back, an odd thought occurring to him. What if he had developed his relationship with his ex-wife with this kind of care? Would it have been possible to have avoided the pain and humiliation? The idea of still being married to her gave him a cold feeling in the pit of his stomach, but he had to admit that her unfaithfulness might have been partly because of his own insensitivity. He should have anticipated her needs and realized what the loneliness was doing to her. He frowned and scribbled Laura's name on a pad of paper.

Could he be making the same errors with Laura, he wondered. She'd made it very obvious how she felt about him. No words of love, actually, but he didn't need that to know that her feelings were deep—deep enough for her to express desire for him. He would be willing to bet any amount of money that that wasn't the sort of thing Laura Jensen went around telling guys.

He got up from his chair and walked around the littered desk to the watercooler. He drew a cupful of the cold water and sipped at it slowly.

She had said that she hadn't wanted to further their physical intimacy until she was sure about her decision for the future. But was that really what she wanted. He remembered the times they had kissed and realized that not once had she resisted him. And it had always been his move, his words, that had kept things from going farther.

Sometimes, Hawthorne, he told himself, *you can be ten times a fool. The lady has been sending you green lights for weeks now. Is your personal ambition more important than your relationship with her?*

No, he decided, it wasn't. Tonight he would show her how much he did care, how important she was to him. He would quit trying to manipulate her and would lay all his cards on the table.

A nervous shock hit his stomach. Suppose that she politely, coolly refused his advances? What then? He rubbed damp palms together.

Okay, he thought. It was like the sixteenth or seventeenth green putt. The game could go smoothly and then be blown to hell and gone, on that one stroke. The nerves that took him through those moments would stay with him for this one. He sat back down at his desk.

She would be working late today, he knew. Her schedule showed her taking late rounds at the hospital, which meant it would be nine or even ten before she could finally call it a day. How, he wondered, had she managed to maintain such a pace before she had gone on his system. Through sheer willpower, probably.

But she wasn't on call, and that meant he had a clear field all night. All night long. Nick's lips curved in a wicked smile.

LAURA SIGHED WITH WEARINESS and opened the front door of her house. She had finished rounds early and had raced over to the health club to catch the last aerobics class of the evening. It had been a mistake, since she was exhausted from the sleepless night before. In fact, she had dozed off in the whirl-pool. She was making the mistake of trying to do too much, just as she had in the past. But she did know that her body was handling the stress much better now. A few months ago she would have been aching with fatigue, hardly able to drag herself into the bedroom.

She flipped the light switch, annoyed when the living-room lamp didn't go on immediately. The wiring throughout the entire house could use an overhaul, and she reminded herself to mention it to her landlord the next time she paid the rent. A soft, glowing light was coming from the kitchen, and she assumed that Nick must have been over and left a hurricane lamp lit for her. He wouldn't have bothered to stay around in a dark house this late in the evening.

"I hope that's you, Laura." His big frame appeared in the kitchen doorway, a shadow against the glow. "Sorry about the lights, but I seem to have blown every fuse in the place."

"Don't worry." She bent down to slip her shoes off. "I've done it dozens of times myself. What are you doing here so late?"

"Waiting for you." His voice was an invitation. Laura straightened and walked into his embrace.

His kiss was long and leisurely, filling her with a gentle fire and making her forget her weariness. Laura pressed herself against him and ran her hands along his shoulders and back. The material of his coat felt strangely familiar.

"What in the world are you wearing?" she asked when he released her slightly. She touched his chest and felt a silky ruffled fabric. "This isn't your usual polo shirt or sweats."

"No, it's not." Nick placed a kiss on her temple. "This is a special evening, and I dressed for the occasion"

Laura turned him so that the golden light from the kitchen illuminated him. "You're wearing your tux, for goodness sake!"

Nick bowed. "It's appropriate. I'm introducing you to a new man tonight." He smiled, and he looked exactly as he had the first time she had seen him.

"New man?" she repeated, puzzled.

Nick took her elbow and steered her toward the kitchen. "You know Nick Hawthorne the lecher, the con man, the bully, the businessman. I thought tonight you might enjoy getting to know Nick Hawthorne, your lover."

Laura gasped. The kitchen had been transformed into an intimate dining place. White cloth on the old table. Shining silver, gleaming crystal and gold-rimmed china that she had never seen before. The glow of candles made the entire scene shimmer with elegance.

"Nick, where did all this come from?" Laura put a hand on the edge of the counter to steady herself. After the first stunning impression, she could see that it was still her old kitchen, George was still on top of the refrigerator, and the counters were still the same old chipped formica. But fragrant aromas of food cooking filled the air, and an arrangement of roses had been placed at the side of the table, lending a warm perfume of their own.

"The table setting's mine," Nick explained. He helped her off with her jacket, his hands moving seductively down her arms as she slid the garment off. "I have tons of stuff like this in storage. Until now, I didn't have anyone to share it with."

"And you're sharing it with me?" She turned to look at him. What did all this mean?

"Indeed I am." He picked up a candle in a silver base. "There's something in the bedroom I'd like you to take a look at as well." He handed her the light. "Something I want you to decide if you'd like to share with me."

Laura hesitated. "Nick...?"

"Go on." He shooed her gently toward the door. "I've got a few last-minute things to do with dinner. Don't take too long, but don't rush either."

Her curiosity at an all time high, Laura walked into the bedroom. Like the kitchen, it had been transformed. From what she could see by the light of the candle, there were flowers on the bureau and on the bedside table. Soft music played from a small tape deck set on the floor. The bed was turned down, and it didn't look as if it was made up with her old cotton sheets. She ran a hand over the pillow case. Satin.

Across the foot of the bed lay something that looked as if it was made from fine material. Laura set the candle down on the bureau and picked the thing up.

It shimmered in her hands, the silky fabric feeling like cool water as it flowed across her fingers. Laura found the shoulders and held the garment up.

It wasn't quite a nightgown. The pearly gray material wasn't sheer enough. It was more of a dressing gown, a lounging gown. Laura held it up to her face and sniffed. This hadn't been in storage. It was brand-new, chosen especially for her.

A thousand questions tumbled in her mind. Why this sudden turn of events? Why had he suddenly assumed a lover's role? She felt her palms dampen. Was she ready to accept this change? In spite of her bold words, she was nervous at the prospect of going to bed with Nick. There were so many unanswered questions.

From the kitchen, she could hear his deep voice humming and singing in his usual off-key style, and a wave of warm affection replaced the anxiety. She had been open about her feelings, and he was responding. She started to remove her clothing. She wasn't going to back out on him now.

The gown fit as if it had been tailor-made for her. The silky folds fell from her shoulders to her ankles and were caught up at her waist by a thin line of elastic. Laura brushed her hair, carefully applied a minimum of makeup by candlelight and dug a pair of dress sandals out of the back of her closet. Then she smoothed the gown over her hips and headed for the kitchen.

Out of the corner of his eye Nick saw her enter, and he turned the gas down under the dish he was heating. When he looked up at her, he felt the breath catch in his throat.

She was more than beautiful. She was a vision. The silk gown was perfect and made her look like an angel. Her dark hair floated loose around her sculptured face, and when her gray eyes gazed into his, Nick realized that he had never seen a woman so lovely.

I'm in love! The thought rose in his mind like a silvery bubble, both terrifying and exalting him. He stood frozen, watching her, knowing that she held the key to his future in more ways than he had imagined.

Laura smiled and snapped her fingers. "Earth to Nick," she said in a light tone. When he had glanced over at her, he had seemed to be stunned. She knew the gown was becoming, but his continued stare concerned her. She had expected an appreciative leer, maybe a kiss, but not this spellbound fascination.

Then the enchantment was over. He grinned in apparent approval and waved her into her place at the table. "You look marvelous," he said, giving her a kiss on the cheek and helping her into her chair. "When I saw that gown, I knew it was just right for you. It reminded me of the one you wore the first night."

He talked on, praising her beauty and telling her about the meal as he served it. Laura accepted the compliments and food with equal relish, but through it all she felt deeply puzzled. At times, she was certain she was hearing him speak from his heart, but other times, she suspected he was running a much-practiced love scene.

But he was charming and attentive and amusing, and except for the nagging feeling that he wasn't being totally open with her, she could find nothing to complain about. No one had ever treated her so romantically before, and after a while she slipped willingly into the scenario Nick was creating.

After the dinner was over, completed by an icy, minty sherbert that made her tongue tingle with its freshness, Laura offered to do the cleanup, since Nick had gone to such lengths to make a memorable dinner. She wasn't surprised, however, when he insisted that the dishes could wait until morning.

"I have a far more important activity in mind," he said, coming around to help her out of her chair. His hands touched her shoulders and slid down her arms to gather her hands in his. "Let's say good-night to George and go to bed."

Laura smiled. "You know, you didn't need to go to all this trouble, Nick. A simple 'I need to sleep with you' would have done."

He shook his head. "I did this so you'd know that I don't want to put any pressure on you. That this was purely a romance I wanted to start. It has nothing to do with our other involvements."

His words brought a warmth to her heart. Maybe for once he was being sincere. Maybe his own feelings were starting to deepen, and this staged seduction was the only way he could express himself.

"Well, then," she whispered. "If it's romance you want, then let's get on with the show." She put her arms around his neck.

Nick scooped her up and drew her against his chest. His kiss was warm and tender, and Laura felt an excitement building inside her. Tonight would be the best night of love she had ever experienced.

He turned around and blew out the candles, then he carried her into the bedroom and placed her on the satiny sheets. The light of the candle Laura had left behind softly illuminated the scene.

"One little thing," Nick murmured, reaching behind the bedside table. He gave a short jerk of his hand and raised the unplugged telephone cord. "I don't give a damn if you're on call tonight and the mayor himself wants your personal attention. Tonight, Laura Jensen, you're mine."

"The mayor's a *her*self," she said, laughing softly. "And if anyone could see the look on your face right now, I'm sure they wouldn't dare interfere."

"I need you, Laura," he whispered, his voice as intense as his expression. His features were as handsome as ever, but there was something new... something almost frightening in his eyes.

He took his shoes off without looking away from her, and Laura felt her heart start to beat wildly. For a moment she experienced an unreasoning sense of panic. His desire seemed too strong for her. Too overpowering. Then she remembered that the man sitting on her bed was her friend, not some strange lover who sought her out in the darkness. If his passion was powerful, so was hers. She reached out and caressed his face.

"Undress me," he said, catching her wrist in his hand and moving her fingers to the front of his shirt. "Take your time and do whatever you want to do." Show me, his eyes said, how you feel about me.

She sat up, kneeling in front of him, and began to remove his tie. As her fingers brushed his skin, she saw that his muscles jumped slightly and that the vein at the side of his neck was pulsing strongly. She pulled the tie away and flipped open the first studded buttonhole. Then she lowered her head and kissed the hollow at the base of his throat and up the side of his neck to a point just below his ear.

"Oh, God!" he gasped, clutching at her shoulders. "I don't think I can stand it. Let me..."

"Be quiet, Nick." She put her hand on his mouth. "You gave me a job to do, and I intend to finish it. Without any help from you, understand?" She raised herself up until she was looking down at him, and Nick Hawthorne, big and strong enough to crush her in his arms, nodded in submission, his eyes fired with barely controlled emotion.

Laura slowly slid the coat from his shoulders and arms. She folded it carefully and set it on the floor beside the bed, realizing that if she tried to get up, she might break the spell. Then she gave his chest a little push, and he lay back on the bed.

His socks came next, and she stripped them off without haste. His arches were covered liberally with soft hair, which shone reddish-gold in the candle-light. She caressed instep, toes and ankle and heard him groan in pleasure.

Nick watched through half-closed eyes as Laura moved around the bed. Her touch was driving him to a fever pitch, and he was sure that any moment his passions would break free of his control and he would find himself ripping the gown from her body and ravishing her. He took deep breaths and forced himself to lie still as her hands gently removed the studs from his shirtfront.

Her fingers were feathers on his chest as she parted the shirt. He closed his eyes as she fluffed the matted hair then opened them wide when her lips kissed his nipple. The sensation sent a thrill all through him, and he started to wrap her in his arms, stopping a fraction of a second before crushing her to him. *Control yourself,* he thought. *You told her this was her show. Leave it that way.* He settled for stroking her soft hair and her silk-clad back.

Laura continued to caress his skin, pleased that her touch was so exciting to him. She drew her fingers over the fastenings of his waistband and then over the swollen mound that strained against the front of his formal trousers.

"Okay." Nick's voice was thick. "I think it's my turn." His fingers tangled in her hair, and his other hand gripped her hip.

"I'm not finished," Laura complained, and she started to unfasten his pants.

"I know you're not!" Nick moved suddenly, pulling her down and positioning himself above her. "But if you keep on, *I'm* going to be in just a matter of moments. I need something to take my mind off the way your touch makes me feel!" He lowered himself onto her and began kissing her with a fierce tenderness.

Laura responded, her own passion rising. Touching him had been good. Having him touch her was heaven.

He kissed her throat and slid the gown down to her waist, baring her breasts. He teased and caressed with his lips and tongue until the excitement within her became a burning sensation. Then he slid the gown the rest of the way off.

Laura cried out his name as he explored every inch of her body. Her skin seemed to be on fire, and his caress only made the flame burn hotter. She was aware only of her need and his touch, and she began to cry out for fulfillment as her body began a deep throbbing that made her almost frantic.

"It's okay, love." Nick's legs moved against hers, and she realized that he was completely naked. His arms slipped beneath her, and he lifted her hips to meet his.

Laura cried out as they became one, and the throbbing within her soon grew to an overwhelming pulsation of pleasure. She held Nick tightly as the wave subsided, willing him to feel every degree of delight that she had. But rather than continuing to move as she expected him to, he lifted his upper body and looked down at her, a devilish smile on his face.

"That was a pretty impressive earthquake for such a cool lady," he said. "How'd you like several more of the same?" His hips pushed hers down into the mattress. Laura laughed and declared that she had been completely satisfied, but something in his eyes told her there was more to come. Much more.

He proved to be as good as the promise in his eyes. His strong body and loving hands and lips took her to levels of physical delight she had never known before. His skin grew hot and wet beneath her hands, and the sound of his whispered words of passion set her mind on fire.

Finally, when she was certain she could feel nothing more, she sensed that he was unleashing himself. The muscles in his back began to swell, and his arms wrapped around her so tightly she could hardly breathe. Then his grip eased.

"Look at me, Laura," he said, his voice barely recognizable. She complied and found herself looking into a face strained with passion. His gaze caught and held hers, and she was swept along with him as he spoke her name repeatedly, thrusting deep within her. Her body tingled and she was released on a wave of pleasure that crested just as Nick shuddered and called her name.

For a moment she felt her self-identity slip, and she was one with the man who held her and whose eyes told her of the passion he had spent and the pleasure he had known. He smiled and kissed her. Laura kissed him back, then drifted into a dreamless sleep.

CHAPTER TEN

THE FIRST THING SHE NOTICED on awakening was the sweet smell of an almond herbal tea. The second was that she was alone in the bed. She was naked, but the sheets were tucked neatly, and they were her old cotton ones. Had the entire experience only been a wonderful dream?

"Good morning, sleepyhead." The sound of Nick's voice put an end to her fears. "Or should I say, good afternoon?" He entered the room carrying a tray loaded with cups and bowls that emitted swirls of fragrant steam.

"Afternoon?" Laura sat up, holding the sheet to her chest.

"Yep." Nick cleared the bedside table and set the tray on it. "I don't know if I should be flattered or upset. You went out like a light, and you've been dead to the world ever since. I even changed the sheets...."

"My God, the hospital! The clinic..." Laura swung her legs over the side of the bed.

"I called in for you." Nick put a hand on her bare knee. "It's okay. Have some tea." He handed her a cup.

She took a sip, feeling the warmth spread through her, bringing life to her still-sleeping brain cells. "I didn't sleep night before last," she said, not looking at him. "I had a lot on my mind."

Nick sat beside her and put his arm around her bare shoulders. "After last night you seem to have made up your mind about some of those things."

"I guess I have," she said, turning to look at him. His kiss was tender.

"But remember," she said, sipping her tea, "you said there were no strings attached...that this would be one thing, and our other involvements would be entirely separate."

"I know what I said." He released her shoulders and picked up a bowl of cereal. "But after everything that happened..."

"Everything that happened was wonderful, Nick." Laura put the tea cup down. "And I appreciate your taking care of things for me today. But I'm not sick, and I'm not a child who needs to be fed in bed." She pointed at the cereal bowl. "I'll eat some of that in the kitchen after I've showered, but I'm really not feeling hungry at all."

"But after last night...." He looked hurt.

Laura struggled against relenting. She was convinced he was trying to pull her strings again, using the passion they had shared to get her into line. She stood up, wrapping the sheet around herself, unwilling to be naked when he was dressed.

"Last night made you more dear to me than ever before," she said softly. "But, Nick, it gave you no right to take over. You've taught me how to take care of my body very well. Now, ease off and trust that I'll use what you've taught me to best advantage." She turned and went into the bathroom.

Nick stared at the closed door, then down at the warm bowl in his hands. What had he done wrong? The last thing he expected her to do was turn cool on him! He'd given her everything he could, and what did he get back? Thanks, Nick, but no thanks. Well, two could play that tune!

He slammed the bowl down and stalked into the kitchen. She was a heartless woman, he concluded, gathering up his tuxedo and the bundle of satin sheets. She wanted no more from him than sex, and he had actually believed last night and this morning that he was in love with her. Self-disgust rose in him. He tossed his jacket over his shoulder and headed for the front door.

"The cereal's good, Nick." Her voice from the bedroom pulled him up short. "Did you use a new recipe?"

What the hell was going on? He hesitated. She sounded friendly, pleasant, as if nothing had happened. Curiosity overcame anger, and he turned around.

"Don't leave just yet." She appeared in the doorway, wearing her old terry cloth bathrobe and spooning up the cereal. "I need to talk to you about some business."

"Business?" He let the clothes and sheets slide to the floor.

"Yesterday I started a project involving four of my patients." Her tone was crisp, and she didn't seem to notice his confusion. "I need your advice on preparing diets for them. We're hoping to show that certain kinds of food can help reduce excessive weight gain during pregnancy."

Nick listened to her, amazed. Instead of shoving him to one side of her life, she was actually bringing him closer. For her to have gone ahead and started an experiment that could help him was proof that she was involved with her mind as well as her body. The question was: where was Laura Jensen's heart?

Laura continued to talk while she went into the kitchen for more tea. When she had seen Nick at the front door, a sullen angry look on his face, she knew she had overdone the distance bit. He was bruised, and she was responsible. She hoped that letting him know how much she respected what she had learned from him would soothe his feelings.

Except for the breakfast dishes, the kitchen was clean. While she had slept, he must have worked like a fury. In the cage on top of the refrigerator George dozed peacefully, probably replete with sunflower seeds.

"I don't know how comfortable I'd be, drawing up diets for expectant women." Nick leaned against the doorway. "Aren't there all kinds of complications you have to keep watching for?"

"That's why I'll monitor the program." Laura smiled at him. "You know far more about food than I do, I know more about body chemistry. We're a team."

Nick's grin lit the room. "A team," he repeated. "Partners." He looked heavenward and snapped his fingers. "That's it," he yelled. "Partners for Life!"

Laura found herself swept up in a bear hug. Nick swung her around the room, repeating the phrase over and over. Then he stopped, holding her close and gazing into her eyes.

"That's what we'll call the program," he said. "Partners for Life." His hand stroked her hair. "That's what we'll be," he murmured.

Laura heard the last words as if they were an electric shock. Was this a proposal of some sort? The idea of marriage, especially coming from Nick, seemed completely out of line with reality. She held her breath, praying that he wouldn't make the proposal. She couldn't trust him to mean it yet.

"You don't like the idea?" He held her away from him and studied her a moment. "Partners for Life? I think it's pretty darn catchy."

Laura sighed. He had only meant to refer to his system. "It is a good name, Nick," she agreed. "Now you've got even more to present to Mr. Selkirk."

"I sure do." His expression was delighted. "When he sees you and hears you giving the sales pitch...."

"Hold on." Laura raised her hands and pushed away from him. "Salesmanship's your line, not mine. I'll just keep in the background, thanks."

"Okay," Nick agreed easily. But there was something in his eyes that made her realize the subject wasn't closed yet.

Laura dressed, and they spent most of the next hour seated at the kitchen table making notes and discussing how Nick could best get his proposal for Partners down on paper. She told herself that even if things didn't work out between them romantically or professionally, she did owe him her help for now.

But as they worked, it became apparent to her that they were more than two people with a few ideas. Their approaches meshed perfectly, and the concepts that Nick began to write out were far-reaching.

"You know," she said, "what you're talking about is nothing more than a total remake of society. Don't you think that's pushing it a bit?"

Nick gave her his usual smile, but she could detect the seriousness underneath it. "I admit I get carried away," he said. "I know that the world won't beat a path to my door. But if I can reach even a few people, and they find their lives improved, I'll be satisfied."

"A *few* people." Laura looked at his notes. "Nick you've got a nationwide campaign mapped out here."

He shrugged. "Why think small?"

Laura tried to frame a reply, wanting to slow him down without actually throwing a wet blanket on him. She could see the possibility of his opening a center in a largely populated area, and maybe even expanding to more than one city. But what he seemed to be envisioning was far too ambitious for one man—even one man accompanied by a woman, she mused. The sound of the doorbell cut through her thoughts.

Anne Vance stood at the door, a tureen in her hands. "Pete told me you called in sick," she told Laura. "I was making soup, and I thought you'd like some."

"I wasn't sick." Laura showed her into the kitchen. "I'm playing hookey. Nick and I are doing a little work on his project. But we'll enjoy the soup anyway."

Nick greeted Anne and motioned for her to sit in Laura's chair. While Laura heated the soup, he revealed bits and pieces of his ideas to Anne. Her reactions were interesting.

"It sounds like you have a life's work cut out for you," she commented. "As long as there are people who become aware of the possibilities and are willing to make a change in their life, you'd never run out of clients, would you."

Laura served the soup. Nick tried to offer her his chair, but she declined, saying she'd rested enough. The soup was a thick rich vegetable, and she sipped it with gusto while she leaned against the sink.

"I want to tell you again," Anne said, "how much I appreciate what both of you did the other night. It was so stupid of us to fight like that."

"It happens." Nick put his spoon down. "Marriage is a tightrope at best. I hope the two of you can figure out how to walk it together."

Anne smiled. "You don't sound very encouraging."

Nick's expression darkened, and Laura hastily changed the subject. "I did mention to my dad that you might be interested in looking at the situation in Advance," she said. "You ought to plan to take a weekend and go up to check it out with the kids."

"Oh, no, Laura." Anne looked down at her soup. "We couldn't...I mean, it sounded so good the other night, but it's your..."

"Take her up on it." Nick leaned back in his chair, his eyes intent on Anne. "You'd be doing us both a favor. Laura isn't quite convinced yet, but her future lies with me." His tone was confident.

Anne glanced at Laura. "I heard through the grapevine that you'd picked up an application for the ER job."

Laura saw the look of triumph on Nick's face. "I haven't filled it out yet. I'm still thinking."

"Keep on thinking," he said softly. "I like the direction your mind's taking you in, these days."

Anne left after a few more minutes, and Laura turned to face Nick. "Don't go thinking I've made up my mind," she warned him as she took in his smug expression. "I'm not committed to anything but finishing up the six weeks."

"Of course you aren't." He took a plastic container out and put the rest of the soup in it. "Good soup," he commented. "Has a bit too much salt, though. I want you to drink several large glasses of water over the next hour to flush out the sodium."

"I'll flush it!" she snapped. "And you'd better flush, too. Your car's been out front for the better part of twenty-four hours, and the neighbors are probably having a great time talking about it."

Nick came up behind her and put his arms around her. "Well, then, why don't we give them something to talk about?" He began to kiss her throat.

Laura felt a warm melting sensation, but she didn't want to succumb. It would only give him more evidence of the control he had over her. She should insist that lovemaking be on her terms at times.

"Not in the middle of the afternoon," she protested, hearing the lack of conviction in her own voice. Her mind might say that giving in was strategically foolish, but her heart and body were eagerly succumbing.

Nick eased her hair aside and licked her ear. "Give me one good *honest* reason why not," he whispered, sending shivers through her body.

"The lights," Laura said frantically. "We have to call an electrician to get the lights fixed."

"Wrong." Nick's hand moved gently down her body. "It was just a fuse. I reset it this morning while you slumbered in your bed of sloth." He touched her and began working his magic.

Laura groaned and turned into his embrace. "I'll show you sloth," she hissed, wrapping her arms around his neck and kissing him for all she was worth. Beneath her hands, she felt his back shake with laughter, and then she was lifted and carried into the bedroom.

IN SPITE OF NICK'S PERSUASIVENESS, Laura refused to agree to sharing domestic quarters. She was having enough trouble sorting out her feelings, and she knew that if he was around constantly, she would never be able to get a clear perspective on the situation. And the idea of living with a man when there was no marriage potential did bother her in spite of her liberal outlook on life and love. They were lovers. She could not deny that any more than she could deny that his touch inflamed her, but she determined to keep some distance, some independence. If she wasn't careful, Nick would suck her life into his like a sponge soaking up a puddle of water. Then who would she be, and what would she do when he got tired of the relationship and decided to squeeze her out of his life?

She was convinced that she was no more than a romantic interlude to him. His interest in her professional help outweighed any other considerations. She had only to look at the history of their relationship to be convinced of that. Sex had been secondary, and although it was fantastically satisfying, he never mentioned love unless it was in the

standing, they were also chances for him to cut out on her, if he were so inclined.

His arm tightened around her. "Come on, Laura. You've been working hard and you could use the holiday. I need you, remember?"

"I'll have to see if I can arrange it," she mumbled, holding her teacup near her lips.

Nick tilted his head and tried to study her face. Although she had been unbelievably loving and compliant in bed, her attitude still chilled him at times.

He loved her, there was no doubt in his mind about that. Each time they were together she wove her spell more tightly around him. The way she looked. The things she said. Each graceful move she made. He was hopelessly hooked. But he had felt that way once before, and it had only lead to heartbreak.

What he should do, he realized, was get down on his knees and confess his feelings outright. He demanded honesty from her. He ought to be willing to give the same back.

But the idea that she might look at him with her soft eyes and tell him that she was sorry, the feeling wasn't mutual, kept him quiet. Sooner or later her actions would give him clues to the truth. Until then his pride made him wait.

"Try hard," he said softly, lowering his head to kiss the side of her mouth. "Because I'm not going without you. I'm not putting myself through what happened last time."

She protested, but he sensed that underneath she was pleased. She set her cup down and turned in his arms until her legs were across his lap.

"You know," she said, narrowing her eyes seductively, "I figure about half of everything you tell me is blarney, but I like to hear it anyway." She put her arms around his neck and kissed him until his toes tingled. Nick remained passive for as long as he could, then took over.

Laura found herself pressed backward into the sofa, her blouse and jeans magically unbuttoned, and Nick's skillful touch beginning to set her on fire. She laughed and pulled the tail of his polo shirt out of his pants.

"You are a lusty wench," he growled as she teased his skin with her fingertips seeking the spots where she knew he enjoyed being touched. "Will I never be able to satisfy you?"

"Give it your best shot," Laura challenged, and Nick willingly complied.

MUCH LATER he was jerked out of a well-earned slumber by the sound of a ringing telephone and the movement of warm limbs untangling from his own. The top sheet was hopelessly twisted into a long, satin rope, and he flung it aside as Laura fumbled for the phone.

Watching her through half-closed eyes, he thought about the fact that he would have to get used to this sort of interruption. She was a doctor, after all. They were going to live together someday, and he would have to learn to adjust.

She hung up the phone. Her dark hair swung forward to veil her face, and her slender limbs looked so delicate and fragile in the soft light of the bedside lamp it was difficult to believe that only hours before they had been wrapped around him, almost squeezing the breath from him. Nick smiled at the memory and felt desire for her rising again.

"I've got to go in," she said, looking at him quickly then getting up from the bed. "One of my patients is having a difficult labor, and even though I'm off the rotation, I think she needs me. We've established a good rapport." She gave him an apologetic glance.

"I can vouch for your ability to establish good rapport, my love." Nick lay back and waved at her. "Go on, give the lady your help. I'll be right here when you get back."

"All right." Her smile made his heart do a flip. Had she expected him to fuss at her leaving to do her job? No way!

In fact, he thought, as he watched her move around the small room while she dressed, he felt proud of her. To think that this beautiful woman could be so many things, had so many talents and gifts, and she was his. Maybe not completely, but he had made great progress. Nick relaxed and let vague plans for the future drift through his mind.

Laura ran a comb quickly through her hair and pulled on her gray jacket. She blew Nick a kiss, not trusting herself to get too close to him. She wasn't obligated to go in, and the temptation of his warm body might be too much for her to resist if she touched him.

"Don't wait for me," she said. "I have no idea how long this will take. You might as well go on home, if you want."

"Nothing short of a cataclysmic event could get me out of your bed," he murmured. "Even if it takes the rest of the night, I'll wait right here for a repeat performance of this evening's loving.''

His words brought a glow to her heart, and as she drove the few blocks to the hospital, Laura began to wonder if her feelings for Nick Hawthorne were getting beyond the like-and-lust stage. Could it be that she was in love with the man?

Once on the job, however, her mind became occupied with giving help and relief to the young woman struggling with her first delivery. Laura's presence obviously gave her renewed courage, and although the process did go slowly, the result was the birth of a healthy baby girl.

Laura resisted the urge to call Nick and report, but she wasn't sure he would share her enthusiasm at four in the morning. She spent time helping the young father calm down and tactfully suggested things he could do to make his wife's first days at home with the new baby easier. Around five, she drove home.

She had rented the small house because of its proximity to the hospital, but now that she and Nick were obviously going to be spending much more time with each other, she wondered if she should look for a larger place. She had never seen Nick's apartment, and though he had been hinting that they should live together, he had not suggested his place would be more roomy. She turned the corner and almost ran into a fire truck parked across the road. She slammed on her brakes and stared in horror at the scene in front of her.

Her house was in flames. The truck blocked her way, making it difficult for her to tell how much actual damage had been done, but she felt as if the world had ended.

Nick! Had he been trapped inside? Dead from smoke inhalation? Or worse, by burning? An icy fear gripped her heart.

She managed to get out of the car and walk around the big truck toward the burning house. A fireman reached out to stop her, but she shook his hand off.

"That's my house," she cried, the words tearing at her throat. "My...was anyone...?"

"No one was hurt, ma'am." The fireman smiled reassuringly. "It looks a whole lot worse than it is. What's burning is the old wood siding on the outside of the house. The inside will have some smoke and water damage, but most of it can probably be salvaged."

Laura groaned in relief. Then another thought hit her. No one would have any reason to know that Nick was in her bedroom. He hadn't driven over, preferring the exercise of a walk. Since her car was gone, the neighbors would presume that she was at work, and no search would have been made for any occupant.

"I've got to get inside," she said, whirling around. "There's a man...."

"No, there isn't." The sound of Nick's voice made her turn again. "I got out, Laura, and I got George out with me."

Laura clapped her hands to her face, undecided whether to laugh or cry. Nick stood barefoot on the wet street, the gerbil cage tucked under one arm. He was clad toga-style in one of the satin sheets.

"It was all I could manage to grab on such short notice," he said, grinning.

"Oh, Nick! I love you!" Laura threw her arms around his neck. "I thought I'd lost you."

"It won't ever happen," he said softly, embracing her with his free arm. Then he kissed her fervently, and Laura knew that from now on, she would have to live by his side. Her feelings were too strong not to be love. Even if he didn't reciprocate, she was committed, heart and soul.

CHAPTER ELEVEN

"YOU AND GEORGE will have to bunk in with me," Nick said after they had reached the relative seclusion of Laura's car. The firemen had besieged Laura with questions once they had found out she was the official resident in the house, and Nick had stood off to one side, shivering in his makeshift clothing and turning her startling declaration of love over in his mind.

She had said she loved him! That in itself was enough to make him want to shout for joy. But the circumstances were unusual, to say the least, and he wanted to find out if she had really meant it when things were calmed down and they were alone together.

In any event, he thought as he buckled on his seat belt, the problem of getting her to agree to live together was solved. The fire had been one lucky break, even if it had nearly killed him. He sneezed and caught the cage, which was balanced on his bare knees, just before it fell.

"Oh my gosh," Laura exclaimed. "I didn't think about you standing around in the cold." She started the engine. "We've got to get you in a hot shower as quickly as possible."

Nick sneezed again. "I've got a double bed," he said. "You can minister to me there. You're a hell of a lot hotter than a shower."

Laura didn't reply, and when he looked over at her, he saw that her lips were pulled into a tight line. What now? Had he been too flip? Said something that had made her mad?

"What's the matter?" he asked, reaching over to touch her. "I'm safe. George is safe, and your belongings aren't a total loss. My apartment isn't much, but it is roomier than the house was. What's bothering you?"

Laura blinked back tears. It was silly, but she felt like bawling her eyes out. Nick was safe, but the near miss still frightened her, and her blurted declaration of love embarrassed her now that the heat of the moment had passed. He had made no reply except to kiss her. Did that mean he didn't *want* to make a response? She wasn't sure she needed to find out.

Well, until she knew where she stood with him, she would be far more careful from now on not to expose herself. Nick was a competitor, and he could be one of those people who lost interest once the game was won.

"I just don't know about moving in with you," she said carefully, driving the car in the direction of the apartment complex where he had told her he lived. Dawn was beginning to turn the air from darkness into grayness, and she could tell that the day was going to be overcast. It would suit her mood.

"Don't be silly." Nick waved his left hand in the air. "It doesn't make any sense for us to live apart. We have Partners to work on. We have each other."

He paused. "People set up households on much less." His tone was ironic.

His marriage again, Laura thought. Had his experience been so bitter that he would never consider going through it again? Would he never take a chance on making a different woman his wife?

And if he was willing, would she be? Was love enough to make a relationship last a lifetime? She thought of her parents and the way the two of them lived and worked as a team. Could she and Nick ever operate with such harmony?

"I suppose I don't have much choice right now," she conceded. "It'll be weeks before the house is habitable, and I hate the idea of looking for another place to live. I'd probably have to take out a longer lease than I'd like..." She lapsed into silence. Beside her, Nick was quiet. Only the sound of the car moving along the street and the scrabbling of the upset gerbil in his cage were audible.

She followed Nick's earlier directions and pulled into the parking lot next to his station wagon. Without a word she took the cage from him and let him lead her into the apartment building.

It was clean and neat but far too sterile for her taste. The hallway was carpeted in an undistinguished brown tweed, and the only touch of decoration was a tall rubber plant standing in front of the window at the turn of the staircase. Nick bent and dug in the dirt with his fingers.

"I keep my key in here," he explained. "That way I always know where it is." He stood, adjusting the sheet with an air of great dignity.

In spite of her depressed feelings, Laura had to smile. "You look really funny," she said. "I think we'd better get inside your place before someone comes out and decides to call the cops." Nick smiled and made a sweeping gesture with his bare arm. "It's *our* place now," he said. "And if the neighbors don't like it, that's just too bad. There's no law against wearing a sheet or having a roommate."

Laura didn't comment, but she did let out an exclamation of astonishment when she saw his apartment. It was the barest, starkest place she had ever seen. There were no carpets or curtains. Just bare wood floors and metal blinds. The furniture was all vinyl, glass and wood. No softness, just angles and lines. "You actually *live* here?" she asked.

Nick laughed dryly and strode past her. "You don't recognize the decor? My allergies, remember?" He went into another room, and she could hear drawers opening and closing.

She found the kitchen and set the cage on the counter. In contrast to her own, the cupboard and counter area was spacious. Glass containers, neatly marked, stood in long rows, and everything gleamed. He might be many things, Laura thought, but one of them was an excellent housekeeper.

She heard the sound of water and assumed that he had gone ahead and taken a shower. Good. She needed the time to think.

However, Nick reappeared before she had much time to sort through her feelings. Dressed in faded jeans and a white T-shirt, his auburn hair combed back from his tanned face, he looked so devastatingly handsome that she asked herself how she could seriously consider life without him. He made her blood sing and her heart beat faster. She loved him. There was no way around it.

"Okay." He rubbed his hands together. "First order of business is to get this place fit for you. I need to get more food for starters."

"Nick." Laura decided she had to try one more time, but her heart wasn't in it. "Maybe I should take a motel room until—"

"Listen to me!" Anger flared in his eyes. "I *heard* you say that you love me. Was that a lie, or just a statement in the heat of the moment?"

She shook her head. "I meant it. I think I've felt that way for quite some time, but it took thinking I'd lost you to make me realize it."

Nick nodded slowly. "Okay, then. Don't go giving me any more grief about not living with me." He reached for her and gathered her into his arms.

Laura melted into his embrace, and the tears started. She was flooded with them, uncontrollably shaken by the emotions that ran through her. Nick held her tightly, and when she had cried herself out, he led her to the bedroom, undressed her and made her promise that she would try to get some rest. He told her he was going to go out and get a few clothes for her and some provisions. Laura didn't protest. She was too exhausted.

When the telephone rang sometime later, Laura woke with a start, disoriented at first. Nick was still gone, so she took the call.

It was the fireman in charge of investigating the blaze at her home. The cause, he told her, was old and faulty wiring. Until the landlord fixed the problem, the building would have to remain empty. So much for moving back in a few days, she thought uneasily.

She called the Center and explained her absence. She was allowed to work shorter hours for the rest of the week and arranged to take days off the following week to accompany Nick to his tournament. Then she called her parents. Her father was gone, but she and her mother talked for a while.

"You're in love with this man, aren't you?" Adele asked, obviously trying to find a logical explanation for her daughter's unusual behavior.

"I think so," Laura admitted. "It's crazy, but I've never felt this way about any man before."

Adele laughed. "That's the way I felt about your father. I'll never forget the looks on my parents' faces when I told them Walt and I were going to get married and live in Wyoming."

"Do you and dad mind very much...I mean, is dad upset with me for not...?"

"Honey, don't you worry. We both want you to be happy, and if it means that you have to live a different life than the one we thought you had planned, well, that's the way it's going to have to be. He's already talked to your friend, Peter, and he seemed to like the young man."

After the conversation with her mother, Laura took a long shower in Nick's spacious bathroom, reveling in the luxury of a full stream of hot water, and considered her situation.

For almost all of her twenty-nine years she had been sure of what she wanted. Nothing and no one had deterred her from her set path. Now, here she was, tossed around by circumstances and fate and the strong will of a man she believed she loved. *Come out of the fog,* she scolded herself. *Make up your*

*own mind about what you want, and quit letting
things just happen to you.*

She dried herself and dressed in a bathrobe she
found hanging on the hook behind the door. It was
yards too big, but she had no desire to get back into
her own clothes. Nick had promised to pick up a few
things for her, and later she could go back to her
house and see what could be salvaged from the fire.

Then, feeling a bit as if she was snooping, she set
out to explore the apartment.

Nick was inordinately tidy, she discovered. If they
were going to live together in harmony, he would
have to loosen up and she would have to get used to
putting things away instead of letting them pile up.
Her style of house cleaning was once-a-week-maybe.
Nick's was clearly minute-to-minute.

It was also clear that he lived in the present. She
could find no references to the past. No pictures, no
trophies. He had a small collection of paperback
books on his bedside table, but no television. In the
living room was an expensive-looking radio system,
but no records or tapes. If she had walked in, not
knowing who lived in these stark rooms, she would
never have placed the electric spirit of Nick Hawthorne within the undecorated walls and bare floors.

Hunger pangs reminded her that she had had
nothing to eat since the feast Nick had prepared the
night before. She also remembered that she needed
to get over to the laboratory soon for the tests that
would show how her metabolism had reacted to his
six-week makeover. But that would have to wait for
a less hectic morning. She went into the kitchen and
rolled back the sleeves of the huge bathrobe. When

Nick finally returned, she was cleaning up the remains of a large breakfast.

He was laden with packages and good humor. His smile widened as he took in her bathrobe-wrapped form and the messy kitchen. "Making yourself at home, I see."

"I'm cleaning it up," she replied, not sure if his comment implied censure or satisfaction.

"Don't worry." Nick set his armload of packages down on a clear section of the counter. "It's good to see a little homey clutter." He turned and put his hand under her chin. "You look wonderful," he said softly. "You must have rested all the sad feelings away."

"I rarely come unglued like that," Laura admitted. "I guess it was a reaction to all...all the changes and things."

"And things," Nick repeated in a whisper. He kissed her tenderly, undemandingly, then stepped back. "Come on into the living room," he said, grinning. "I've got some surprises for you."

The surprises turned out to be an entire new spring and summer wardrobe. Laura was aghast and protested that she couldn't accept such a generous gift from him, but Nick insisted.

"If you can't bring yourself to take it outright," he said, "then think of it as an investment I'm making. When I show you off to potential investors next week, I need you properly packaged." He gestured toward the bags and boxes of clothing. "Think of all this as decoration for the product I'm trying to sell."

He seemed so determined that Laura finally gave in, but privately she decided to find out the cost of the clothes and pay him back. Her insurance would eventually cover the loss of her damaged items. She could reimburse him then.

The next issue at hand was the matter of food and rent. It took more arguing, but she finally beat him down.

"I'm *not* your wife," she pointed out. "I'm in no way dependent on you, and now that the six weeks is up, you have no obligation to feed me, much less house me. If you don't let me carry my share, I swear I'll find a place of my own!" His expression darkened for a moment, then he agreed, promising to keep tabs on the grocery bills and to let her pay half the rent when it came due.

For the remainder of the week she juggled her time training at the Center, salvaging her belongings, loving Nick and learning to live with him. The results of her tests came through, and they spent hours working them into a presentation for Partners. The combination of not smoking and the aerobics had done wonders for her heart rate and blood pressure, and Nick joked that her heart would probably outlast the rest of her. Laura agreed privately that it might if he didn't break it.

She continued negotiating with her father and Peter and accepted the fact that she was going to stay with Nick, no matter how things went between them romantically. As they worked together and planned, she realized that her love went beyond infatuation. She believed in Nick and what he wanted to do. What his true feelings were for her, however, she had no idea.

He seemed to enjoy the changes she brought to his living space, although she kept expecting him to have a neatness fit at any moment. By Saturday she felt comfortable enough, however, to hang some pictures and buy a few bright cushions for the stark chairs and couch. When Nick returned from the club late in the afternoon, he expressed only delight.

"I couldn't ever bring myself to make this a home," he said, hugging her. "You've done it in just a few days."

Laura felt his praise wrap around her like a warm blanket. They were going to make it. Living together would help them iron out any difficulties in the relationship, and down the road she could see marriage. Marriage, a family....

"I have a treat for you tonight," Nick said, breaking into her thoughts. "Isabelle's invited us over for dinner. We're in for a fine feast and a social treat."

"Social treat?" Laura eyed him askance.

"Isabelle's dinners are legendary and exclusive. It's kind of like being invited to the White House, only on a smaller scale. In spite of all the years I've known her, this is the first time I've gotten an invitation." His face lit up with excitement. "I think it's because of you."

"Me?"

Nick nodded. "Isabelle loves me, but she's never approved of the way I've lived. You, she approves of."

He turned out to be right. The party was large and formal, but Laura found herself monopolized by Isabelle from the first moment she and Nick entered their hostess's magnificent home. It was less of a dinner party, Laura observed, and more of a debut for herself and Nick as a couple. She enjoyed herself thoroughly, however, until Isabelle asked Nick directly when they planned to marry.

Nick's laughter had an uneasy ring to it. "You know my feelings about matrimony, Isabelle," he said, taking Laura's hand in his. "We're friends and we're partners. We don't need anything else to bind us."

"Oh?" Isabelle's thin white eyebrows rose. "And how do you feel about that, Laura?" she asked.

Laura hesitated. Almost any answer she gave would be a no-win. "I hadn't given it much thought," she finally replied. "Beyond getting Nick's system out to the public..."

"Well, give it some thought," Isabelle said sternly. "Nickie needs to be married to you, even if he's too blind to admit it."

The conversation shattered the pleasant mood of the evening. Laura watched as Nick grew withdrawn and sullen. He cleared his throat and coughed frequently, and if she hadn't known better, she would have sworn he was coming down with a bad cold. When the coughing gave way to difficulty getting his breath, she became thoroughly alarmed.

"It's all the perfume and smoke and dust," he claimed after she had drawn him aside and demanded to know what was wrong. "This house is decades old, and I always get allergic reactions in places like it."

"Do you have any medication with you?" Laura noted the strained lines near his mouth and eyes. If she was any kind of diagnostician, he was on the verge of a severe asthma attack.

"In the car. Glove compartment."

Laura took his arm. "Let's step outside for a minute, Nick."

A few breaths from his Medihaler seemed to do the trick. Within seconds he was breathing normally again, and a smile had replaced the strained and sullen expression. "I'm sorry," he said. "I should have loaded up on antihistamine before we came. I forgot what a wet blanket my allergies can be."

"It wasn't your allergies, Nick." Laura looked straight at him, challenging him. "You were just fine until Isabelle backed you into a corner about marriage. What is it with you, anyway?"

Nick avoided her eyes. "It's a long story. I'm okay now. We'd better go back inside.

"No!" Laura grabbed his arm and pulled him around to face her. "Nick, I want to know now why you're so weird about marriage. Why you have nothing around your apartment to remind you of the past. If I'm going to commit my love and my career to you, I have a right to know!"

He gazed at her for a long moment. "Okay," he finally said. "Let's go tell Isabelle good-night. I promise to come clean with you."

He was as good as his word. An hour after they had returned to the apartment, Laura was struggling to absorb the chilling story. He told her of Caroline's loss of love under the realities of marriage to a touring golf pro, of her cheating affair and of her schemes to destroy his life. If his ex-wife had been more subtle, his friend less loyal and Nick less perceptive, he could be in prison for an assault conviction. Now she understood his complete aversion to marriage.

"I got unlucky," Nick stated, his voice flat and emotionless. "I managed to pick a piranha. Please, don't take it personally, but I vowed once the divorce was final that I'd never let myself get into a situation where I could feel that kind of pain again."

"I understand," Laura said. It didn't help the feeling of rejection, but at least she knew that his problems were nothing she had caused. "I really appreciate your honesty. As far as I'm concerned, the issue is history. Don't let yourself get upset about it anymore."

Nick stared at her. He had taken off his jacket and tie and loosened his collar. Nervous sweat dampened his face, and when he had gestured with his hands, Laura noticed that his fingers shook slightly. Telling her his story had cost him a great deal, she realized, and she was determined to put him at ease as quickly as possible.

"You're really going to let me off without an argument?" he asked, his expression incredulous. "No protestations that you'd be a better wife than Caroline was?"

Laura forced a smile. "I never said I wanted to get married."

"No," he agreed slowly. "You haven't. But I figured..."

"Don't figure." She took his hand. "It might serve to get you stirred up again. I've known chronic asthmatics who could conjure up an attack just by brooding. Don't let yourself be like that, Nick. It isn't necessary."

He pulled her close and put his arms around her. "I know," he said softly. "And I feel one hundred percent better now that I've told you about it." He kissed her temple. "You're the best medicine I've ever had, Laura."

She snuggled against him, vowing to herself that she would be content to be that for him as long as he needed her.

Later, as they lay together on his bed and Laura slept in his arms, Nick did brood for a while. He had hoped he would never have to tell her about his wife's betrayal. It somehow made him feel less of a man. It wasn't logical, but that was the way he felt.

Laura, hadn't seemed to be bothered though. She had come into his arms willingly enough, and her words had reassured him of her love. He had tried to tell he that he loved her in return, but the words stuck in his throat. It had seemed wrong to tell her of a ruined love and then turn right around and mouth trite protestations of devotion to her. So he had kept quiet about his feelings.

A strand of her hair tickled his bare chest, and he gently smoothed it back. Her soft even breathing and the beat of her heart against his side soothed him, and he gradually relaxed.

Maybe things would work out, he thought as sleep drifted over him. She was working with him and seemed to have abandoned her old plans. She said she loved him and understood his bitterness. What more could he ask?

You could tell her how you really feel. The thought stung him back into wakefulness. He wrestled with it for a while then decided against complete honesty. Laura seemed content with things the way they were, and he didn't feel strong enough to risk rocking the boat. After they had been together for a while longer, maybe. But not now.

He took a deep breath, releasing the air out of his lungs slowly. Damn his weaknesses, anyway. They constrained his life and betrayed his emotions. If he couldn't depend on his own body, what was left?

Laura stirred against his side. He wrapped his arms more closely around her and eventually sleep came.

CHAPTER TWELVE

LAURA WOKE to the sound of Nick's off-key singing coming from the bathroom. The rush of the shower provided a counterpoint to the melody. She rolled over and stretched, feeling her muscles pull pleasantly. Sunlight streamed in through the open window.

Nick was obviously over the emotional upset of the previous night, she decided. He was in full, if not exactly melodious, voice. Laura smiled to herself.

Opening up to her about his past had explained a great deal and given her insight into his attitude toward their relationship. Nick's behavior was directly tied to his past hurts. She could afford to wait until they healed completely.

Meanwhile she had plenty of work to get done today if they were going to fly out tomorrow. She got up and pulled on jeans and a sweatshirt and padded barefoot into the kitchen to start breakfast.

In a few minutes Nick joined her. "It's a beautiful day," he announced. "I'm going to spend all of it on the course. Want to come along?"

"I can't." Laura set the bowls of cereal on the table. "I have to go through the records of the OB patients I put on your modified diet. I have to finish charting the results of my test. I have to set up a schedule for the week after next for my clinic hours.

I have to pack." She sat down and reached for the honey.

"You work too hard," Nick said in a teasing tone. "I prescribe at least an hour out this afternoon. The fresh air and sunshine will do you good."

"I don't have time."

"Take time."

"Listen here," she retorted, annoyed. "I've been running the clock backward trying to get everything done that I have to before we take off for *your* tournament. It's like working two jobs at once, and I don't appreciate your nagging me to waste what little time I've got."

"I'm not asking you to waste it," he said quietly. "I'm only asking you to share it."

Laura considered his words. She could keep herself busy all day and half into the night with things that she felt needed to be done, but was that what she ought to do? Maybe he was right. Maybe she ought to spend at least part of this April day at the side of the man she loved.

"I hear the wheels turning." He was smiling, the laugh lines cutting deeply into his tanned skin. "Have I convinced you to play a little?"

"Yes, you win." She returned his smile. "I'll try to cut out for an hour or so this afternoon."

Nick's eyes gleamed with pleasure. "It'll be good for you," he repeated.

But Laura was sure he meant more than that. He was telling her that her decision to put time with him into her busy schedule made him glad, and it reminded her sharply that her days of total devotion to her career were over. As long as love existed between them—at least on her part—Nick's needs would have to come first.

That afternoon, however, as she walked on the grass and smelled the fresh odors of spring and felt the warm breeze in her hair, she had to admit that the outing was doing her a world of good. She had spent the morning bent over charts and scribbling notes, and when she had finally driven over to the club, her neck, back and shoulders ached. Nick had greeted her with a kiss and a smile, and her pains had fled. Now, walking at his side, she felt so lighthearted she was sure she could float right off into the blue spring sky if she tried.

"This is a pretty interesting hole," Nick was saying. He pointed with the end of a club. "Water hazard. The fairway narrows in the center, and cottonwoods along the creek obstruct a clear view of the green."

Laura peered into the distance. "If you didn't know the course, how would you know how to aim?"

"I'd have walked it before I played." Nick set up his ball. "But I know this course like the back of my hand. Stand right there and watch."

Laura did, noting that once his attention was on the game, he became a different man. His energies seemed to turn inward, and he looked almost dangerous as he positioned himself to strike the ball. His eyes narrowed. Then he took a deep breath and swung the club.

The thwacking sound reverberated like a shot from a gun, and Laura jumped slightly. Golf had always seemed a vaguely effete sport to her in the past. Obviously she had been wrong. The power Nick had put into his attack had been awesome.

He held the follow-through pose for a second then lowered the club. "Let's go see how I did."

"I think you made it into Nebraska." She took his hand. "Now I see why you're so dedicated to weights. Your strength must help your game."

"It doesn't hurt." He squeezed her hand. "But you don't need to be strong to play. With some lessons and a little practice, even someone like you could become a fair player."

"No thanks!" She looked up and caught the teasing glint in his eye. "I've learned enough from you already, to last a lifetime," she added in a warmer tone.

"But there's so much more I want to teach you." His expression was calm, but his voice was sensuous and full of promise.

"Will I enjoy the lessons?" she asked.

"Every single moment of them."

His ball lay just a few feet from the cup and Nick putted it in effortlessly. Laura felt a thrill as the ball dropped into the hole. Maybe being a spectator at the tournament would be more exciting than she had thought. There was something very satisfying about seeing Nick doing his thing and doing it well.

THE TOURNAMENT took place at a resort island off the coast of the Carolinas, and Laura did find the time she and Nick spent there interesting and educational. She learned much more about the man she loved, and she learned a few things about herself, too.

Nick was popular. Even with Laura in tow, he was swarmed by women, at first. Lovely, tanned, soft-spoken women whose attentions to her man made Laura's blood boil. But she held her peace and waited to see how he would handle his "fans."

He did it with an aplomb that amazed her. No sooner had a group of women come up to him than his arm was around her shoulders, a move that brought looks of disappointment to every pretty face that saw it. The closer another woman tried to come to him, the closer Nick got to Laura. His behavior didn't vary for the entire four days. He was pleasant and polite to everyone, but his actions made it clear that the only woman he was interested in was Laura. This brought her a renewed sense of security.

His attitude toward the game, however, did cause her some uneasiness. As soon as they had checked into their room, he announced that he had to walk the course. She was welcome to join him, but she had to promise not to distract him. "I've played here before," he said, "but it's been a few years, and it was before my allergies got bad enough to force me off the regular tour. I want to see how things have changed, and..."

"And I want to see how you react to the local foliage." Laura opened her bag and took out a bottle of pills. She shook one into her palm. "Here, take one of these before we go out."

"No." Nick pushed her hand and the pill away. "Let's wait and see how I do. I play better unmedicated, and I'd rather stay that way if I possibly can."

Reluctantly, Laura agreed, but she made certain that she carried his Medihaler and enough medication to treat a massive allergic attack, just in case.

She also had to promise not to bother him, a caution she found to be a little annoying.

Nick's concentration was so intense as he paced the course that she decided she could probably have crawled all over him and he would have paid her no more attention than a gnat. It miffed her until she realized she was simply experiencing the same muddled emotions she had suffered during the first weeks of their relationship, when he had seemed interested in her only as a case study. She had got herself under control and reminded herself that it was silly to be jealous of a game. Nick was still her man. He was only doing his job—and doing it with admirable zeal.

Other golfers were walking the course, too, but he paid no attention to anyone. He made notes on a piece of paper, bent down to feel the grass now and then, muttered to himself and generally appeared absorbed in what he was doing. Laura paced behind him, watching for signs of allergic reaction.

But he reached the last hole without a sneeze. The green had an expansive view of the ocean, and as he stood on it, he seemed to break his concentration for the first time. The late afternoon sun made his hair appear almost reddish, and when he turned and smiled at Laura, his skin had an extra bronzy glow.

"I've got a good feeling about this one," he said. "I don't have the game I used to, and I don't expect to win, but I'm going to play it well." He held out his hand, and she took it. "I want to impress you," he added.

"I'm already impressed."

He lifted her palm to his lips. "All right then," he murmured. "I want to overawe you. Knock your socks right off." He kissed her palm, and then he started to sneeze.

Laura kept him inside for the rest of the afternoon and evening, hoping that the air-conditioning would filter out whatever irritant was attacking his system. She examined her collection of drugs, praying she had brought the right ones and was dispensing them to him correctly. "Sometimes medicine is an art, not a science," she told him. "One of the things you learn in school is that sometimes you have to drop back and punt for it. Try one of these." She gave him a capsule.

It seemed to do the trick. By bedtime he was drowsy but no longer seriously congested. "I only need one more thing," he announced sleepily. Laura put away the book she had been reading and got into bed with him.

His loving had a gentler quality than usual, and he was unusually silent, giving expression to his feelings by sighing contentedly when his pleasure reached its peak. As she drifted off to sleep, Laura wondered if it had been the medicine that had subdued him or if it had been anxiety about how he would play in the morning.

When she awoke she found that she was alone. A note on the dresser told her that he hadn't wanted to wake her. Tee off was at eight, and she could pick up on the play whenever she wanted to. The note said nothing about his taking any medicine.

She scrambled into her clothes, frantic at the thought that he might be out there sneezing the game away. But when she reached the course, she saw he was fine. Not a sign of even the sniffles.

It had rained during the night and the air was much cooler and fresher than it had been the previous afternoon, and she decided that perhaps whatever had bothered him needed the warmer, more humid air to do its dirty work. She relaxed and went back to the clubhouse for a breakfast of orange juice and a roll. Nick was doing his thing, and there was no reason for her to starve.

She was almost finished when she saw a strange man approaching her table. He had gray hair but appeared to be in good physical shape and sported a dark tan. Laura prepared to repel an advance.

But the man's smile was only friendly. "You're Dr. Jensen, aren't you?" he asked, extending a hand. "I thought I recognized you from Nick Hawthorne's description. I'm Andrew Selkirk."

Laura took the offered hand. So this was the vitamin baron who might be backing Partners, she thought. He looked fit enough for the role. Wasn't anyone Nick Hawthorne knew overweight or out of shape?

"I'm happy to meet you, Mr. Selkirk," she said. "You say you recognized me from Nick's description?"

"I caught him just before he teed off." Selkirk took the chair she indicated. "He told me to be on the lookout for you."

"Oh." Laura patted her lips with her napkin. Now what, she wondered.

"Tell me about Nick's program," he said.

For the next hour, Laura talked. She explained every detail about Partners she could think of, and the older man seemed fascinated. When she had finished, he leaned back, a speculative expression on his face.

"Let me ask a question or two, doctor, if you don't mind," he said. "Nick's enthusiasm tends to color any conversation I have with him, and I'd like to have your opinion on a few points." Laura agreed.

"If I decide to bankroll him," Selkirk asked, "do you think he'd be willing to devote himself full-time to Partners, or will his golf get in the way?"

"I...I really don't know that I can..."

"How about his relationship to you?" Selkirk leaned forward. "Is that stable enough to ensure that you'll be a team for as long as necessary to make the system a profitable business? Are you two getting married?"

Laura felt herself blush. "Really, Mr. Selkirk, I don't think that's any of your business," she retorted.

"Yes, ma'am, it is." He settled back in his chair. "You see, if I agree to go with Partners, I'll be committing a great deal of money. It's going to take lots of it to set up a nationwide system. I don't know Nick very well, although I did know his father. The man was a genius, but not completely dependable. I'm concerned that his son may be the same. I like everything I've heard, don't misunderstand me. But I do have these reservations."

"Isn't any investment a gamble, Mr. Selkirk?" Laura folded her hands in her lap and gave him a cool look. "And as for dependability, isn't that what contracts are for?"

"Well-taken point." The older man smiled. "You aren't easily rattled, are you. I think Nick Hawthorne's got himself a good partner."

Laura mumbled an acknowledgment of the compliment but decided that the idea of spending the rest of the morning sparring with this high-powered businessman was more than she was willing to do, even for Nick's dream. She managed to excuse herself by saying she wanted to watch him play for a while. Andrew Selkirk made no objections and in fact seemed pleased by her loyalty.

"We'll be having dinner together anyway," he told her, "so we can continue our discussion. Maybe Nick will be willing to shed some light on his personal plans then."

She started to caution Selkirk about the connection between Nick's emotions and his allergies but thought better of it. If Nick was unable to take heat, now was the time for both of them to find out—before any clear agreement involving money and time had been made. She bid Selkirk a cool but courteous goodbye and went down to the course to find Nick.

It wasn't difficult. All she had to do was locate the golfer with the most attractive young women following his play. She settled in with the rest of the gaggle and watched the show.

Nick looked at ease, confident and very handsome in his yellow polo shirt and green slacks. If she were a golf groupie, Laura thought, she'd be on his trail, too. He was a magnet and the ladies were drawn to him.

After a while he spotted her, acknowledging her presence with a wink and a smile before turning back to the business at hand. Laura flushed with pleasure. He was her man, and she was proud of the fact. *Come what may,* she thought, *I do love him.*

Nick finished the eighteenth hole with a risky, dramatic putt that could have cost him another point but instead brought cheers from his gallery. He knew that he was probably showing off in vain, since Laura couldn't appreciate the finer points of the game, but it gave him a deep sense of satisfaction to play extraordinarily well in front of her.

He had finished with a seventy-four, only two over par for the course. He hadn't played so well in years! And he knew he owed it to his ministering angel. Just the sight of her had given him a boost of confidence. The day before she had given him the space he had needed without question. No nagging. No intrusion when he withdrew to study the course. So different from the way Caroline had behaved.

He saw her waiting by the clubhouse for him, but his way was impeded by a flock of fans asking for his autograph. He obliged good-naturedly but didn't linger. Instead, he broke gently through their ranks after a few minutes and hurried to Laura. Her smile was radiant as he approached.

"I guess you did all right," she said as he took her hands in his own. "You look happy and so do all your fans."

"I was only two strokes over par," he said. "That means I'm a cinch to make the cut and play tomorrow. Does that make the only fan who matters to me happy?"

"I'm happy you aren't showing any signs of respiratory problems, if you're talking about me," she replied. "You took a chance, coming out here without any protection."

Nick chucked her under the chin. "What the doctor did last night seemed to give me all the protection I needed. I feel terrific. Did you meet Andrew?"

Her expression changed. "I sure did. Are you aware of what you might be getting into with a man like that? He seems to want a lot of control."

"Andrew's okay." Nick put his arm around her shoulders and hugged her briefly, reassuringly. "He's a successful businessman, and if his style is a little abrasive, just remember that if he's on our team, we'll get the best advice and assistance possible."

"I hope you know what you're getting into." She sounded concerned. "The man is asking if you're ready to make a serious commitment and give up everything else."

"I know." Wishing he could take her back to the room and love away her concerns, Nick leaned over to give her a light kiss. "And I'm more than willing. I love what I'm doing, but if Partners can become a reality, I'll relegate the game to leisure time and go for the gold. I want the system to succeed."

Laura looked at him searchingly. "I hope you really mean that, Nick."

"I do." He gave her another kiss. "Now, let's go into the clubhouse. I need to hang around for a while and see how my score rates. The we'll have time to change for dinner. I guess you know that we're—"

"Having dinner with Selkirk," Laura finished for him. "Be sure to bring your Medihaler. You're liable to need it."

But to her surprise and relief, Nick handled himself as well at the dinner as he had during the day on the course. He fielded the older man's questions with skill and didn't trip up at interrogation over his intentions. He was thoroughly committed to the idea of Partners, he said, and Laura was an integral part of the system.

"Without a physician's input," he explained, "I'd be afraid to take responsibility for anyone's future health. I know the system, and Laura knows medicine. We'll always have to work together."

"Pardon my asking, but—" Selkirk scratched his chin, and Laura braced herself "—what if you and the lovely doctor, uh, cease to have a social relationship? What happens to Partners then?"

"Our relationship," Laura said, "doesn't affect—"

"Our relationship," Nick interrupted, taking her hand, "is based on friendship and trust. You don't need to worry about it coming to an end, or that either of us would deliberately sabotage Partners."

There was steel in his voice, and though Laura saw Andrew Selkirk's eyebrows rise slightly, she knew that the older man wouldn't pursue the subject any further.

No formal agreement was made that night, but handshakes were exchanged all around, and Laura knew it was an important step. The prospect excited her.

Nick played well for the next two days of the tournament, coming in sixth in the final round. Not too shabby, he declared proudly, for a has-been who had been off the regular circuit for several years. His allergies acted up late in the afternoon but didn't get out of control, and he submitted to Laura's pills in the evening without any argument.

She and Nick spoke with several other potential investors for Partners, but Laura sensed that Nick had made up his mind to go the route with his father's old acquaintance. When she alluded to Selkirk's expressed opinion of the elder Hawthorne, Nick merely agreed.

"My father was a genius," he explained, his tone both loving and wry. "He had a real head for dreams but couldn't keep his feet down on earth solidly enough. Mother tried, but she wasn't strong enough to help." He looked into Laura's eyes. "I know I won't have that problem."

Laura struggled with his words. Had she not made a vow to herself to let him find his own way out of his emotional tangle over the subject of marriage, she would have taken the opportunity to bring it up. But it wasn't words Nick needed. He needed love in actions and love over time. Only love, generously given, would heal him.

Meanwhile, she enjoyed what was for her the first vacation she had taken in years aside from trips home. She lounged in the sun and acquired a light tan, which Nick declared made her body all the more exciting because the pale places were the most interesting. She followed his game but didn't hang on his every stroke, and he seemed to like her casual attitude. They swam in the ocean, made love in their room, attended numerous parties and became well established as a couple. In fact, several times Laura heard herself referred to as Mrs. Hawthorne. If Nick overheard, he gave no sign, nor did he correct the speaker. Laura took the occasions in stride, emphasizing her own name and professional status when discussing Partners.

The end of the holiday came as a disappointment to her. Going back to Wyoming meant leaving the

mild spring climate of the south and returning to
unpredictable weather, which would probably last
until at least June. It also meant facing the possibility that the Vances had decided not to go to Advance. Although her future was not unquestionably
with Nick, she still felt guilty about abandoning her
father. If Peter didn't want the job, she'd have to
hustle the ranks of upcoming graduates from the
Family Practice Center to find another candidate.
She wouldn't feel completely at ease until that situation was resolved.

"You've enjoyed this," Nick murmured as they
lay together the night before they were to leave.

"More than enjoyed," Laura admitted. "In fact,
I sort of dread going back. This has been such a
treat. Such a change."

"I told you it would be good for you." He stroked
her hair slowly. "But why the reluctance to go
back?"

Laura explained her feelings about the situation in
Advance. Nick listened quietly.

"I think there's more to it," he said when she had
finished. "Want my opinion?" Laura said she did.

"You've never had a vacation like this before,"
Nick explained. "Sunshine, leisure, no demands or
responsibilities. You've always been beautiful, but in
the past few days you've grown beyond ravishing. I
think I'll have to insist on a holiday like this with you
at least once every six months. It should be an integral part of your program."

Laura laughed softly. "I can't afford it, Nick. I
found out today what the rooms cost per day. I paid
just a little more than that per month for my old
rental."

"We don't always have to come to expensive resorts," he replied. "There are plenty of places where you and I can escape for a little while that are quite reasonable." He talked on, describing some of them, and Laura fell asleep, dreaming of endless vacations with him at her side.

THEY ARRIVED back in Linville Springs on Monday afternoon during one of the heaviest rainstorms Laura had ever seen. By the time she and Nick had made it into his station wagon in the airport parking lot, they were both soaking wet.

"It never rains like this here," she grumbled, shaking water out of her hair. "Snow I can handle. But this stuff gets you wet."

"And you're beautiful when you're angry," Nick quipped, reaching over to buckle the seat belt around her. "Let's hurry home so I can dry you off." A brilliant flash of lightning punctuated his words. Laura winced, waiting for the thunder.

"Let's just get home," she pleaded. "I don't mind blizzards, but I hate thunderstorms." Nick chuckled and suggested they could hide under the bed together until it was past. He could, he was certain, take her mind off her fears.

Laura didn't respond to his teasing. As they started down the highway into town, she felt a growing sense of alarm. The storm made the afternoon almost as dark as night, and the wind was blowing hard, forcing Nick to make an extra effort to keep his blocky vehicle on the rain-slicked road. The rain was falling so fast that her side of the front window seemed to be a solid sheet of water in spite of the rapidly swooshing windshield wipers.

"Can you see at all?" she asked, trying to peer through the gloom. There were other cars on the highway, their headlights yellow ghosts in the dimness, and she began to be concerned about the possibility of someone running into them.

Nick slowed down, and she noticed when she glanced at him that the good humor was gone from his face. "I can't see much," he admitted. "I think I'm going to pull off until this lightens up a bit." His voice sounded tight with tension, and he rubbed his hand across the condensation that had built up inside the windshield.

"Here, let me." Laura undid her seat belt and reached into her purse for a tissue. She leaned forward and started to clean the window so that he could see more clearly. Nick signaled a right turn and slowed even more. He glanced into the rearview mirror, and his startled intake of breath made her turn to look at him.

"Get down!" he yelled, grabbing her and pushing her onto the seat with his right arm. "There's a truck coming right up our tail pipe!"

Laura felt a tremendous jolt that threatened to throw her to the floor, but Nick's arm kept her protected. The station wagon lurched, and she heard him curse as another thudding jolt came from the rear.

The station wagon swerved and Laura heard the squeal of brakes and the honking of horns. She shut her eyes tightly, certain they would crash against another car at any moment. But Nick wrenched the wheel around, and she felt them leave the highway. His arm still held her down.

The station wagon slowed, the wheels seeming to bog down in the dirt and mud. Laura screamed for Nick to let her go and take the wheel with both hands, but he only pressed her more firmly to the seat. They slowed down some more, and she began to hope that they might get out of the situation with no more than a few bruises. Then the car suddenly lurched downward, tipping toward her side.

Only Nick's tight hold kept her from sliding. She heard him shout, and there was a terrible crashing sound. Something hit her head, and she heard Nick yelling again from a million miles away. And then the world disappeared.

CHAPTER THIRTEEN

WHEN SHE OPENED HER EYES AGAIN, Laura was no longer in the station wagon. She was lying on her back, looking up at a vaguely familiar ceiling with white acoustical tile and recessed fluorescent lighting. The air was no longer filled with the smells of rain and fear, but with a bitter sharp medicinal odor. Every inch of her body hurt.

"Nick?" she whispered, trying to sit up. Her head felt as if someone was pounding it with a sledgehammer.

"Just take it easy, doctor." A small hand pressed her shoulder, making her lie back down. Laura blinked and managed to focus her gaze. The face she saw belonged to one of the emergency room nurses.

"You took a hit on the head, Doctor Jensen," the petite woman told her. "Some other minor bruises and scratches, too. Please don't try to move. We're getting ready to take you up for X rays."

Laura raised a hand to her head and felt a sizable bandage. Her traveling clothes were gone, and she was wearing a hospital gown underneath the sheet that covered her.

"The man who was with me...Nick Hawthorne. Where is he?" she asked, a terrible fear rising in her chest.

"He's in surgery," the nurse said. Her smile faded slightly. "But don't you worry. He's going to be just fine."

Laura closed her eyes. That was one she had heard before. A line she had delivered herself when trying to keep one patient from feeling anxiety about a more seriously injured loved one. Nick *wasn't* going to be just fine.

"Where's Garrison?" she demanded, asking for the emergency room chief physician. "I want to know exactly what's going on."

But the nurse skillfully sidestepped her commands, reminding Laura gently that she was a patient now, and her first need was to be checked for possible injury. Realizing she would get nowhere by being unpleasant, Laura submitted to the X rays and other tests. Once her own condition had been established, then she would find out about Nick.

She held her peace until the tall, gray-haired Dr. Garrison came into her room. Ignoring the pain in her head, she struggled to a sitting position. "I want to know," she said in careful, measured tones, "what has happened to Nick Hawthorne."

"He's in good hands." Bob Garrison glanced down at her chart. "Don't worry about him. I'm sure we'll hear in just a little while..."

"Listen, Bob—" Laura swung her legs over the side of the bed, ignoring the dizziness in her head "—if I don't get some straight talk right now, I'm going to go up to OR myself and see what's wrong with him. Don't try to patronize me. Remember, I can recognize a snow job, since I'm pretty good at giving them myself."

"I'm sorry, Laura," Garrison said slowly. "I really can't tell you anything. The man took a bad mangling from something that came through the window. We did what we could to stop the bleeding, and then passed him right up to surgery."

"Mangling?" Laura whispered the word.

"Just on his arm." Garrison gave her a reassuring smile. "Nothing vital was hit, so he wasn't in danger except for the blood loss. It looked like he had raised the arm to fend off something that broke the window. Probably the same thing that gave you that bump on the head."

"It was a steel fencepost." Peter Vance, wearing green surgical garb, came into the room. His lean face was drawn, but the expression in his blue eyes gave Laura hope. "It tore his arm up, but he's going to be okay."

Laura started to shake. "T...t...tell me everything, Peter."

"Only if you lie down." His tone was firm.

She obeyed, feeling a rush of gratitude as the nurse tucked a warm blanket around her. Then she listened as Peter filled her in on the details of the accident.

Nick's station wagon had been rear-ended by a truck that hadn't seen them in time to jam on the brakes. They had swerved into oncoming traffic, but Nick's driving had been skillful enough to avoid other cars. He had turned them back to the right and had driven off the road, but he hadn't been able to see far enough to know that the shoulder dropped abruptly. There had been a fence just below the drop-off, and one of the steel posts with torn metal mesh had broken the window on Laura's side. She had been hit on the head, but Nick had used his own body to deflect the wire that would have lacerated her to ribbons. His arm had absorbed most of the punishment instead.

"He came through the surgery like a champ," Peter told her. "You know better than I how damned healthy the man is. But I've got to warn you, he may never have full use of that arm again."

A picture of Nick taking his golf club through a full, powerful swing came into Laura's mind. He wouldn't be crippled, she thought fiercely. Somehow, someway, she would see to it that he was healed!

But later that evening when she spoke to the surgeon who had performed the operation, she felt less confident. Damage to the muscles had been severe, but it was the nerves that would carry the day. Or lose it. If they had been too severely damaged, nothing would ever restore the limb to full use.

"Take me to see him," Laura demanded.

His room was down the hall from hers, and after a bit of bullying, Laura received permission to be taken there in a wheelchair for just a few minutes. She grumbled at being treated like an invalid, claiming that the dizziness was over and all she had was a bad headache, but the nurse refused to budge from hospital policy. It was the wheelchair or no visit. Laura got into the chair, her temper barely in check.

When they reached Nick's room, she persuaded the nurse to at least let her go in alone. She promised to stay in the chair and come out in just a few minutes. After a moment of awkwardness with the chair, she propelled herself inside, stopping to shut the door firmly behind her. Then she wheeled herself over to his bedside.

Nick was the only patient in the room. The other bed was made but empty. Except for the IV connected to his uninjured arm and the bandages around his wounded one, Nick didn't appear to need to be in the hospital at all.

He seemed asleep, his dark lashes making soft crescents on his cheeks. His color was good, and his face showed no signs of pain. Laura bit at her lip to force back tears. She reached out to smooth back a lock of hair that had fallen across his forehead. At her touch, his eyes opened slowly.

"How's your noggin?" he asked, slurring the words. "I wouldn't let 'em take me away until I found out you just had a rap on the head." He smiled crookedly. "Knew then you'd be okay. Too tough a nut to crack."

Laura began to cry. "You saved my life, Nick." Was he aware of what it had cost him?

"You're my partner." His smile widened. "I had to."

"Nick..." She hesitated. It wasn't her place to discuss his condition with him. That was reserved for his surgeon. "How are you feeling?" she asked instead, hating the shallowness of the question but unable to think of anything else to say. "What can I do for you?"

He looked at the wheelchair, his face showing a trace of pain for the first time. "Are you really okay? The nurse told me you had a mild concussion, but..."

"That's all it is." Laura got out of the chair and stood by the bed. "The only reason I'm not home is that Garrison doesn't like to let concussions go until he's had twenty-four hours observation. He's very old-fashioned.''

"Good." Nick's eyes closed. "I don't want anybody takin' any chances with you. Too precious to me.''

Laura took his left hand gently into hers. "I love you, Nick," she whispered, and kissed his lips softly. He seemed to have fallen asleep, so she remained only another moment, looking down at his face. Then she wearily got into the chair and wheeled out of the room.

Nick lay still until he sensed she was gone. He smiled as he heard her voice from the hallway arguing with the nurse about the foolishness of her having to ride the few yards to her room in the wheelchair. She would be fine after a good night's sleep, he decided, relieved.

About himself, he had no such hopes. All his dreams had seemed to be coming true, and now everything had been slammed right out of the ball park by one lousy, unlucky accident. He clenched his left hand into a fist and pounded slowly on the sheet.

He hadn't needed to hear the surgeon's grim forecast to know that his right arm was shot to hell. After the first searing pain as the metal wire had bit into his flesh, he had felt nothing. The arm was dead, or as good as dead.

And that meant he was finished as a golf player, much less a professional. Undoubtedly Selkirk would withdraw from Partners, once he learned that the founding member was going to be less than physically perfect for the rest of his life. Laura? Well, Laura would feel obliged to care for him and take on the responsibility for their household herself. And when his savings and insurance ran out, she would probably try to support him fully. Damn! He hit the sheet again.

There was no way he was going to let her ruin her life and her career. He had offered her a good thing, but the offer was now dead, and the kindest thing he could do was to let her off the hook. Let her go. Tell her he didn't...

But he did love her. That was the problem. If she were just a friend who was also great in bed, he could somehow manage to let her go. But he wasn't sure that he cared about living at all if it meant being without Laura.

The nurse came in, interrupting his tortured thoughts. She checked his IV and asked how he was feeling. Nick mumbled a reply, which she seemed to find acceptable. Then she turned out his overhead light and left him to seek what sleep he could.

Laura got little rest that night. Because of the nature of her head injury she was given no sedative and only a mild painkiller. When she sat up, her head throbbed. When she lay down, it ached sharply. She finally opted for a half-raised position on the bed but was unable to do more than catnap. She was cranky and uncomfortable, and concern for Nick kept her mind in turmoil.

Regardless of how serious it was, she knew his injury would eventually be more trouble to him psychologically than it would physically. His lifelong drive for physical perfection would seem to be a shattered dream until he came to terms with his handicap. She would have to be more than just a lover. She would have to help him adjust, help him to see that he could still be as valuable as ever. And if it meant she had to agree to sign her entire life away to Andrew Selkirk, she would see that Partners didn't go down the drain because of the accident. Nick would need the dream to keep his hope alive.

She finally slept a little near dawn, but her dreams were filled with disturbing reenactments of the accident and gave her little real rest. When the nurse on morning shift came in to check her temperature and blood pressure, Laura had to struggle with herself not to be as gritty and bad tempered as she felt. She inquired about Nick and was told that he had spent a comfortable night. At least one of us did, she thought.

Breakfast helped her attitude a bit, as did a call from her parents. Peter had let them know about the accident and had reassured them that their daughter was all right, only a little shaken up. Both Walt and Adele wanted to know about Nick, whom Peter had evidently billed as a hero for saving Laura's life.

"He's hurt," she said. "I don't know how badly yet, but it's certain his career in golf is over." Her voice caught on the last words. "I got to see him play this week, you know. He was really good."

"Honey, do you want to bring him up here?" her father asked. "When he's recuperated a bit, I mean. We'd be, well, broadminded about your relationship."

Laura started to laugh. "Oh, that's sweet of you two. I'll keep it in mind, but knowing Nick he'd insist on sleeping in the guest room." They talked for a little longer, and when Laura hung up, she felt much more cheerful.

Bob Garrison came in shortly after seven to check her over. He pronounced her fit for discharge as long as she kept a close watch on her own symptoms and called for help at the first sign of dizziness or nausea. After he had left, Anne Vance appeared with toiletries and fresh clothing for her.

"I peeked in on Nick," Anne told her after reporting that George, whom Laura had left in the Vance boys' care, was thriving. "He looks just great, considering. He told me to tell you to quit hiding and come up to keep him company."

"That's just what I plan to do," Laura announced briskly. "I intend to keep him company, then go down and submit my application for the emergency room job, then go over to Physical Therapy and learn all I can about rehabilitation. I intend to get him back into being as close to one piece as I possibly can!"

After Anne left, Laura set out down the hall to see Nick. He seemed to be expecting her.

"I can't promise you anything anymore," he began, his usually bright eyes a dull, dark gold. "You'd better plan on going up to work with your father. I'll tell Andrew that Partners is out of the question now, and..."

"The hell you will!" Laura flung the words at him, pleased when he winced slightly. "Nothing's changed, Nick, except for the fact that you're going to have a lot more time to give to the project. In fact, this might be a blessing in disguise. Since you won't have any other demands on you, you can make Partners a reality sooner than any of us dreamed."

He seemed to digest her statement. "I hadn't thought of it that way," he began. "I only..."

"Well, keep on thinking of it that way," Laura snapped. "You've got too much to give to waste it feeling sorry for yourself."

A smile appeared on his face. "Yes, ma'am," he drawled. "That bump on the head seems to have changed your sweet, submissive personality. What are you now? My drill sergeant?"

"If necessary." Laura put her hands on her hips and glared at him.

Nick felt his heart fill to almost bursting with the love he had for her. But the emotion was almost immediately undercut by the realization that she was crusading for a hopeless cause. He pushed the button that raised the head of his bed.

"Let's stop playing like we're characters in a movie, Laura," he said, stopping when he was upright enough to look her straight in the eye. "I understand and appreciate your attitude, but it won't change the facts. The fact is that I'm going to be crippled for..."

"For as long as you decide to be." Isabelle Franklin's breathy voice interrupted him. The small woman appeared in the doorway and made her way stiffly but steadily to the foot of his bed. "You can't seem to stay out of trouble, can you, Nickie."

"He got into this one saving my life," Laura said, relaxing her indignant pose and looking to Nick as if she was on the verge of tears.

"I know," Isabelle said. "I got the whole story before I came over. Nick, that was a very heroic thing you did."

Nick found himself unable to meet either woman's direct gaze. "It was instinct," he said, shrugging as best he could. "I refuse to take credit for what my body did out of reflex action. I couldn't let my lady get all chewed up by a damned cyclone fence could I?''

"You were protecting me from the first instant of danger," Laura said hotly. "Don't tell me you were acting out of instinct all of the time!"

Isabelle raised her thin hands. "Simmer down, you two. I didn't drag my old bones all the way up here to listen to a lovers' quarrel. I came here to tell you, young man, that I called Andrew the moment I had all the details, and we both agreed that unfortunate as the accident was for your golf career, it might have actually been a sign that you were ready to move into a different direction." She paused and looked at Nick with more pride and love than he had ever seen in Isabelle's blue eyes before.

"Andrew says a grant contract, with a tentative figure of two million dollars to start with, will be on its way to you by tomorrow," Isabelle continued, her eyes now sparkling.

"Two *million*?" Nick sank back on the pillow. It was more than four times what he had expected as an initial allotment. Laura, he noted out of the corner of his eye, looked as stunned as he felt.

"Andrew said for you to consider it seed money." Isabelle smiled. "My late husband's corporation is matching the sum, with the proviso that you both grant yourselves reasonably good salaries from the income investment the money will bring you. I think something approximately what you both would have been making if you had gone on with your intended careers would be a good guideline."

"Isabelle, I don't know what to say," Nick said, his voice tight with emotion. Laura came over and took his hand.

"Try saying thanks," she whispered. "Try saying this is more than either of us hoped for or ever dreamed of," she added in a normal tone. "Try saying that this will give you added incentive to get up and get on with your plans."

Nick nodded. If all these people believed in him, he would be a pretty miserable excuse for a man if he just lay here and continued to feel sorry for himself. "I'll be up and out of this joint by tomorrow," he declared. "And I'll learn to putt with one hand."

"The first thing you'll have to learn is how to sign checks," Isabelle said. "Now, I have a favor to ask of you both."

"Ask away." Nick laughed. "I can't think of any favor I wouldn't do for you after what you've done for us." Laura gave his hand a squeeze, signaling her agreement.

Isabelle left the foot of the bed and walked over to the window. "I'm going away for an extended period," she said. "I need someone I can trust to stay in my house, to take care of my property." She paused and looked back over her shoulder. "Maybe make a home of a place that was once full of love and laughter and seems so empty to me now."

Nick released Laura's hand and pushed the button so the head of the bed lifted higher. "Isabelle, where are you going?" Isabelle turned back to the window. Her narrow shoulders were too stiff beneath her neat suit coat, and he knew that whatever he heard next would be a lie.

"I have a yen to travel," she said in a tone that he knew would brook no questions. "I'm not sure exactly where I'm going, but it would be a great comfort to me if I knew that the home I spent so many wonderful years in was in your care. What do you say?"

Nick looked at Laura. Uncertainty was written all over her face. "Isabelle," she said, "wouldn't one of your children...?"

Isabelle turned, a sad, proud smile lifting her wrinkled features. "My children are all old enough to be your parents, my dear. They have their own homes in places far from here, and none of them have ever expressed a desire to return." She looked directly at Nick. "You're still young enough to make a home out of a house. Will you please...stay in mine?"

Nick wavered for a moment. He knew what Isabelle was asking, but he couldn't bring himself to refuse the woman. It wasn't the money, and it wasn't the mansion. If she had asked him to take over a log cabin for her, he would have done it. But Laura... Laura owed neither of them such responsibility.

"You know my answer, Isabelle," he said finally. "But I think we need to talk about it before we give you our mutual consent." Laura's hand came to rest on his shoulder.

Isabelle looked from one to the other, then nodded. "Of course. I understand you can't make a decision like this on the spur of the moment. However, you should consider that you would be doing me a service, and yourselves, as well."

"How's that?" Laura's voice was quiet.

Isabelle's eyes twinkled. "You'll be able to take care of most of Nick's therapy right at home," she said, waving a thin hand at Nick. "There's a room full of equipment that my late husband used. There's even a whirlpool bath. And once he's fit for it, there's a study that will serve nicely as an office for Partners. Until you get to the point when you're ready to expand, it'll give you a base of operations."

Laura looked at the elderly woman and then at the man on the bed. There was a strong rapport between them that she was being left out of, unspoken emotions. She suddenly felt like a stranger gaping at a private family matter.

"Isabelle, why don't you sit down and keep Nick company for a little while," she said briskly. "I've got to go run downstairs and get some things done. It would help me out if you'd stay." They both seemed surprised by her words, but Isabelle agreed.

Laura made it almost to the elevators before a wave of dizziness hit her. It wasn't the concussion, she told herself. It was the sense of being caught up in affairs far beyond her comprehension. After she pushed the call button, she leaned against the wall and shut her eyes.

Four million dollars. Soon she would be partly responsible for more money than she had ever imagined. She had looked forward to a life much like her parents—comfortable but hardly affluent. Nick had been right when he'd assumed she had never vacationed at a resort. The few family outings she had taken as a child had been camping trips in the Rockies. Her life had always been simple and predictable. Now...

She got onto the elevator, feeling sick to her stomach as it started to move downward. She could understand Isabelle's request that they house sit for her, but she suspected there was much more to it. Isabelle seemed healthy for a person of her years, but she was elderly. Was her offer more permanent than she had indicated.

And what of Nick? His attitude toward his injury had seemed negative until Isabelle had come in. Once she was gone, in spite of the promised fortune, would he sink back into despondency? Could she help him pull out of it, or would her own emotional involvement only serve to make things worse? Perhaps, she thought, the best thing for him would be for her to step aside.

She got off the elevator and stood in the hallway for a moment, trying to remember why she had come down to the first floor. Hospital personnel moved by her, hurrying on the way to appointed tasks.

"Laura, are you all right?" Peter's tall form suddenly appeared before her, a concerned expression on his face.

She drew a shuddering breathe. "I thought I was this morning," she said. "But now I don't think so."

NICK HELD ISABELLE'S FRAIL HAND in his own. The skin was soft, dry and as thin as old parchment. Knuckles and veins stood out from the meager flesh. His own hand looked like that of a giant's.

After Laura had left, Isabelle had taken the chair by his bed, and they had simply joined hands, communing in silence for a while. Nick felt strangely peaceful, even though his heart was brimming with emotions.

Finally he cleared his throat and spoke. "How long do you think you'll be traveling?" he asked, turning his head and trying to catch her eye.

Isabelle smiled but continued to stare out the window. "It's estimated that the journey could take as long as a year."

"Oh." Nick looked down at the small hand again. He wanted to ask outright what she meant, what she was hiding behind a dignified lie, but if her pride dictated that she cover the truth, then he wouldn't pry.

"Then again," Isabelle said, suddenly standing up. "It could be as short as six weeks, but that won't matter to you and Laura. I must tell you, Nicholas, that at first I thought you were leading that young woman down another garden path. I sensed her strength of character and was sure she would only go with you where she wanted."

"You were right." Nick closed his eyes for a moment. A dull ache was beginning to spread along his injured arm. "But she fell in love with me somewhere along the way. Now look at what she's doing. Giving up everything for..."

"Nick Hawthorne!" The bite in Isabelle's voice made his eyelids jerk open. "If she does love you," she said, pointing a finger at him, "she's not giving up a thing. Not even if you'd been crippled for life. I think that woman will stand by you in spite of anything that could ever happen, and I think you are a damn young fool for not asking her to marry you and make an honest man out of you."

"Isabelle..." Nick began.

"Don't try to hand me any of that stuff about your first marriage!" She made an angry gesture with her hand. "If you're really honest with yourself, you'll admit that was a mistake in character judgment on your part. That woman wanted only to take. She wanted you at her beck and call constantly, and when you weren't, she reacted like a spoiled child. Laura Jensen would never, never behave in such a selfish manner, and you know it."

Nick sighed. "We don't need marriage, Isabelle. It would ruin everything. We're with each other because we've both chosen freely to be. Not because some legal..."

"Oh, you are confused, young man." Isabelle's eyes sparked. "Marriage isn't a legal thing. It's a relationship made in heaven or hell. You lived in hell during your first one. With Laura, it would be different."

Nick hesitated. Something deep inside of him agreed with his old friend, but something else shuddered at the thought of taking such a risk. After all, he hadn't known her for very long, only a little more than two months...

But he did love her. That was undeniable. "I can't ask her now," he said, hoping Isabelle would understand. "Not while I'm..."

"Nicholas, Nicholas," Isabelle chided, moving back to stand at the foot of the bed. "If I didn't care for you as if you were my own child, and if you didn't look so silly, trying to be pitiable, I think I'd just leave and let you stew in your own juices. But you need to listen to someone with a little perspective on life."

"And that someone's you, isn't it." Nick held out his hand. "I promise to think very seriously about everything you've said."

Isabelle came around to the side of the bed and let him pull her into a brief hug. Her small shoulders felt like those of a child against his arm. "I'm going to miss you," he whispered. "Who's going to give me a quick kick in the seat if you go away?"

Isabelle stepped back, and he could see tears in her eyes. "Give me a call when you and Laura decide about the house," she said, her voice breathier than usual. "I'll be at home, preparing for my trip."

"I love you very much, Isabelle," Nick told her softly.

She lifted her small chin, smiled at him and left the room.

CHAPTER FOURTEEN

"I'M ALL RIGHT," Laura protested. Dr. Hester Mcfadden, the neurologist, nodded in agreement.

"You check out just fine," the gray-haired specialist said. "But I think Dr. Vance is right. You should stay in another day and let us run a few more tests on you."

"It's a waste of time." Laura shook her head. "I have too much to do."

"You know what your trouble is?" Peter, who had been observing the examination, spoke up. "You have absolutely no professional perspective on yourself."

"That's not so," Laura snapped. But he could be right, she thought. The enormity of the responsibilities that lay before her was frightening, and she might be ignoring symptoms in her haste to tackle her new life. "I...I just need to go home and get things ready for Nick." She didn't mention Isabelle Franklin's offer. It would only make matters murkier.

"Ah," Peter intoned. "Nick. Now, he's the primary reason you ought to let us run those tests."

"Who's Nick?" Mcfadden asked.

"A serious complication in Dr. Jensen's life," Peter explained. "Could I talk to her alone for a minute."

After the neurologist left, Laura sat up and glared at her friend. "There was no reason to bring my personal life into this," she said. "What Nick and I..."

"Nick and you have managed together to shake up quite a few people, Laura." Peter folded his arms across his chest and leaned against the closed door. "Not necessarily for the bad, you understand. But you have to admit that since you met him, things haven't been the same."

Laura shrugged. "So?"

"I'm your friend, Laura." Peter's expression was concerned. "Hell, I feel like I'm your brother, and I know that if I decide to go to work with your dad, the feeling's going to be even stronger. I don't want to see you hurt or unhappy."

"Peter, what has that got to do with...?"

"I want you to have another X-ray series and a CAT scan." He hesitated. "But before that, I want to have a pregnancy test run on you."

"Pregnancy?" Laura drew the word out. "It's not possible. I'm not idiotic. I took...precautions."

Peter's eyebrows raised. "As a doctor, you should be the first to acknowledge that nothing's a hundred percent reliable if two people are very actively in love."

Laura felt herself blush. "You're right," she admitted. "I'll take the tests. But I won't check back into the hospital. You'll have to do me on an outpatient basis."

"Fair enough," Peter said. "Let's get started."

It was late in the afternoon before Laura had a chance to get back to Nick, and when she did, she found him in a foul mood.

"Where the hell have you been?" he barked. "People have been in and out all day, poking and prodding me." His face was drawn, and there were dark patches under the skin around his eyes. "One of them, a Hester something-or-other, got real interested when she saw my name. 'Oh, *you're* Nick,' she said. Never explained it, either."

"I can." Laura sank into the chair next to his bed. "I got a little dizzy after I left here this morning, and Peter found me standing dazed in the hallway. He insisted that I go through some more tests."

"For what?" Nick sat up, scowled at her, then winced in obvious pain. "You're okay, aren't you?"

"I'm fine." Laura stood and helped him ease back down onto the pillow. "Everything turned out negative, including the pregnancy test. Now, tell me about Isabelle."

"Pregnancy?" Nick looked as if she had hit him in the stomach.

Laura smiled. "You of all people should know there was that possibility." She smoothed his hair back from his forehead.

"Pregnancy," Nick repeated in a whisper, his amber eyes staring at her.

"The test was negative." Laura sat back down. "What about Isabelle?"

Nick rubbed his hand over his face, and his expression became sad. "I think Isabelle's dying," he said, blinking rapidly. "She didn't come right out and say it, but I felt as if she was saying goodbye the entire time we talked.''

''And the house?'' Laura felt her throat tighten.

''I think it's meant to be a legacy.'' He sounded choked up. ''I won't be surprised to find the place deeded to us after she...after she...''

Laura got up and put her arms around him. His grief affected her deeply, and she thought she understood his feelings. Losing Isabelle would be like losing a parent to him.

''Laura,'' he said after a while, ''I believe we ought to think about getting married.''

''What?'' She straightened and stared at him. ''What did you say?''

Nick looked confused. ''I...it would make Isabelle happy, and I...''

''Oh, no.'' Laura shook her head. ''I'm not getting married for somebody else's sake, no matter how dear they are.'' She backed away from the bed. ''You're still not yourself yet. Get some sleep, and I'll come back in the morning.''

''Don't go!'' Nick eased himself back on his elbow, cursing himself for his choice of words and timing. She was right about his not being himself. The events of the past twenty-four hours had left him staggering mentally, but having blurted out the word ''marriage'' had started a tremendous flow of juices in his mind and emotions. He and Laura really should get married. Form a family. Have some kids. He had been blind to the truth. ''I love you, Laura,'' he said.

''You're all mixed up,'' she replied, running the words together. ''Try to rest. I'll come back—''

"No!" Nick threw the covers aside and swung his legs over the edge of the bed. "I mean it, Laura. Come back here and talk to me, or I swear I'll get out of this rack and chase after you."

Laura hesitated. Nick's expression told her that he meant every word. Corded muscles stood out along the sides of his neck, and his wide shoulders were bunched. The injured arm had been bandaged to his bare torso, and all he wore was a pair of hospital-issue pajama bottoms. He looked vulnerable and formidable both at the same time. Love battled with logic inside her, and love won. She turned back to him.

"I won't go," she said, "if you promise you won't talk any more crazy stuff about marriage. We both have enough on our minds without adding trouble."

He seemed to weigh her words. "You're right," he agreed after a moment. "No need to go complicating things, is there." Pain etched his face, and he started to lie back down.

Laura hurried over to help him, every nerve in her body hurting with him and for him. She would, she promised herself, see this man well and whole again, no matter what it took.

NICK'S RECOVERY was swift. Surprising to everyone except Laura. Knowing about his strength and self-discipline, she had expected to see him putting textbook predictions to shame. By the end of a week he was doing things with his arm and hand that had the hospital staff amazed.

He didn't mention marriage again, and Laura put the incident down to his emotional state at the time.

He did continue to declare that he loved her, and Laura believed him. His actions had already proved so.

They did agree to accept Isabelle's offer of her house. Laura knew that Nick would do anything to please the elderly woman, and she was willing to go along with him, up to a certain point. Isabelle reacted to their decision with delight, saying that now she could go off on her "trip" with a clear conscience about her home. Laura tried a little tactful probing in an attempt to discover what she could about the older woman's motives, but Isabelle neatly sidestepped her comments and questions. Nick remained convinced that she was hiding a fatal illness, but Laura wasn't so sure. Isabelle was acting mysteriously, but not like a woman resigned to death.

By the end of April, Laura decided that the ship of her future was fully launched. She and Nick were living in Isabelle's home—the problem of dust and his allergies solved by a series of strategically placed air purifiers. Because of the generous amounts of money they had received for the project, she decided not to worry about getting a position after her residency was over in July. Living quarters were free-and-clear, and Nick's insurance checks covered most of his medical expenses plus a small compensation income until his injury healed completely. If the two of them lived a simple life-style, she knew they could manage. It was more important for her to have the time to work on Partners.

Her decision convinced the Vances and her parents that she intended to stay with Nick and had pledged the future of her career as a physician to turning his dream into reality.

"We're going up as a family this weekend to check out Advance," Peter told her one afternoon early in May. "You and Nick want to come along?"

"Not this time." Laura experienced an inward rejoicing. Peter had thawed considerably in his attitude toward Nick, and she hoped that eventually the two might become friends. The invitation was an indication that her wish might be coming true. "I'd like my parents to meet Nick," she said. "But this should be your visit. We would just clutter things up."

"I thought you might like to fill your father in on exactly what you're planning to do," Peter replied. "I've talked with him a number of times on the phone, and he does seem confused."

"I know." Laura sighed. Her mother had seemed less concerned, saying that she trusted her daughter was doing what was necessary for her happiness. But Walt, understandably, was having difficulty adjusting to the idea that his doctor daughter wasn't going into practice. "I want to wait a little longer," she told Peter. "Until Nick and I have Partners fully launched. Then Dad can see something concrete and not just a bunch of papers and a string of ideas." Peter considered her words, then said he thought he understood.

"But you should get Hawthorne to meet them," he added. "If I had a daughter and she... Well, you know what I mean, I think."

Laura nodded. "Yes, I do."

She had deliberately put off getting her lover together with her parents, fearing such a meeting would reignite Nick's ambivalent feelings about marriage. He did not, she believed, need any more pressures on him than he already had.

Since his release from the hospital, he had worked religiously with physical therapy on his arm. From whirlpool baths to graduated weights to careful massages designed to restore elasticity to the scarred tissue, Nick pursued healing himself with an awesome single-mindedness.

He had also pursued the programming of Partners with the same intensity. Laura worked with him as much as she could while finishing up her obligations at the Family Practice Center, and by the end of May, between the two of them they had designed dozens of basic profiles for prospective clients. Nick purchased a computer and spent long hours putting the profiles into the system. "Now," he declared, "we have the product in tangible form." He pushed several buttons, and Laura's original program appeared on the screen, complete with her measurements, diet and exercise needs. "There you are, my love," he said, the old mischievous light in his amber eyes. "Mine at the touch of a button."

It was true, Laura often reflected. She was his at a touch. The intensity with which he strove for health and success was nothing compared to the energy and ingenuity he put into his lovemaking. He seemed to draw strength from it, and Laura found the same need within herself. She remembered her former addiction to cigarettes and smiled. She had been able to kick the habit with his help, but the craving she had for Nick would never end.

The only negative she was aware of in their lives was Nick's premature mourning for Isabelle. He was convinced he would never see his friend again, and that caused him pain and sorrow.

"I've fought against death all of my life," he told Laura one evening as they were taking a stroll and enjoying the warm spring air. "And I hate to think of Isabelle off somewhere surrounded by strangers while she fights her own last battle."

Laura looked at him. The twilight darkened his tanned complexion and made the lines in his face seem deeper. He wore a light yellow, V-necked, long-sleeved cotton sweater, a garment that covered most of the scarring on his right arm. He still seemed very powerful, she noted, but there was definitely a vulnerable edge to him now.

"Nick," she said gently, "Isabelle is, what, eighty-two? Eighty-four?"

"I'm not sure." He jammed his hands into the pockets of his jeans. "She was always too vain to be pinned down to a definite age."

"She still *is*." Laura linked her arm with his. "If she weren't, we'd have been notified, don't you think?"

"Nobody knows where she is." Nick gave a frustrated sigh. "I've called all her kids. They don't know. And her lawyer's not talking. I've tried everything with him short of violence. It's as if there's some kind of conspiracy."

"Maybe there is." Laura remembered the look on Isabelle's face when she had left. It had not been the look of a woman who was facing death, but rather a challenge. "You've known her a lot longer than I have, but I think you're overreacting. Like all of us, Isabelle will eventually die, but I have a hard time believing she's ready for it to happen yet."

"You out to know nobody gets to punch their own ticket." Nick stretched out his right arm, and there was bitterness in his voice. "I sure learned that the hard way."

Concerned about his state of mind, Laura suggested they scrap plans to work on Partners for the rest of the evening. "Let's go see a movie," she said. "A comedy, something to take our minds off things."

Nick seemed to brighten. "I want to see a romance," he declared. "Something with lots and lots of steamy sex."

They settled for the latest science-fiction flick, which had little to laugh at and virtually no sex, but which did serve the purpose of removing them temporarily from everyday worries. As the story progressed, Laura felt Nick relaxing beside her. After a while, his arm went around her shoulders, and his right hand moved slowly over to capture hers. She held it tenderly, knowing how hard he had struggled to make that hand operational again.

As they left the theater they ran into Bob and Ellen Patterson, and to Laura's surprise, Nick said yes to their invitation to join them for a drink. They walked around the corner to a bar that Bob declared was a nice, quiet neighborhood place and found a table for four.

"So," Bob Patterson said after they were seated. "We keep hearing exciting things about you two." The heavyset stockbroker leaned forward in his chair. "Are you going to be taking investors in whatever it is you've been cooking up?"

Nick chuckled. "Don't miss a thing, do you, Bob?"

"How did you find out about it?" Laura asked. "We didn't intend to publicize it until we had it better organized."

"Simple." Bob waved a big hand at Nick. "When the pro here tendered his resignation, he mentioned that he wasn't quitting just because of the busted wing. He said that he had a big iron in the fire, and I made it my business to find out what I could."

"I've been dying to call you," Ellen interjected. "But I've been, well, sort of embarrassed..."

"It's all right." Laura watched Nick's eyebrows rise questioningly. "Ellen tried to warn me about your reputation with the ladies," she explained, laughing.

"Little good it did you." Nick grinned and covered her hand with his.

They ordered, Nick requesting a soft drink but making no objection when Laura asked for a beer. The conversation moved along easily, and Laura was pleased to find that her old friends seemed to have accepted her relationship with Nick. Perhaps, she thought, because they were going into Partners together and not just having an affair.

Bob and Nick began talking finance, and Laura filled Ellen in on the changes in her life, telling her friend of the improvements Nick's program had caused.

"You do look much better," Ellen admitted. "Healthier, somehow."

"I can walk up a flight of stairs without gasping for breath. And I haven't had a single cigarette since the night I met him."

Ellen rolled her eyes. "Do I remember that night! I was so worried you were walking right into the worst mess of your life."

"It may be a mess," Laura confided, "But believe me, it's a very pleasant mess."

"Excuse me." Nick leaned over and spoke softly into her ear. "You did too have a smoke after our first date. The next morning, remember? When you got uptight about submitting to the measuring."

"You weren't supposed to be listening," Laura said in mock anger. "Excuse me if I stretched the truth a little." She put her hand on his face and pushed him gently away.

Nick laughed and grabbed her wrist with his left hand. "I'm just trying my best to keep you honest," he teased.

"Let go, Nick. I have to use the bathroom." Laura tried to free her arm, but he held her easily.

"Ah," Nick said, turning to Bob and Ellen, "you see, you two have caused her to slip into a state of nostalgia. We first met in a bathroom, you know." He began to explain the details of the way he had trapped Laura in the ladies' lounge, and Laura covered her face with her free hand in embarrassment.

"So after I got her name from you, Bob, I inked up a little sign that said out-of-order and proceeded to snare Her Loveliness alone in the john. You might say that our relationship began with a flush.''

''Nick, that's positively tacky.'' Laura finally freed herself from his grasp. She pretended to be disgusted, but she was actually pleased to see him in such good humor again. She made a note to make sure that they both got out in good company again soon.

Ellen declined a trip to the rest room, saying that the whiskey she was drinking didn't affect her kidneys the way Laura's beer did. Laura left as Nick launched into a lecture on the value of natural diuretics. He never missed an opportunity, she thought wryly.

A few minutes later, after a final check of her appearance in the washroom mirror she started to head back to the table. But as she passed the cigarette machine that stood outside the ladies' room, a tall, unfamiliar figure blocked her way.

''Excuse me,'' Laura said, glancing at the man. He was suntanned, blond and handsome, and he was deliberately standing in her path.

''Excuse *me*, ma'am,'' the man drawled. ''But I couldn't help noticin' you seemed to be having some trouble with that fella who brought you in.'' He grinned. ''Happy to help out a lady in distress. Name's Danny Howard. What's yours?''

Before Laura could answer, Nick's sturdy form loomed behind the man. She saw him tap the cowboy on the shoulder. ''Your mistake, friend,'' Nick said in a quiet voice. ''The lady wants to come back to her table. How about standing aside.''

The blond man turned, and Laura could tell that he had had one or two drinks too many. His grin broadened as he looked at Nick. "You gotcher brand on this 'un?" he asked, pointing at Laura with his thumb.

Nick's smile was friendly, but Laura saw the ice in his eyes. "Don't do this friend," he advised. "It won't work out for you, I promise."

"Listen to him, Danny." Laura tried to sidle by the man and lessen the tension at the same time. "I appreciate your concern, but I live with..."

"You ain't married." The man grabbed her left hand. "I don't see no ring." His fingers grabbed her wrist too tightly, hurting her, and involuntarily Laura cried out.

Nick moved so quickly that she didn't see how it happened, but one second the stranger held her and the next his face was slammed against the wall, the offending hand twisted high between his shoulder blades. Nick held him with his left hand, his right hand balled loosely into as much of a fist as he could make.

Laura resisted the urge to interfere. She didn't want Nick to be hurt, though she was sure he would be if the situation deteriorated any further. He was strong, but in a fight he would be at a terrible disadvantage with only one good arm. Yet something kept her from doing or saying anything. Bob Patterson came up behind her, but she shooed him back.

"Let me show you something, Danny-boy," Nick whispered, letting up on the pressure he had exerted on the man's arm. "Hold real still now, because it's real important, understand?'' His prisoner quickly nodded agreement.

The man was too loaded to be much of a problem, Nick decided. He was big, but his coordination and good sense had been dulled by one too many brews. Psychological warfare would do the job. After seeing the man treat Laura like a cheap piece of meat, he yearned to pound the stuffing out of him, but his peaceful nature showed him a more satisfactory way to get revenge.

He released the man's arm and turned slightly to the side, ramming his shoulder into the taller man's back and pressing him hard against the wall. Then he held up his right arm and slowly pushed the sleeve of his sweater up to reveal the long, deep scars.

"See these," he said. Danny nodded, his eyes bugging slightly at the sight. Inside, Nick felt his laughter rise, but he kept a macho scowl on his face.

"Last animal tried to mess with my woman," he said, keeping his voice low, "was a grizzly. Came after her when we were up in Jackson camping. Know how I got these scars?"

Danny shook his head, his expression indicating clearly that he didn't want to know. Nick paused for effect.

"I reached down his throat and yanked his heart out," he said in a low voice, sounding as savage as possible. "Got a little cut up on the way, but it was worth it. You see, *nobody* touches my lady."

"I didn't know." Danny began to look rather green. Nick released some of the pressure on his back. "I'm sorry," the man added.

"Tell her." Nick barked the words and straightened. He shoved the sleeve back down over his scars and nodded toward Laura. "Apologize to the lady, son," he commanded.

Laura managed to accept the man's stammered excuses for his behavior without cracking a smile. But when he disappeared into the men's room, a look of queasy desperation on his face, she was unable to keep the laughter back.

"That was just *beautiful*." Bob clapped Nick on his shoulder. "I've never seen a drunk cowboy handled better."

"It was a better show than the movie," Laura added.

"Were you really hurt?" Nick reached for her hand. "Because if you were, I can still tear that guy apart."

"I was only startled," she reassured him. "And you scared him badly enough. I thought he might have a heart attach. A grizzly bear! Do you have any idea how mean those animals can be?" She put her arm around his waist and led him back to the table, where Bob was regaling Ellen with the tale of what had happened.

"I was inspired." Nick slid down into his seat but kept holding her left hand. "When he asked if I had my brand on you, I knew I wasn't dealing with a man of a liberated turn of mind." He rubbed her bare ring finger absently.

"Hey, I am sorry about all this," Bob said. "This is usually a nice place to have a quiet drink. Guys like your cowboy generally hit one of the bars farther downtown."

Nick smiled. ''Don't worry about it. Maybe he was an angel in disguise, sent to shake me up a little.''

''What in the world do you mean?'' Laura asked.

''Nothing.'' Nick smiled, released her hand and changed the subject.

Later, when they got home, she tried to question him, but she learned nothing more. Nick wasn't in the mood for talking.

''I love you,'' he said huskily, pulling her into his arms. Laura made no objection as his lips covered hers and his tongue tasted her hungrily. His passion inflamed hers, and she ran her hands up under his sweater, enjoying the feel of his skin and muscles beneath her palms.

''You make me crazy,'' he whispered, gently biting at her neck and shoulder, sending shivers of delight all through her at the touch of his hot breath on her skin.

''You don't need me,'' Laura told him, laughing. ''You're certifiable already. A grizzly bear, indeed!''

Nick reacted by growling, then he bent down and scooped her onto his shoulder. Laura objected vigorously, fearing he would hurt himself. But Nick mounted the stairs rapidly, ignoring her protests. He entered the master bedroom and dumped her on the king-sized bed.

''Strip, woman,'' he commanded. ''I'm gonna put my brand on you but good.'' He pulled off his sweater and kicked off his loafers. Then he started to unfasten his jeans.

Still laughing Laura hastened to obey. By the time he stood before her naked, she was down to her underwear, and her laughter had become breathless.

Even scarred, he was magnificent. His body seemed sculpted from solid oak, and the marks on his arms only accentuated his barbaric beauty. Laura held her arms open to him.

He knelt on the bed beside her and removed the rest of her clothing, his fingers shaking with suppressed passion. When he finally touched her, it was with such skillful tenderness that Laura felt her body flame with an immediate yearning for him.

"Love me, Nick," she whispered, pulling him onto her. "Oh, love me now!"

He slid inside her, and she wrapped herself around him, longing to show him with her body how much she cared for him. He moved with a slow, surging rhythm, and Laura crested and faded and crested again, until she heard herself crying out with the pleasure of it.

Nick called up every reserve of willpower he possessed to resist spending himself until he was certain she had reached the very limit of her desire. Then he gave himself over to the tidal wave that had been building within him. Passion shuddered through him, and he forgot everything but the joy of being as close to one with his love as possible. The pleasure stayed with him long after his body relaxed, and he continued to hold her, resting his head on her shoulder and breast and letting his weak hand stroke slowly down her side and thigh.

Her skin was silk, and the beat of her heart heavenly music to his ear. This was his woman, he thought, and he was her man. No brands, no labels, no documents were needed to prove it.

But as he felt sweet rest coming on him, a determination grew in his mind. Laura pushed him gently, and he rolled to one side, letting her get up and turn off the light. He listened as she padded into the bathroom, and he knew that he could never be any closer to another person. When she returned to adjust the bedclothes and snuggle against him, he whispered a request in her ear.

"I want to meet your parents," he said.

CHAPTER FIFTEEN

LAURA WAITED until Nick was actually nagging her before she called. His desire to meet her folks unsettled her, and she wasn't quite sure what to make of it. Her parents, on the other hand, sounded delighted and eager. Laura wondered if they really knew what to expect, if Peter and Anne had given them an accurate picture of the man she was living with.

When she confronted Peter at the hospital, he only added to her feeling of uncertainty. "Your dad and I got along famously," he told her. "I don't think there's any question about our getting along professionally. Anne and the boys love the town. Kids are all set to get horses..."

"I've got a horse they can have," Laura offered, thinking that Buster might as well go the way George had. When she was alone, a pet had seemed necessary. Now, she reflected, she had Nick. That was quite enough.

Peter accepted her offer with delight, and Laura told him that she would make arrangements to have the horse's ownership papers changed while she was in Advance over the weekend. "The woman who's keeping him is an old friend of mine, and she also happens to be a Justice of the Peace. Once she gets the papers in order, no one will be able to accuse you of horse stealing."

"You're sure you want to do this?" Peter's expression changed to one of concern. "You could lend him to the boys, Giving him away seems a little drastic."

Laura shrugged. They were walking together along the few blocks that separated the hospital from the Center. The day was sunny and pleasant, full of June's promises of a long good summer. "I seem to need to shed myself of all the ties to my past," she confessed. "I'm still not sure exactly how Nick plans to market Partners, but whatever he has in mind, I need to be able to move freely with him."

"Sounds more like slavery than partnership." Peter hunched his shoulders slightly.

"You still don't approve of him, do you?" Laura was amused by her friend's attitude.

"I like him a lot more than I used to," Peter admitted. "But I don't see that he's set you up as good a deal—"

"Translation—you think he ought to marry me."

Peter stopped walking. "Yeah," he said belligerently, "I do." He pointed a finger at her. "And you ought to be upset that he isn't going to. I mean, the man's used you, used your knowledge, your professional standing, your...your..."

"My *body*." Laura widened her eyes in a look of exaggerated horror. Then she started walking again. "Different people do things different ways, Peter," she said.

He caught up to her. "Don't be a fool, Laura," he said. "Some things don't change, no matter how much pop-culture sociologists try to trumpet liberation. If Nick Hawthorne doesn't want to marry you, then he must be planning somewhere down the line on dumping you.''

"That's an awful thing to say!" Laura stopped to face her friend. "You've got no reason to believe that. *I've* got no reason to think it."

"You don't want to think it."

Anger rising, Laura started to walk again. She heard Peter's footsteps behind her, but he didn't try to catch up. She walked faster.

Peter was being old-fashioned, she told herself. That was the problem with people around here. Everyone was so...so rooted in the old values. Like Ellen. She had practically tarred and feathered Nick because of nothing more than rumors and gossip. Thank goodness she had been a witness to the scene in the bar. At least now Ellen knew that Nick was ready to defend her, ready to fight for her.

Come to think of it, that had been pretty old-fashioned of him. She debated telling Peter about the incident.

No. He would have to come to terms with their relationship himself. She wasn't going to explain or apologize. And the same went for her parents. She loved them both dearly, but Nick was her life now. If they found it awkward that she and Nick...well...

But he had insisted on the meeting. It was cowardly of her, Laura knew, but she would have preferred to wait until Partners was going. Until it looked a little less as if...as if Nick was using her. Angrily she shoved the disloyal thought aside.

"Laura." Peter was at her side again. "You know I'm your friend. All I'm trying to do...." His words were interrupted by the blatting sound of a horn.

"What in the world?" Laura watched, astonished, as a big motor home pulled up beside them. A man she didn't recognize was at the wheel, but it was Nick who pulled open the side door and stepped onto the sidewalk, grinning from ear to ear.

"Glad I caught you," he said, taking her elbow. "Chased you all over the place before I found someone who told me you were walking back to the Center. Hi, Pete."

"Nick, what is this thing?" Laura gestured at the oversized vehicle. "Have you hijacked the Queen Mary?"

"It's our home away from home." He put his hands on her waist. "I talked to Andrew this morning, and we hammered out a plan. Partners will go city to city, setting up clinics and workshops and eventually centers. We'll train personnel...."

"You bought this thing?" Laura felt a little dizzy.

"Selkirk Enterprises bought it," Nick explained. "After Partners gets going, we can pay it back, if we want." He reached into the vehicle and took out a briefcase. "Here. I need your signature on these papers."

"Hold on a minute." Peter stepped up to the curb. "Aren't you being a little highhanded with her, Hawthorne? I mean, she had no part in the decision process, and here you go, shoving papers at her."

"He's right," Laura agreed, suddenly defensive. "You gave me no idea this morning that you were going to be making such plans, much less accepting the responsibility for an investment in a thing like this.''

An exasperated look crossed Nick's face. "You were at the hospital. I couldn't stop talking to Andrew and call you, could I?"

"Couldn't you have waited until I got home? Does every decision have to be made right this minute?" Laura felt a deep sense of injustice. For all his talk, maybe she was just a figurehead. Maybe she was being used.

"Did you feel you had to come running to me when you started those women on my diet?" Nick's mouth pulled down at the corners. "Those times that people in the hospital commented about my progress being partly due to the system—you had told them about it without consulting me first."

"Yes." Laura gestured widely. "But this! This is a major—"

"It's a major decision," Nick agreed. "And it makes sense. As long as we sit here on our great ideas, Partners will get nowhere fast. We're going to take it to the public. There are people in Selkirk's offices right now starting to make arrangements, itineraries, speaking schedules. Listen, Laura, this is going to be big business!"

Nick's eyes were alight with a jubilation she had missed seeing in them since the accident. His excitement and enthusiasm were contagious, and Laura felt her sense of outrage weakening. From a business and publicity viewpoint, what he had done made sense.

"Let me see the papers," she said. Grinning, Nick dug into the briefcase.

"Don't let yourself be run over," Peter remarked. Then he turned and started walking away.

"Wait a second, Pete." Nick handed her a pile of papers. "I need to talk to you." Peter looked back, a puzzled expression on his face.

"Check things out." Nick guided her into the doorway of the motor home. He indicated the driver. "Have Leon here show you how the boat steers. Take it out on the highway and see what you think. I'll wait for you back at the Center."

Laura hesitated, giving him a searching gaze. Then she nodded. If this really were one big con game and she was the ultimate victim, she would still go along with him. She loved him. "I can't be gone long, though. I have to attend a lecture in an hour."

"I'll take notes for you." Peter didn't look pleased, but his offer reassured her.

Nick gave her a quick kiss and mumbled something about love. Then he shut the sliding door, and through the window she saw him walking away with Peter, talking a mile a minute.

"You're the captain, ma'am. Where to?"

Laura turned. The man in the driver's seat didn't look old enough to have a license, much less to be piloting such a mighty machine. She set the papers down on the table and moved toward the passenger seat.

"Take us out on the highway, I guess," she told him. "It looks like I'm going to be living in this thing, so I might as well get used to it."

"You're gonna love it, ma'am." The kid cranked the engine. It sounded muted but powerful. "This is the finest home on wheels you can buy. Your old man's got good taste.''

My old man. Laura considered the words. Did the kid think they were married? She excused herself for a minute and went back to explore.

The vehicle was ideally equipped. There was a small cooking area and lots of storage space. The table could be used for work as well as dining, and there was even a recessed area where Nick could set up his computer. The bathroom was cramped, but no worse than the one in her old rental had been. And everything gleamed and shone with newness.

The bedroom was wall-to-wall mattress. Laura smiled wryly and tested the spring. It would do. She walked back to the table and picked up the papers, noting that she had no trouble keeping her balance even though the vehicle was moving. Nick had chosen well. Probably the best.

The papers all seemed straightforward and clear. She was a little surprised to find herself listed as co-signer, and that he had waited for her signature. All right, she thought. That was one for him. He hadn't totally gone off and done this on his own.

''She gets pretty good mileage,'' Leon was saying. ''Not in town, of course. But if you keep her at a steady pace on the road, gas bills won't eat you alive.''

''I'll try to remember that,'' Laura said. They entered the ramp onto the interstate, and she looked around at the green countryside spread under the endless Wyoming sky.

Traveling with Nick would be an adventure, she told herself. To see places all over the country. It would be an opportunity she would never have had if she had gone back to Advance. Something in her leapt with delight, and she realized that she yearned for the adventure.

NICK PACED UP AND DOWN on the sidewalk outside the Family Practice Center. Laura had been gone almost an hour, and he was becoming steadily more nervous. His conversation with Vance had made him edgy about her state of mind, and he was anxious to talk to her.

Everything was coming together for them. In a few weeks, perfectly coordinated with the end of her residency program, Partners for Life would be on the road. Selkirk's people would have taken care of all the planning headaches. All he and Laura had to do was sell the program.

They would do it well, too. Nick had outlined several different kinds of presentations, depending on the audiences, but, as Andrew pointed out, it was the magic of two of them together that would be the key to winning over an audience.

And it was the magic of the two of them together that had made him talk to Peter Vance. A phone call that morning to the county licensing office had informed him that simple blood tests and paperwork were all that were necessary for a marriage license. From Vance, he had learned that Laura had already had the test as part of routine physicals. He'd had his own done a little while ago.

He shook his right arm, wincing a little as the scar tissue pulled. It would never be as serviceable as before the accident, but he was definitely not crippled.

A few more months of therapy and he might even try swinging a club again. Or better yet, teach his wife to play the game.

He was determined to marry her. He'd gone full circle and now was as sure as dusk follows dawn that it was right for both of them. It hadn't only been Isabelle, or the hints from Andrew. The idea had been growing in him for some time. Laura openly loved and trusted him. Her gentleness and patience with him had gone beyond anything he had known from another human being in his entire life. She made no unreasonable demands, simply gave and gave and gave....

The instinctive bonding he had felt so strongly when they first met had been real. Only his own cowardice, his unwillingness to let himself be vulnerable, had kept him from accepting his feelings immediately. Instead, his recognition of their special bond had had to grow slowly over the weeks and months. Now he was sure.

But he knew Laura wasn't likely to believe him. She had given him enough clues for him to realize that deep down she might want a traditional relationship, but for his sake had accepted their situation. The best thing would be to do all the groundwork and present her with an almost complete package. The blood work was taken care of, and so was most of the paperwork. When the time was right, he'd spring everything on her.

Maybe this coming weekend in Advance. If he asked her father for her hand first, it would add even more weight to his sincerity. And Pete had mentioned that the Justice of the Peace was an old buddy of Laura's.

Vance had been delighted to learn of his intentions, and Nick hoped he would keep the news to himself, as he'd promised. This was a gift he wanted to give to Laura from his own lips, with no warning. That was the way it should be.

His heart started to pound, and he wiped his damp palms on his trousers as he saw the motor home turn the corner with Laura at the wheel. Her pleased expression cheered his heart. It was all going to work!

LAURA HESITATED over her choice of clothing for the weekend. Usually she just threw a few things in a bag and took off, knowing that the chance of having to dress up was remote. But Nick, humming away in that off-key manner of his, had carefully stowed a dress suit in the motor home closet and had also packed a good shirt and tie. Was something up that she wasn't aware of?

His good humor had continued unabated since the day she had agreed to the motor home. She had expected him to grow moody at the prospect of meeting her parents, but instead he had been acting like a kid anticipating Christmas. It seemed odd.

Then there was Peter. After the lecture he had given her the other day, he had made no further mention of his contention that Nick was using her. Whatever Nick had said to him while she had been trying out the new machine had apparently smoothed the waters. That was odd, too.

Well, she thought, she couldn't be wasting her time trying to figure out the behavior of the men in her life. Maybe it was simply the pleasant summer weather and the fact that both Nick and Peter were looking forward to new directions in their life. That must be it. She stopped worrying about what Nick was packing and tossed her usual weekend jeans and shirts into her bag.

"What? No pretties?" Nick came up behind her and put his arms around her waist. His warm breath tickled against her neck.

"Advance isn't a place you do much dressing up in." Laura patted his hand. "Just clean jeans and a couple of changes of underwear—a blouse and skirt for church, maybe. I don't want to have to ask Mom to do laundry."

"Do me a favor." His voice was low. "Put a pretty dress in the motor home closet. You never know."

"Nick," Laura said, turning to look at him. "What are you up to? We're just running up for the weekend. Believe me, there's no reason to carry good clothes."

He pulled her tight against his body. "Humor me."

Feeling slightly annoyed, she finally agreed. He was in one of his stubborn moods, she decided. Argument would be futile.

Laura drove, and Nick lounged happily in the passenger's chair, entertaining her with tales from his years on the professional tour, a subject he hadn't mentioned much since the accident. It seemed that more than his arm was beginning to heal.

They reached Advance around four in the afternoon, and Laura felt nervous anticipation growing inside her as she eased the big vehicle carefully down the street toward her old home. Nick sat up and cleared his throat.

"Sleeping arrangements," he said abruptly. "I get the motor home, and you get your childhood bedroom."

"Nick, my parents understand…."

"I won't abuse their hospitality." His tone was firm, and when she glanced at him, she saw that his jaw was set. "We sleep separately."

"That's silly," she protested. "They know we…that we're lovers, for goodness sake."

Nick looked at her, and a world of feeling seemed to dance in his eyes. "Trust me on this, will you, Laura? It's for the best."

It's a lie, she thought, her spirits dashed. *He wants to put on a show of false morality.* Disappointment filled her. She was willing to live the way he wanted, and now, under the slightest bit of social pressure, he was planning to deny the kind of relationship they had. That hurt.

But she determined to put on a good front for her parents. It was enough that she had chosen Nick over them. She wouldn't let them know there were any problems in the relationship.

Her mother came out of the house the moment she pulled into the driveway. Her father, she noted, followed more slowly behind. As she got out of the motor home, she heard Nick clear his throat again and cough.

Oh no, she thought despairingly. He couldn't have an allergy attack right now! She put on a fake smile and embraced her mother warmly. When she looked up, she saw to her great relief that Nick was striding purposefully toward her father, his hand outstretched. No sign of difficult breathing.

"Nick Hawthorne, sir," he said, taking her father's hand. For a moment, the two men seemed to be measuring each other. Then the tension broke and there were smiles and greetings all around.

"Where'd you get the ship?" Walt asked, pointing the end of his pipe at the motor home. "Last time I saw you, honey, you were driving a car like the rest of us."

"It's for Partners," Nick explained. He quickly outlined the plans Andrew Selkirk had for them.

"Sounds like the two of you are likely to be kind of famous in a few years," Walt commented. "Going from place to place like that, spreading the gospel." His tone was dry.

"It's a possibility," Nick admitted. He coughed again.

"Why don't we go inside," Laura suggested quickly. "I'll get my stuff and be right in." The look on both her parents' faces was one of surprised relief. Maybe Nick's insistence that they sleep apart was a more sensitive one than she had thought.

She hurriedly gathered her bag, leaving the dress hanging in the closet. When she went into the house, she found her mother waiting.

"Your young man and your father are taking a walk," Adele told her. "Laura, is something going on I should know about?"

Puzzled, Laura shook her head. "Beats me. He's been acting funny all week, but I suppose that meeting you had made him nervous. He should settle down in a little while."

But Nick was far from settled when he and her father returned more than an hour later. He kept up a pleasant flow of conversation all through dinner, but she sensed an antic spirit in him. His eyes seemed to spark, and he coughed or cleared his throat frequently.

Her parents, however, didn't know him well enough to realize that he was like a coiled spring. All of Walt's reserve had disappeared, and he treated Nick with warm friendliness. The change bothered Laura a little, and she wondered what the two of them had discussed on their long walk.

The evening passed without unusual incident, in spite of her apprehensions. Nick volunteered to help with the kitchen cleanup, a gesture that astonished Adele. Laura took the opportunity to speak to her father in relative privacy. They retired to the living room, and Walt stoked up his pipe.

"I like the man," he told her quietly, a small smile on his face. He looked at her with an expression Laura couldn't read and added, "I think you've made yourself a good choice, honey."

"We do work well together," Laura replied, feeling that there was something wrong with her father's words. It sounded as if he was talking about a husband rather than a business partner cum lover.

"I spoke with young Vance today," Walt said, emitting a thin stream of smoke from between his lips. "He's definitely going to come up here."

"Oh, that's wonderful!" Laura got up and hugged her dad. "I know you two will like working together."

Walt smiled at her, and his blue eyes twinkled. "Funny how some things seem to work out, isn't it."

Nick and Adele brought coffee into the living room, and Laura watched with amusement as Nick pointedly opened a window and fanned the pipe smoke out of the room. Walt seemed equally amused.

"Passive smoking," Nick intoned darkly. "It can be as dangerous as inhaling directly."

"Listen, kid." Walt leaned forward and pointed at him with the end of his pipe. "I've got a patient who lives out on the range, winter and summer, in a sheep wagon. The man has smoked hand-rolled for almost seven decades, and his lungs are as clear as a bell. I'm not claiming it's good for you, mind. But I intend to continue using my pipe, and if we're going to get along, I expect you'd better show me a little tolerance."

Nick grinned. "Agreed, but it works both ways." He sat on the couch next to Laura. "The coffee you're getting is a special blend I brought along. The flavor's great and there's no caffeine at all."

"Nick's been giving me all kinds of ideas about how I can adjust my cooking to help your blood pressure, dear," Adele interjected.

"Health nuts," Walt grumbled as he accepted the coffee. "Give 'em an inch, and they want to reform your life."

The conversation continued in the form of good-natured banter until late in the evening. After her parents retired, Nick and Laura sat quietly on the couch holding hands.

"They like you," she said, running her fingers over the top of his hand, teasing the sprinkling of soft reddish hair.

"I like them." Nick turned his hand over so that she could stroke his palm. "Walt and I are going to be a bit like two bulls in a pasture, but I expected that."

"Why?"

He grinned. "You had to get your stubborness from somewhere, love, and I didn't figure it was from your mother." He caught her fist before she could punch him in the stomach.

That night, alone in her old bedroom, Laura thought about her feelings. Coming home could have been an uncomfortable experience, but everyone seemed to get on so well. In fact, at times during the evening, she had had to remind herself that she really wasn't married to Nick. It had seemed so *family* with the four of them chatting in the living room.

She rolled over, missing Nick's presence. It was a good thing they hadn't come for a week's visit, she thought. She wasn't sure if she could stand the deprivation. Tomorrow she would have to get him out in the brush and seduce him. She would load him up with antihistamines, borrow a gentle riding horse for him and take Buster out one last time. She fell asleep dreaming of making love with Nick.

In the motor home, Nick paced the narrow floorspace nervously. He tossed a gold wedding band up and down in his left hand. His talk with her father had gone better than he had dared hope. He had convinced Walt that, given his past and the way he had put down the idea of marriage, the best strategy to follow would be to confront Laura once all the arrangements for the wedding had been made. Walt said he would fill his wife in after they went to bed.

But Nick was worried. Laura was quite capable of jumping either way. He tossed the ring into the air and caught it. She might be madder than a scalded cat that he had gone ahead with everything and not consulted her. He could only hope she would understand he'd done it out of love.

Out of love, he thought, remembering the telegram he had ordered sent to Isabelle's lawyer. If she was still alive, and if the closemouthed attorney who handled her affairs delivered it, his old friend would know of his plans tomorrow. Wherever she was, whatever was wrong with her, Nick knew the news would bring her happiness. He could only hope that by tomorrow evening the marriage would have taken place.

He toyed with various ways to tell Laura of his plan. Maybe at breakfast he could suggest they go for a hike or something, anything to give her parents a few hours to set things up. When they returned he could suggest they get dressed for dinner, and...

He should have made better plans, dammit. He slammed the ring down on the counter and stripped off his clothes. A hot shower would help him get to sleep. Maybe it would even help him come up with a more plausible scheme.

The water calmed him, but the empty bed made him restless. He rehearsed a thousand speeches in which he explained that his aversion to wedlock was a thing of the past.... That he loved her too much not to make her his in every possible way.... That he hoped she would understand he wasn't trying to be high-handed by setting it all up without telling her....

That he would turn himself inside out for the love of her.

The last thing he saw before finally falling asleep was the gray light of dawn starting to fill the small window on the wall of the motor home.

CHAPTER SIXTEEN

"WAKE UP, SLEEPYHEAD." Laura shifted the break-fast tray to her left hand and pulled open the side door of the motor home. Nick hadn't responded to her knocking, so she decided to invade his privacy and wake him personally.

It was already eight in the morning, but when she went into the bedroom, she saw he was still sound asleep, his face half-buried in the pillow he clutched.

She almost hated to wake him, he looked so deep in slumber, but she had already called Myra and made arrangements for Buster and a mare suitable for Nick to be ready by ten. If his system hadn't had time to absorb the medication, it would be unfair to expect him to get within a hundred feet of a horse.

"Up and at 'em," she crowed, laughing when he looked up from the pillow with an expression of sleepy astonishment. "Come on, lazy, the rest of us have been up for hours." She presented the tray to him.

Nick blinked and rubbed his eyes. "What's that?" he asked suspiciously, regarding the breakfast.

"Eat it." Laura sat on the edge of the bed. He looked scruffy, his face unshaven and his auburn hair uncombed. But the sight of his bare torso made her itch to take the tray into the other area of the motor home and put the wide bed to good use. Only the knowledge that her mother anxiously awaited Nick's empty dishes as proof that he enjoyed her cooking kept her from giving in to the temptation. "Mom made it especially for you, and her feelings will be hurt if you don't give it a try."

He sniffed the offering. "What the hell is it?"

"She made it from an old family recipe. I think it's supposed to be some kind of cereal, but she put all kinds of dried fruit into it. I had some. It isn't bad."

He took a tentative taste. "Not bad," he agreed. "But it tastes a little...stale."

"I think some of the ingredients have been in the pantry for a while." Laura leaned back on the bed, watching as he ate. "Are you ready to play cowboy today?" she asked.

Instead of the roguish look she expected, Nick's expression was puzzled. "Cowboy?"

"I'm taking you riding." She reached into a pocket and took out an antihistamine capsule that was a little stronger than his usual dosage. "This'll protect you, and we'll have a great time. She handed him the pill.

"We're leaving town?" His smile was slow and incredulous. "Going out into the countryside?" He sounded delighted.

"Unless you have strong objections." She rolled onto her stomach and propped her chin on her hands. "I know of a beautiful remote place down by a creek. And I don't know about you, but last night I discovered that celibacy isn't all it's cracked up to be." She tickled the sheet over his thigh.

Nick gobbled down the rest of the cereal. "Let me grab a shower," he said. "I'll be ready in less than five minutes." He scrambled from the bed and headed for the bathroom.

Laura smiled as she heard him start to yodel. She gathered up the tray and started out of the bedroom.

But as she walked by the counter, the shine of something gold caught her eye. She balanced the tray on her hip and picked the object up.

It was unmistakably a wedding ring. Laura frowned and held the ornament up to the morning sunlight. It looked new. She squinted and tried to read the inscription that ran along the inside of the band.

NBH...LJH...PFL... What in the world...? She heard the shower stop and hastily tossed the ring back onto the counter. Her mind full of questions, she hurried out of the motor home.

Whose ring was it? Whose initials? She carried the tray back to the kitchen, absentmindedly responding to her mother's questions about Nick's enjoyment of the special dish. Nicholas...B?...Laura Jensen...Hawthorne? PFL?

"Laura, is everything all right?" Her mother's voice broke into her thoughts, and Laura turned, smiling.

"Everything's fine, mom," she replied. "I was just puzzling something out, that's all." She continued to chat, but her thoughts were whirling.

The idiot had brought a *wedding* ring and had their initials engraved in the thing. PFL had to stand for partners. What a crazy, romantic thing to do. Was it his plan to have her wear the ring while they were on the road—a sort of reputation-protection device? Something that would prevent the kind of episode that had happened with the amorous cowboy in the bar?

Or was the ring for another, more serious purpose? She felt herself stiffen inside, then took a good long look at her mother for the first time that morning.

Always cheery, Adele fairly sparkled. She hummed as she washed the dishes from Nick's tray, and her voice seemed to bubble with joy. Laura leaned against the counter and raised an eyebrow.

"Mom, did dad ever tell you what he and Nick talked about yesterday?" she asked, watching for her mother's reaction to the question.

"Hmm?" Adele scrubbed busily at a pan. "No, honey, I don't believe he did." She didn't look at Laura.

"Mom!" Laura pushed herself off the counter. "Don't fib to me. I can always tell." She put her hands on her mother's shoulders. "Come on, now. What's going on?"

"I...I promised not to tell." Adele smiled, but still didn't look at her daughter. "Your father swore me to secrecy."

"Whose secret?" Laura persisted.

"Good morning, ladies!" Nick's hearty greeting interrupted her probing. He entered the kitchen, filling it with his presence, and came over to give Adele a kiss on the cheek.

"That's for the special breakfast," he said, sending Laura the shadow of a wink. "It gave me an extra jolt of energy, which I understand I'm going to need. Laura's got plans for us to go horseback riding."

"I made a lunch for you." Adele wiped her hands on a dish towel. "The weather should be wonderful all day, so you two can stay out as long as you want. I won't plan dinner at any particular time."

"That's great," Nick replied enthusiastically.

Laura listened as he and her mother chatted away like old friends. There seemed to be even more warmth between them this morning than there had been last night, and her suspicions were fired to a white heat. He couldn't have had the gall to arrange for...

No, it was impossible. Marriages had to be planned at least a few days in advance. There were the blood tests, the paperwork...

"Excuse me just a moment," she said, interrupting a story her mother was telling Nick. "I left my jacket in the motor home. I'll be right back."

Nick felt a rush of relief. He had been hoping for a chance to talk to Adele alone. When Laura had left, he reached into his pocket and gave her the wedding ring.

"Keep this safe," he said, whispering conspiratorially. "I accidentally left it out on the counter last night, and I'm scared to death she might see it before I'm ready to give it to her. Walt filled you in last night?"

Adele slipped the ring into her apron pocket and nodded. "He's talking to Myra Black right now. He told me to tell you to keep Laura out as long as you possibly could. When you get back, we'll tell her that there's a special meeting at the church tonight, and..."

Nick raised his hands. "Don't make it too complicated. I still don't know if she'll go along."

"She will." Adele nodded firmly. "She loves you."

Laura searched the countertop for the ring, not surprised to find it gone. She took her jacket from the closet and started to close the door when she caught sight of Nick's briefcase stuffed in a corner. Biting her lip, she ran over to the window and looked out. No sign of him. Apparently he was still talking to her mother. She went back to the closet.

Rummaging through his papers would be wrong, she told herself. She would just take a peek....

In the kitchen Adele handed Nick a weighty saddlebag, which she declared was full of enough food to last them a week. Nick draped it over his shoulder, took the blanket roll and one of Walt's old straw cowboy hats, which Adele offered, and headed out the front door. Laura was waiting for him at the foot of the walk, her arms folded across he chest.

"It's not too far to Myra's," she said, studying him through narrowed eyes. "We'll walk, if you don't mind."

"I never mind, if you don't," Nick joked. When she didn't respond, he pushed the brim of the borrowed hat back on his forehead. "What's the matter, little gal?" he asked. "Ain'tcha lookin' forward to our ride? Your ma packed a truckload of goodies for us." He hefted the blankets, "And thoughtfully provided some protection from sand and cactus."

Laura gave him a strange look. "If I didn't love you so much..." Her words trailed off, and she started to laugh.

"What's so funny?" Nick jogged in front of her, running backward so that he could look directly into her face. "Come on, Laura. You know I hate it when I don't know what the joke is."

She wiped tears of merriment out of the corners of her eyes. The scoundrel! To think he had set her up for a wedding, and had apparently enlisted not only her parents but her friends. He would have had to have used Peter to get at her medical file for the blood test. The rat!

And here he was, dancing along the sidewalk in front of her, a silly, quizzical grin on his face and her father's old hat pushed back on his head. All she could feel for him was love.

"I was just thinking," she lied, getting control of herself again, "how your fluttery little golf fans would react if they could see you now. All you lack for the John Wayne look is a gun at your hip."

"Hmm." Nick dropped back to walk beside her, satisfied, it seemed, with her explanation. "I've never learned how to use a gun. Maybe I ought to try."

"You're too dangerous as it is," Laura commented dryly.

Myra's oldest boy, Rob, had the two horses ready when they arrived at the stables. Laura watched Nick carefully, but he showed no allergic reaction. He did admit, however, it had been decades since he'd ridden, and that had been English-style, not Western.

"Just sit on her," Rob instructed him. "Let her follow Buster. She's a good trail horse, long's you don't make her go someplace on her own."

Nick eyed the animal with a doubtful expression. "A female with no mind of her own? I find that hard to believe."

Laura swung up onto Buster's back. "We can't all be feminist trailblazers, Mr. Hawthorne. Mount up. Time's a-wasting."

"Yes, ma'am!" He mounted with his usual physical grace, but settled somewhat gingerly into the saddle. "There's sure a lot of hard surface area here," he muttered as Rob handed him the reins.

"Buns as tough as yours should have no problem with a saddle," Laura said as she turned Buster's head and led them out of the corral area. From behind her, she heard Nick's mare clop slowly along in pursuit.

"Go, horse," Nick urged.

"Her name's Maude," Rob called after him.

"Go, Maude." Nick sounded impatient.

Laura followed the familiar trail that led back into the low foothills west of town. The air was warm, with a hint of a breeze and a promise of the heat that afternoon would bring. Spending a few hours under the cottonwoods by the stream would be just the ticket.

"Can't you drop back and walk beside me?" Nick complained. "Much as I love looking at your backside, Buster's does leave a lot to be desired in spite of Maude's apparent fascination with it."

Laura pulled back on her reins. "She's a dude trail horse," she explained, holding Buster until the little mare's nose was almost by her knee. "Unless she sees another horse in front of her, she's liable to turn and head back to the barn."

"You knew they'd give me a dude horse?" He looked indignant.

Laura suppressed her laughter. "I want the day to be as peaceable as possible. You plus a horse with any amount of pizzazz would be an accident looking for a place to happen."

"Thanks a lot," he muttered. Then he gave his horse a kick with his heels. "Giddup, Maude." Maude only huffed.

After a while, however, Nick seemed to relax into the leisurely pace. He would let long minutes pass without saying anything, and Laura felt herself lulled by the soothing sounds of softly creaking leather and the gentle clopping of the horses' hooves. She let her body relax and her mind wander.

Marriage to Nick was something she hadn't let herself think about too much. She had been so sure that it would take a long, long time for him to give up his prejudices from his first experience that she hadn't wanted to think about it. But here he was, pushing her into it the same way he'd done with his exercise and diet program. The way he did everything.

"I'm beginning to see the charm in all this." His voice interrupted her musings. She slowed Buster, and Maude pulled up alongside.

Nick's face reflected a quiet pleasure. He looked around at the countryside, then back at Laura. "It's so damned peaceful," he said, gazing into her eyes. "Makes me think how lucky I am."

"Lucky?" Laura cocked her head to one side.

"Lucky," Nick repeated. "Lucky to have a wi—to have a woman like you." Laura smiled tightly and let Buster take the lead again.

Nick settled back in the uncomfortable saddle. Something was eating at her, that was for sure. For a moment he wondered if her mother could have spilled the beans, then he dismissed the thought. From the way Adele had talked, he couldn't believe she had let the secret out.

But something was definitely wrong, and he intended to find out what it was.

Laura led the way without speaking for another hour, taking the long path that meandered through the low hills and shallow valleys paralleling the creek. The water bubbled and tumbled along, running high because of the spring rains and snowmelt.

"I suppose it's too chilly for skinny-dipping," Nick called.

Laura turned around and have him a hard look. "It depends on how hot the day gets."

"Laura, what...?"

She didn't give him a chance to finish. She clicked to Buster, who turned his ears back at the signal and broke into a trot. Behind her she heard Nick yell for his horse to slow down. Then he was quiet. She glanced back and saw that he was intent on learning how to ride a trot Western-style.

After a few more minutes she had pity on him and slowed back to a walk. She heard him groan with relief.

The spot she had had in mind came into view. By the creek, a stand of cottonwood formed a natural canopy of shade, and the wild grass was a thick carpet beneath the trees. She reined Buster to a halt and dismounted. Maude stopped, too, but Nick stayed put.

Laura walked over to him. "Get down, Nick," she said. "We need to talk."

"I'm not sure I can." His tone was aggrieved. "Get down, that is. Whoever designed these torture racks didn't seem to have the male anatomy in mind." He slapped the side of his saddle.

Laura felt a smile tugging at the corners of her lips. "You have to get used to them. Come on, now. I've got a lot on my mind."

Groaning, he slowly dismounted and limped around in an exaggerated manner while she tended the horses. But when she came back, carrying the saddlebag and the blanket roll, he sobered and straightened up. "Okay," he said in a serious tone. "What do you want to talk about?"

She dropped her burden onto the grass. "Nick, I've never lied to you, and I don't think I've ever kept something important a secret from you."

"Who blabbed?" He looked uneasy. "Pete? Your mom?"

"You did!" Laura turned on him, suddenly feeling furious. "You and your behind-my-back, sneaky, double-dealing..."

"Hold it." Nick raised both hands. "Just hold it right there, Laura. I..."

"You what?" Her eyes filled with angry tears. "You love me? Well, maybe you do, but you sure have a damn funny way of showing it. If you wanted to get married, why didn't you just ask!"

His shoulders seemed to sag slightly. "I was afraid you'd say no. How did you find out?"

"Like I said, you told me." She wiped her eyes on the sleeve of her shirt. "When I started to leave the motor home this morning, I spotted a ring on the counter. I picked it up—maybe I shouldn't have, but I had the impression that the place is supposed to be mine as well as yours—and I looked at the inscription."

Nick sat down heavily on the grass. "I bought it this week." He covered his face with his hands. "I've been carrying it around like a good luck piece. I couldn't sleep last night, and I was pacing, tossing the thing around in my hand. I thought I'd lost it this morning, but then I found it. I gave it to your mom for safekeeping."

Laura walked over to a cottonwood and sat down with her back resting against the rough old trunk. "Is there anyone else in the universe who didn't know about this before me?"

Nick was silent for a moment. "I don't think so," he said finally. "I even sent a telegram to Isabelle through her lawyer. If she's able, she should have read about the wedding before evening."

"Nick, why? Why?"

He picked up a small stone and tossed it into the creek. "I just figured that you'd take it better if I surprised you. If you...didn't have time to think about it."

"Nicholas Hawthorne!" Laura stood up and walked over to where he sat. "I love you. Why should I have any objection to marrying you?"

He looked up at her, a doubtful expression on his face. "I thought... When I said something about it when I was in the hospital, you objected. I figured..."

Laura stalked over to the edge of the creek. "You know, you do fine until you try to 'figure' what's going on inside of me. For a man who's as smart as you seem to be, you're one incredible idiot when it comes to women."

Nick sneezed.

Laura whirled around. "Oh, no. Don't start that," she cried.

"It's the sunlight!" Nick stood up and flung the cowboy hat to one side. "Sunlight on the water, dammit! I always sneeze if I stare at it too long." He glared at her. "Now, are you going to marry me or not!"

"Yes!" She spat the word out.

Nick took a step toward her, then hesitated. "Why?" he asked belligerently.

Laura stared at him for a moment. "I'll marry you because I love you. I'll marry you because for the first time, I really believe you want to marry me. That it's your own idea and not something you want to do, out of a sense of duty to anyone else."

"You're damn right!" Nick stabbed a finger into the air for emphasis.

The situation suddenly struck Laura as the most ridiculous one she had ever found herself in. Laughter started to tickle inside her, but she was afraid that if she let it out, he would think she was laughing at his proposal.

Well, I am, she thought. For a big, strong, intelligent man, he'd gone at romance like a crazy kid, starting from the very beginning with the lovable, silly trick of catching her alone in the ladies' room and dancing with her to his own off-key melody. And she hadn't done much better, come to think of it. The laughter started to bubble.

"What's so funny?" Nick looked puzzled.

"We are." Laura held out her arms to him. "Have you listened to the past few minutes of mature, adult conversation the two of us have been spewing out?"

Nick hesitated, then he started to grin. "Thank God nobody else heard us," he said, catching her into a tight embrace. "They'd lock us up in a padded cell and throw away the key."

Laura tilted her head back so she could look into his face. "As long as they put us both in the same cell," she said softly, stroking her fingers along the back of his neck. "I wouldn't mind at all."

Nick covered her mouth with his and kissed her thoroughly. He felt almost giddy with happiness, but something inside him stirred uneasily. Something was not quite right. Although he could tell that Laura would be content to go on kissing him, he broke the embrace after a while.

"Come over here," he said, leading her by the hand to the base of the tree she had been sitting against. "Sit down," he commanded.

"What for?" She looked puzzled.

"Just sit." He kissed her temple lightly. "I want you to pretend this moment is taking place days— no—weeks ago."

She eyed him askance, but slid down to rest on the ground, her back to the tree. "Weeks ago it would have been too chilly," she began.

"Hush, love." Nick knelt on the grass in front of her. "Think emotionally, romantically. Not practically."

Laura smiled and reached to push some strands of auburn hair off his forehead. "Do you love me for my mind," she asked, "or my...romanticism?"

"All of the above." He gave her another warm kiss. "I love everything about you, Laura Jensen. Will you please do me the honor of becoming my wife?"

She tilted her head to one side. "Nick, are you proposing again?"

He looked at her steadily. "Will you marry me, Laura?"

"I already said that I..."

Nick shook his head. "This is last month, and I haven't done a damn fool thing like try to railroad you into a wedding."

She laughed softly and leaned her head back against the tree. "Is this like the first time? When I was expected to forget that we were in a bathroom lounge and pretend we were dancing to music instead of your singing?"

The old light of mischief gleamed in his eyes. "Yep. You're a beautiful princess, and I'm just a humble commoner who's lost his heart to you and come to beg for your hand. Will you marry me?"

"Of course I will." She held out her arms. "And I'm not pretending."

The gleam deepened until his eyes seemed almost golden. He reached behind him and picked up the blanket roll. "There'll be no more pretending, Laura," he said. "I swear to you I'll never again go behind your back to do anything." He unwrapped the roll and spread the blanket out. "Well, that is *almost* anything," he added, giving her an unabashedly lecherous grin. He patted the blanket invitingly. "Let me demonstrate."

Love warmed every cell of her body. Laura slipped off her boots and crawled onto the soft, wool material.

They made love and picnicked and slept; loved and splashed around in the freezing creek water, then loved again to warm up goose-bumped skin and tingling muscles. Nick dozed off afterward, his head pillowed on Laura and his arms wrapped around her waist.

Laura propped her own head on a pile of their discarded clothing and watched her love sleep. He seemed completely at peace, the lines that had begun to etch his face since the accident and Isabelle's mysterious departure were gone. Even in slumber he radiated the old strength and energy that characterized him. She gently stroked his silky hair.

It was going to work, she decided. It was all going to work. They would marry, take Partners on the road, and eventually... She thought fleetingly of children, wondering if their commitment to establish the program would stand in the way of starting a family. Well, all good things in time. It was a matter they would have plenty of time to discuss in the future.

She waited until the shadows lengthened considerably before she wakened him. He had confessed to a sleepless night, and she knew the extra dose of antihistamine had to be adding to his drowsiness. But she didn't want to be riding back after dark.

"Come on," she urged, rolling him off her lap and patting his face. "Time to be getting back. Your co-conspirators should be anxiously awaiting our return."

Nick sat up and rubbed a hand across his face. "I was in heaven for an afternoon," he muttered, "and now you're making me come back to earth." He ran a hand through his hair and smiled. "I wish we could stay here forever."

"It would get darned uncomfortable come winter." Laura handed him his clothes. "Maybe once in a while we can take a little time off...."

"We will," Nick promised as he slipped into his jeans. "I calculate we ought to be done with the road tripping within a year. Then I want to settle. Neither of us will see twenty-five again, and I want to start a family as soon as we..."

"Oh, Nick!" Laura threw her arms around his neck. "I was just thinking about that. Wondering if we would ever have time for children."

"Not have time for kids?" Nick's eyebrows lifted. "What do you think we've been practicing for all afternoon, woman?" He kissed her soundly.

They dressed quickly, and Nick splashed the rest of the sleepiness out of his face with cold creek water. Laura packed up the gear and retrieved the horses. She let Nick ride Buster home, a gesture that seemed to delight him beyond all reason.

"It proves you really trust me," he called back to her, and when they hit the flats outside town, he urged Buster into a canter. He was, he told her, in too big a hurry to get hitched to poke back into town at a walk. Laughing at his words, Laura followed on a lurching Maude.

Rob Black was waiting for them at the stable, a strange look on his usually expressionless young face. Nick dismounted Buster agilely and handed the youth the reins.

"We're in a hurry, son," he said, slipping some money to the boy. "Dr. Jensen and I are getting married in a little while. Would you mind taking care of the horses without our help?"

"Thought it was a secret," Rob began. "Mom said…"

"It was a secret." Laura put her arm around Nick's waist. "But Mr. Hawthorne isn't very good at keeping secrets. He ratted on himself."

When they got near the house, Laura slowed down. "What do you think?" she asked. "Should we play this out, or let them all know the game is over and I know what fate lurks waiting for me."

Nick chuckled and pulled her close to his side. "I think…"

But his words were interrupted by Walt Jensen. The gray-haired man opened the front door and waved frantically to them. "Nick," he called. "Hurry up. You've got an overseas telephone call. The operator said it was urgent."

"Isabelle?" Laura breathed. She felt Nick's muscles stiffen and saw that his face paled visibly in the throes of passion. Laura had never said the word at all.

Her doubts about a long-term relationship were increased by a chance encounter with Ellen Patterson late one afternoon in the grocery store. Ellen's telephone calls had come less and less frequently, and Laura had assumed her friend had simply decided that whatever happened with Nick was Laura's business.

"We've been out of town so much," Ellen explained. "With the economy in such a tangle, Bob's been doing a lot of traveling this month to try to keep in touch with what's going on in the major financial centers." Telephones were fine, she went on, but personal contact was better. And speaking of personal contact...

"I asked around about your new friend," Ellen confided. "A lot of people, important people, know him or at least knew his family. And he *does* have a reputation as a ladies man. It seems that after his marriage broke up, he was never with the same woman from one day to the next. No one could believe he was living up here, away from the party scene."

Ellen chatted on, imparting other gossipy tidbits, but Laura barely heard. She felt depressed by Ellen's words, and although she knew it was wrong to rely on rumor, this bit of information didn't surprise her. She would have to be the worst sort of idiot to lose her heart to a man like Nick.

Her resolve to keep a distance between them hardened over the next few days. The weather had taken an early springlike turn, so Nick's schedule was unusually busy. Her own was impossible since she was finishing the obstetrical rotation and preparing to start a final session in clinical diagnosis. They saw each other rarely, and Laura began to feel that she could handle the affair, no matter which direction it took.

Nick had firmly reserved the night that marked the end of Laura's six-week program for the two of them to be together. He wanted to fix a celebration dinner and said there were some important things he wanted to discuss with her. Laura finally agreed, realizing she could put off making a choice for only a little while longer.

The meal Nick prepared was even better than the one he had made the night they had become lovers. Laura ate shrimp, chicken and vegetables until she couldn't hold another bite. While she made tea, Nick cleared the dishes, then they went into the living room.

"I want you to take a few days off next week," Nick said after they had settled down on the sofa. His arm was around her shoulders, and she was snuggled against his side, enjoying the peace she felt whenever they were alone together.

"Why?"

"I'm going to another tournament. It's a bush league warm-up for the big southern championships, but the resort is popular with some very influential and wealthy folks. I want you to come with me, doctor my allergies and help me lobby for some cash commitments."

Laura hesitated. The invitation was a complete surprise. She did know that his late spring and summer schedule included more tournaments, and though the events were important to professional late afternoon sunlight. He grasped her hand tightly, as if seeking support from her, and they hurried into the house.

CHAPTER SEVENTEEN

LAURA WONDERED if she should give him privacy while he took the call, but Nick refused to release her. He held her close while he put the phone to his ear, and she rested her head on his shoulder, willing him the strength to take whatever news awaited him.

"Yes, yes, yes," he said, speaking the words in rapid succession, his voice tense with impatience and anxiety. Then he paused, listening.

Laura closed her eyes. If the news was bad, she would insist they put off any thought of a wedding that evening. Nick would need to mourn, and if he tried to sidestep it by demanding they go on with his plans for a ceremony, she would refuse for his own sake. His emotions were vulnerable, and she would tend them carefully for the rest of their lives.

"Isabelle?" His voice sounded excited. "Are you okay? Where the hell are...yes, ma'am."

Laura opened her eyes and looked at him. Instead of the sad expression she expected, he was grinning widely at what he heard. He was nodding and trying not to interrupt the speaker. There was no question in Laura's mind that the speaker had to be a healthy Isabelle. Nobody else in the world could get Nick Hawthorne to be so silent and obedient. Finally he held the receiver to Laura's ear.

"Best wishes, my dear." Isabelle's voice sounded as if it was coming from another planet. "I'll send up regular prayers for an abundance of patience for you. I know you'll need it, being married to the rascal."

"Thanks, Isabelle." Laura gripped the phone, straining to hear. "Are you all right?"

"Let Nickie explain." Isabelle sounded as if she was laughing. "Again, my best wishes."

Laura handed the phone back to Nick and let him conclude the conversation. She had been right, she realized with a sense of satisfaction. Nick had misjudged Isabelle's actions and words, probably because he was in a turmoil over his own condition and prospects for the future. Whatever it was that Isabelle Franklin had been secretly up to for the past months, it hadn't been dying.

"She's taking the 'waters' at a health spa in Europe," he said when he had hung up. "Says she feels years younger." He looked at Laura with an expression of bewildered delight. "What a crazy thing to do."

"If it makes her feel good, what do you care?"

He shook his head and laughed. "I worried for nothing. Boy, do I feel like some kind of jerk."

"You do seem to have a way of blowing things out of proportion," Laura agreed.

"That's precisely why I need you." Nick pulled her close. "And one reason why I love you." He bent her backward for a dramatic kiss.

A discreet knock at the living-room doorway brought them up and out of the clench. Walt Jensen entered and ambled over to his desk, unlit pipe in hand.

"It's a little difficult not to overhear what's being said in this room when you're out in the kitchen," he said in a disinterested tone. "My pipe went out, and I waited until it got quiet. Figured you two might not notice unless I announced my presence." He started to prepare his smoking material. "Well, what's on the agenda for tonight?"

Laura started to laugh. "We're getting married, you dear old fox."

"Ah." Walt smiled. "Got up the nerve to ask you, did he?"

"Not exactly." Nick rubbed the back of his neck and looked embarrassed. "Laura figured it out first."

"Always was a smart one." Walt lit the pipe. "I was scared to death she would put me to shame if we started practicing together." He puffed, then called his wife.

"You can come on in now, mother," he said when Adele stuck her head around the corner. "Laura's in on the game, and it would appear she's agreeable."

Much laughing and embracing followed, and the elder Jensens told Nick and Laura that Myra Black had agreed to meet them at the community church at seven.

"There's no minister who lives here in town," Adele told Nick. "We have one who comes through on Sundays, but Myra said she could wear a choir robe or something if it would make you feel the ceremony was more official."

"Tell her thanks, but no thanks." Nick squeezed Laura's hand. "I was married once before with all the trimmings, and it didn't last. All I want is to be declared Laura's husband in front of the people who love her. This time I know it'll be for life."

Walt glanced at his watch. "You might find there'll be a few more folks than you expect. I let the word get out that if the lights went on in the church about six-thirty, there might be something more interesting for everybody to do besides sit at home tonight watching television. And we're also expecting my new partner and his family to arrive at any moment. I called 'em this morning."

Nick expressed immediate pleasure. "Great! Vance and I haven't always seen eye to eye, but I don't have a best man, since you have to give the bride away. Think he'd mind if I asked him?"

"I think he'd be tickled pink." Laura put her hands on her hips and gave he father a hard look. "But I want to know why *you* felt so certain I'd go through with this, dad. I mean, I could have said no."

Walt shook his head. "I knew months ago you were going to marry this bird," he said, pointing the end of his pipe stem at Nick. "You got this funny look in your eyes every time you talked about him."

"Your father said it was the same look I used to get when we were courting." Adele slipped her arm around her husband's waist.

"Same look you still get sometimes." Walt kissed her cheek.

The next few hours were busy ones. Laura retrieved her dress from the motor home, thankful she had heeded Nick's advice and had brought it. The four of them had a quick bowl of soup and a sandwich, then went off in different directions to get ready.

Nick showered and dressed, then readied the motor home for his bride. He felt anticipation and excitement, but none of the apprehension that had troubled him in the past. This time, he knew, love was real and would last through anything life threw at them. And his relief at learning Isabelle was thriving knew no bounds.

A few minutes before six-thirty, a knock on the motor-home door took him away from his task of tidying and beautifying the place. When he opened the door, Peter Vance grinned up at him.

"Too late to back out now, sport," the blond man said, holding out his hand. "I just found out I'm your best man, and if I have to hold a shotgun on you, you're marrying her."

Nick took the hand in a firm grasp. "You won't even have to use a cap pistol, friend. Wild horses couldn't keep me from the altar." He rubbed his seat ruefully. "Although certain horses have already insured that I'm not going to enjoy sitting for a few days."

Peter stepped into the vehicle. "Laura told me she'd taken you out for one last ride on Buster. She presented him to the boys a little while ago. They went crazy." Peter paused. "Darn nice of her," he added thickly.

"That's the way she is." Nick reached into his pocket and took out the ring Adele had returned to him. "Keep this until the right time, Peter." He hesitated. "Or better yet, let the little guys bring it up to me. Might as well make them part of the action, too."

Peter declared that nothing would please his sons more.

The bride and groom traveled the few blocks to the church in separate cars, Laura riding with her mother and father and Anne, and Nick wedged happily in between the two blond Vance boys with Peter at the wheel of his car.

"Mr. Nick?" Davy Vance looked up at him. "Remember when we first saw you?"

Nick smiled, remembering the incident clearly. "I do."

"Well," Davy said, shifting his position in the seat, "I've been thinking about what you said. About people being friends and not getting married."

"What about it?"

"Are you and Doctor Laura still going to be friends?"

Nick started to laugh. "Better than ever, Davy," he replied. "Better than ever!"

The small church stood on the back half of a lot on the main street. Grass grew in the yard, and two beds of petunias lined the entrance. The lights were on, even though the light from the summer sun was still strong, and people were streaming into the front door. Lots of people.

Nick got out of the car. "I thought Walt just mentioned this to a few friends," he said to Peter. "Looks like the whole population's showing up."

Peter grinned. "He's their doctor. They've all known Laura since she was born. Looks like you're going to get a sizable wedding, whether you wanted it or not."

"I don't mind." Nick closed the door after the two boys got out. "It's a tribute to the family."

In her parents' car, Laura regarded the crowd with mixed feelings. Suppose Nick was upset by all the attention? What then? She knew her father had only acted out of natural pride, but... The church was going to be filled!

She saw Nick and Pete and the two boys vanish inside. Well, it was too late to change things. If he was upset, he would just have to be upset. She could try to set the tone by showing how pleased she was. It felt good to know that so many old friends and neighbors cared this much.

Anne seemed to feel the same. "I'm already getting teary eyed," she confided to Laura. "This is so...so wonderful!"

"I hope Nick feels the same," Laura replied under her breath.

Anne and her mother went on inside, leaving Laura alone in the yard with her father. "Well, honey," he said, "this is the big moment. Since we don't have any organ music, I guess we can just go on in anytime we want." His blue eyes seemed to shine with a touch of extra moisture.

"I love you, dad." Laura gave him a hug. "I love you especially for understanding why everything's worked out the strange way it has."

"Honey, I don't understand a thing." He kissed her cheek. "I just accept that you love that man who's waiting for you in there, and he loves you. That's what's important. Come on, let's go."

As they stepped through the doorway, Laura was astonished to hear piano music. Someone had sat down at the church's old piano and was playing the Bridal March. She glanced questioningly at her father. He smiled, his head held high.

Then she glanced down to the end of the aisle, and all other thoughts fled. Nick, looking as if he had stepped from the pages of *Gentleman's Quarterly,* waited for her, an expression of expectation and triumph on his face. Her father led her slowly to him.

When she reached his side, Nick held out his hands and took hers. While Myra, a sturdy woman in a dark business suit, performed the brief ceremony, he held her firmly, and Laura could feel the love radiating from him.

It was so perfect, she thought, glancing at his handsome profile. It had all been crazy, and sometimes frightening, but it had also been leading to this perfect moment. Step by step, day by day. Event by event. She and Nick were meant to be married, to be...

"I now declare the two of you to be husband and wife," Myra said in a voice that carried through the crowded church, "under the law of this county and state—" she paused "—and any other higher power that happens to be interested."

Nick turned and took Laura's left hand. He signaled to the Vance boys, and they rushed up to give him the ring. He smiled tenderly into her eyes as he slipped the band over her finger.

"Hello, *Mrs.* Doctor Jensen-Hawthorne," he whispered.

"That's kind of a mouthful," Laura whispered back teasingly. "Maybe I should have two identitites—Dr. Jensen and Mrs. Hawthorne."

"Just as long as both of you are my partner for life, it doesn't make any difference to me what you're called." Nick put his arms around her and drew her into a long, deeply satisfying kiss.

The crowd began to applaud.